PRAISE FOR HELENA HUNTING'S NOVELS

"Perfect for fans of Helen Hoang's *The Kiss Quotient*. A fun and steamy love story with high stakes and plenty of emotion."

— *Kirkus Reviews* on *Meet Cute*

"Bestselling Hunting's latest humorous and heartfelt love story . . . is another smartly plotted and perfectly executed rom-com with a spot-on sense of snarky wit and a generous helping of smoldering sexual chemistry."

— *Booklist* on *Meet Cute*

"Entertaining, funny, and emotional."

— *Harlequin Junkie* on *Meet Cute*

"Hunting is quickly making her way as one of the top voices in romance!"

— RT Book Reviews

"Sexy. Funny. Emotional. Steamy and tender and so much more than just a book. *Hooking Up* reminds me why I love reading romance."

— *USA Today* bestselling author L. J. Shen

"Heartfelt, hilarious, hot, and so much sexiness!"

— *New York Times* bestselling author Tijan on *Shacking Up*

"Helena writes irresistible men. I loved this sexy, funny, and deliciously naughty story!"

— *USA Today* bestselling author Liv Morris on *Shacking Up*

"Fun, sexy, and full of heart . . . a laugh-out-loud love story with explosive chemistry and lovable characters. Helena Hunting has done it again!"
    —*USA Today* bestselling author Melanie Harlow on *Shacking Up*

"With that perfect Helena Hunting flair, *Shacking Up* is the perfect combination of sexy, sweet, and hilarious. A feel-good beach read you won't want to miss!"
    —*New York Times* bestselling author K. Bromberg

"A look into the world of tattoos and piercings, a dash of humor, and a feel-good ending will delight fans and new readers alike."
    —*Publishers Weekly* on *Inked Armor*

"A unique, deliciously hot, endearingly sweet, laugh-out-loud, fantastically good-time romance! . . . I loved every single page!"
    —*New York Times* bestselling author Emma Chase on *Pucked*

"Sigh-inducing swoony and fanning-myself sexy. All the stars!"
    —*USA Today* bestselling author Daisy Prescott on the Pucked series

"A hot roller coaster of a ride!"
    —*New York Times* and *USA Today* bestselling author Julia Kent on
Pucked Over

"*Pucked Over* is Helena Hunting's funniest and sexiest book yet. Scorching hot with pee-inducing laughs. All hail the Beaver Queen."
    —*USA Today* bestselling author T. M. Frazier

"Characters that will touch your heart and a romance that will leave you breathless."

—*New York Times* bestselling author Tara Sue Me

"Gut wrenching, sexy, twisted, dark, incredibly erotic, and a love story like no other. On my all-time-favorites list."

—*New York Times* bestselling author Alice Clayton on *Clipped Wings*

Love on
the Lake

OTHER TITLES BY HELENA HUNTING

PUCKED SERIES

CLIPPED WINGS SERIES

Love on the Lake

HELENA HUNTING

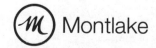 Montlake

For the ones who always put the people they love the most ahead of themselves

CHAPTER 1
WELCOME TO YOUR NEW LIFE

Teagan

"Uh, Dad, I think you need to come here!" I shout. For a panicked moment I question what fresh hell this morning has brought with it.

A moving truck is backing into our driveway.

Less than a year ago we downsized from a seven-thousand-square-foot mansion we could not afford—unless we planned to sell most of our major organs on the black market—to a two-thousand-square-foot home. For nearly two decades my dad used excessive spending as a way to mourn the loss of my mother, God rest her beautiful soul. It took a family scandal for him to realize that he needed to make some very important changes in his life, which included putting an end to spending money he didn't have.

I abandon the care package I'm in the middle of putting together for my younger brother and am halfway across the room when my dad appears in the doorway, his expression reflecting his concern. "What's going on?"

"I don't know. You tell me." I motion outside, where the moving truck continues to beep as it backs up toward the garage. "Please tell me we don't have to move again."

"Oh! Oh no, Teagan." He comes to stand next to me and gives my shoulder a squeeze. "No, we don't have to move. I meant to talk to you about this before today."

The moment of relief is quickly replaced by confusion. My father looks . . . chagrined? "Talk to me about what?"

"Just give me a moment. I need to open the garage door, and then we can have a chat." He rushes off, and soon after, I hear the garage door whir open. One of the movers hops out of the passenger side of the truck, and my dad approaches him.

If we're not moving out, it means that someone else is moving in. It's not either of my brothers—my youngest brother, Bradley, is in prison, hence the care package I'm putting together. Sometimes I wonder if he wouldn't have ended up where he is if I'd been a better big sister. My older brother is living in Pearl Lake with his fiancée—which leaves only one other potential option.

I watch while two men wearing matching T-shirts and old ripped jeans begin carrying boxes and furniture into the garage. I recognize one of the chairs they bring inside. It's in the photo Dad has as his screen saver, of him and his girlfriend of six months.

I go back to packing *Wall Street Journals* and new notebooks into the box. I want to make sure it gets in the mail today so Bradley has it for the weekend. A few minutes later Dad reappears in my doorway.

"Danielle is moving in with us," I say without looking at him.

"She called last night to let me know the movers rescheduled the truck for today instead of Saturday. I meant to talk to you about it before they arrived this morning, but I didn't realize you were already awake, and I didn't want to disturb you. I didn't mean for it to be a surprise, honey."

I glance at the clock on my nightstand. It's nine thirty in the morning. On a Wednesday. It's our work-from-home day, and Dad always tells me I can sleep in. Something I never actually do.

The fact that his plan was to give me a few hours' notice about our new roommate isn't a big surprise. Half of his life choices seem to be afterthoughts.

I force a bright smile. It's not that I don't want him to have someone in his life. If anyone deserves happiness, it's my dad. He's had enough turmoil and strife to last several lifetimes. "You and Danielle have been spending a lot of time together. I think it's great that you've decided to take the next step in your relationship." It's not even that I'm worried about Danielle moving in so soon after they've started dating. The issue is more that I'm in my midtwenties and still living with my dad. I even suggested I get my own place when he downsized. But it was on the heels of my breakup with my long-term boyfriend, and my dad said he would be lonely without me. And that he would miss all my baking, so I moved along with him. And now this.

He gives me an apologetic smile. "I meant to sit down and talk with you. Danielle was worried. I know we haven't been together that long."

"When you know, you know, right?" Six months isn't long, but it isn't short either. And my dad's been on a dating hiatus for the past two decades, so to him, this probably feels monumentally long.

He smiles down at me. "I'm so relieved to hear you say that. I know you and Danielle will get along great."

"We absolutely will." I nod, trying to assuage his concern.

Danielle is a nice lady. She's about ten years younger than my father and also lost a spouse. They met at group therapy and started spending time together as friends. She's been by the house plenty of times over the past six months, usually before she and my dad go on one of their dates. They do a lot of biking and trail walking and going on dinner dates. She and I have made small talk, but that's been about it.

"We didn't expect the truck to get here this early, so she won't be here until after work. I could arrange takeout for dinner? Maybe we could order from that sushi restaurant you two love?"

The thought of sitting down for a "family" dinner on the night my father's girlfriend moves into the house is unappealing. If I were moving into my boyfriend's house, I wouldn't want a third wheel around to spoil the excitement. Especially in the form of an adult daughter.

"Actually, Dad, I'm supposed to visit Van in Pearl Lake this weekend. I was planning to go on Friday, but I could head up there early, and that would give you and Danielle a chance to get things settled." My brother Van casually suggested I come visit him soon, as he does almost every time I talk to him, but I didn't make a commitment to go. Hopefully he doesn't mind me spontaneously dropping by, and in the middle of the week, with a plan to stay for several days.

A furrow creases his brow. "I didn't know you were going to see Van."

"Oh? I thought I mentioned it," I lie.

"I don't want you to feel like you have to leave early because Danielle is moving in."

I wave a dismissive hand in the air. "Van won't mind. He's been renovating the upstairs of the garage into a one-bedroom apartment, and it's nearly finished. Are you okay with me taking a long weekend?"

"Of course—you rarely take time off."

"I'll pack a bag and tell Van I'm on my way up. It's supposed to be gorgeous there this week. Unseasonably warm for late April. I'll take a couple of books with me and enjoy some sunshine and relaxation and time with my brother." And I can fill his freezer with homemade dinners like I did last time. He and Dillion both work long hours, and Van loves having ready-made meals to pull out of the freezer when the two of them are working late.

"You really are the best daughter a father could ask for. Thank you." He pulls me in for a hug and kisses me on top of my head, like I'm six, not twenty-six. "Maybe I'll set up something romantic for Danielle. That would be nice, wouldn't it?"

"Absolutely!" And this is exactly the reason I don't want to be here this weekend. I don't have a problem with my dad doing romantic things for Danielle, but I don't need to witness it.

He nods and spins around, a hop in his step as he makes his way down the hall to his office. I close my bedroom door and sag against it. I rub the space between my eyebrows, trying not to frown or furrow. Portia, my ex–best friend, always used to tell me that I should never show any emotion unless it was happiness if I didn't want premature wrinkles. I blow out a breath. Normally I would call my brother, but if I hear his voice I'm going to want to spill the beans over the phone. This would be a much better conversation in person, so I send him a quick message instead.

Teagan: How close is the garage to being ready for occupancy?

Van: 85-90%. Why what's up?

Teagan: Thinking about taking a couple vacation days if you don't mind a guest for the weekend.

Van: You know you're always welcome. When you heading this way?

Teagan: In an hour or so if that's okay?

The dots appear and disappear a couple of times. I'm about to tell him I can hold off until tomorrow or Friday, but another message pops up.

Van: For sure, you know how to get in. Dillion asks that you bring the stuff for those gin cocktails you make.

Teagan: Will do! See you soon!

Half an hour later I have my bags packed. I put the gin and cocktail mix into a box, along with a couple of bottles of wine, and toss my prescriptions into my purse, checking to make sure I have enough to get me through until the end of the weekend.

I stop by my dad's office on my way out and tell him I'll be back on Sunday night and to have a great weekend with Danielle. And then I'm in my car and on my way to Pearl Lake.

I stop at the post office to mail the care package to Bradley and grab a coffee to perk me up. I pull my hair into a ponytail so I can put the top down on my convertible and enjoy the fresh air and the sunshine. While we had to get rid of most of the cars when we downsized and consolidated my dad's debt, I was able to keep my convertible. But only because I was the one who'd bought and paid for it. I've had it since I was eighteen, and it has sentimental value more than anything.

It's also not super flashy as far as convertibles go. It has a hard top for winter and a soft top for summer. It's probably one of the very few things I still have from our previously lavish and frivolous lifestyle. Over the past year I've gone from weekly spa appointments and expensive dinners out several times a week to painting my own toenails and learning how to cook meals. I had no idea how pampered I was until I wasn't anymore. And honestly, I don't miss it that much.

The highway soon turns into tree-lined two-lane roads, the brush growing thicker and increasingly lush with every passing mile. The farther I get from Chicago, the easier it is to breathe. I try to appreciate the beauty of the drive and not think about Dad and Danielle or what the house is going to look like when I get back on Sunday.

I arrive in Pearl Lake just after noon. A Footprint Construction truck is parked in the driveway, in front of the garage, which isn't unusual. Dillion is Van's fiancée, and they've been living together for months. She often drives into work with her father, who owns the construction company in town, since she and Van live right next door to her family.

I decide I should go ahead and make myself comfortable in the apartment above the garage rather than heading for their love shack. If I don't, there's a chance that they'll try to convince me to sleep in one of the spare rooms in the cottage.

I grab my suitcase from the trunk and heft my weekend bag over my shoulder, along with my purse. It's a lot for a long weekend, but I've never been particularly good at packing light.

Originally, Van planned to convert the garage into a self-contained apartment, but he decided it would be better to keep the garage space as is, and instead he ripped off the roof, added dormers, and turned the space above it into an apartment. That way, the garage still functions as it should.

It has a small workshop, loads of tools, and Van's BMW, which he rarely drives anymore, favoring the ancient pickup truck that once belonged to Grammy Bee, our grandmother, who drove it until she passed away a year and a half ago. She left the cottage and its contents to Van. Turns out there was literally millions in uncashed bonds and piles of cash tucked all over the cottage. I tried to tell him I didn't want any of it, but he set up an investment account for me. I plan to leave it where it is until I retire, or maybe pass it on to my own kids one day, if I have any.

There's a set of stairs inside the garage that aren't as steep as the ones that run up to the second floor from the outside. But I can't remember the code to open the garage door, so this is my only option.

I manage to clunk my way up the outside staircase with my suitcase in one hand and my other bags hanging over the railing. The landing is small and narrow, making it difficult to maneuver with my bags.

I turn the knob, assuming it will be open, since the only reason people lock their doors around here is to keep out the wily raccoons. I step inside and drop my purse and overnight bag on the floor, which I instantly regret because the surface is still plywood—so much for 85 percent finished—and there's a lot of sawdust.

My suitcase is still on the landing and the door wide open when I realize I'm not alone in here. It's also not a raccoon keeping me company. Or a family of squirrels. Or bats.

Beyond the spiders, which I'm fairly certain there must be a few of, is a man. A shirtless man. He's crouched down with his back to me, and he's wearing a pair of huge headphones that look like they came out of the eighties or something. But there aren't any wires, so they must be new. They look clunky. They might explain why he has yet to notice that I'm standing here, gawking at his very bare, very muscled, very tattooed back.

A sun sets over a frozen lake, the watercolor design bright and beautiful; the snow-covered trees hold hints of pink, orange, and yellow, a reflection from the sun peeking through the clouds on its descent toward the horizon. Snow swirls across the landscape, making it seem like the sun is trying to fight its way through a snowstorm. There's script arching over the sun, but it's too small to make out from this side of the room. On his left triceps is an hourglass with only a few grains of sand left in it, as if time is running out.

He's currently laying the floorboards on the other side of the loft. He taps in one of the long pieces, all those muscles flexing deliciously, and then lays another board beside it. He takes a pencil from behind his ear and makes a mark before replacing it.

A moment later he uses his foot to prop up a board and picks up some device with his other hand.

I shriek when it whirs to life and I realize belatedly that it's a saw. The loud noise ceases, and both the board and the saw clatter to the floor.

"What the shit?" The man unfurls from his crouched position, rising to his full and very intimidating height. From the back he's incredible to look at, but from the front—he's just. Wow. He's not a snack. He's a seven-course meal, including the decadent dessert.

His dark hair is covered by a backward baseball cap, the ends curling around his ears and the snapback. His eyes are the color of snow on a moonless winter night, a murky kind of gray that shifts and changes like shadows. His nose is slightly crooked, as if it's been broken and not set properly; his lips are full and ridiculously kissable. He has a scar on his chin, which I only notice because his cheeks and chin are decorated in what I'd guess to be a couple of days' worth of stubble, and a pale, hairless line is evident.

His shoulders are broad, and his chest, defined and thick, has a smattering of that dark-brown hair. His abs ripple and his thick biceps flex as he yanks the giant headphones off. His worn, paint-splattered, and tattered jeans hang low on his hips and are dragged farther down by the tool belt around his waist, exposing that glorious V of muscle, which leads my eye south to the magic wand that is hidden behind his fly.

He will absolutely be starring in my fantasies in the very near future.

Except he won't be angry like he is now.

I quickly drag my gaze back up so I'm not ogling him anymore.

He tosses the huge headphones on the floor. His gray eyes are a storm of shock and annoyance. He motions to the saw at his feet. "I could have cut my fucking foot off!"

"Why would you use your foot to balance the wood anyway? Isn't that unsafe?" What the heck is wrong with me? Since when do I talk back to people I don't even know? But as I look between him and the saw, I realize I *have* met him before.

Months ago.

I made an ass out of myself then too.

"Are you fucking serious? Rule number one in construction: always, *always* make your presence known when someone is handling power tools."

"You were wearing headphones. How was I supposed to make myself known when you can't even hear me? Especially over the sound of that thing." I point at the electric saw thing lying on the floor.

"Those aren't headphones, they're ear protection! And all you had to do was knock loudly and say *hey*, and I would've heard you just fine. The banshee shriek is unnecessary."

"I didn't expect you to be in here! And I certainly didn't expect it to sound like the set of a bad horror movie!"

"Did you not see the truck parked in front of the garage?" He shakes his head and mutters something I can't hear. "Who are you even? And what are you doing up here?" He holds up a hand when I open my mouth to speak. "Wait. Let me guess: you're that new lady from the city that they hired down at the planning department, aren't you? I have permits for everything, so you're wasting your time. You can take your Gaucho-Parade-designer-clothes-wearing butt right back out the door." He points to the door, one thick eyebrow raised.

Gaucho-Parade? Is that some Pearl Lake insult? "My butt does not look like a parade." I pat my bottom, offended, trying to decipher his meaning. Maybe he's referring to Gucci and Prada, neither of which I'm wearing. "And I'm not from the bylaw office. I'm Teagan."

"Is that supposed to mean something to me?" He gives me a look I'm all too familiar with.

It's the one the girls I used to hang out with back in Chicago gave me after Troy broke off the engagement and told me that he and Portia were together.

The one that said that they couldn't wait for me to go away. That they wanted me gone.

"You don't have to be so rude!"

Way to make an even worse second impression than the first one, Teagan, I mentally chastise myself. I'm already embarrassed over the fact that I've scared the crap out of him and could have accidentally caused him to lop off a limb. Now I get to add the humiliation of him not remembering me at all.

I thought our first introduction was pretty memorable, considering how awkward I made things when I told him he had basketball-player hands and made him compare our hand sizes. And when he told me he liked football, I made an even more awkward comment about how much full-body hugging there was in that game.

"I'm Donny's sister. We met last year." I'm not sure reminding him of our previous meeting is going to help my case at all.

"Huh?" He stares blankly at me.

I remember that I'm the only one who calls my brother that, and that it's not his favorite nickname. "Van's sister," I amend. "Last fall. We met. Very briefly. In the driveway." I motion toward the door, as if that's going to help. "You're Aaron. You work with Van's fiancée, Dillion."

His eyebrows lift with something like surprise, maybe because I remember his name and he apparently doesn't recall our introduction at all. "Sorry, I got a shit memory." He rubs the back of his neck and glances at the door. I can't tell if he's thinking about doing a runner or what. But I can say that it makes his biceps flex enticingly.

I wave away the comment and try to do something other than ogle his muscles. "It's fine. Like I said, it was very brief. Anyway, I'm Van's younger sister. He said this place was eighty-five percent finished and that I could stay here for a few days."

"It will be when I'm done laying the floor." He motions to the planks lying at his feet.

"Great! That's just great." I want to do something with my hands, like run them over his chest, so instead I clasp them in front of me. "I don't want to intrude, you know, what with them being recently engaged and all. I know they've renovated the cottage, or maybe that was mostly you?" I don't wait for him to answer; instead I barrel on, powerless to stop my mouth. "Anyway, the walls are thin, and I don't need to hear things I shouldn't."

"Right." Based on his arched brow, that last part was something that should have stayed inside my head.

"I'm going to grab my bag." I thumb over my shoulder.

"Knock yourself out." He turns away, bending to pick up the plank he dropped when I first scared the crap out of him.

In the short time it takes for me to drag my suitcase inside—Aaron does not offer to help—he's covered up all those incredible muscles and his pretty tattoos with a threadbare T-shirt. I put a few things away while he works on the floor.

I know I should probably leave him alone, but for whatever reason, I seem to be compelled to try to make him talk to me.

"How long have you been doing this?" I ask once he's finished cutting another piece of flooring.

"This particular project or this in general?" He taps the board in with a rubber mallet until it clicks.

I wait until he's finished with the saw again before I clarify. "This in general. Have you always worked with your hands? It's obvious you're really good with them."

I get another one-word answer: "Yeah."

Instead of being deterred, I keep asking questions. People love to talk about themselves and what they're interested in and passionate about. So it should, in theory, make him more likely to give longer, more detailed responses. And for a bit it does. He starts going on about the difference between engineered hardwood and regular laminate and how this stuff is better. I have no idea what any of what he's saying means; all I know is that he's talking and I get to stare at his pretty face and listen to his voice.

At least until he abruptly puts an end to my Q&A session. "Look, Teagan, I get that maybe you're bored or whatever, but if you want to have a floor that isn't plywood, you gotta stop with all the questions. I'd like to get this done before midnight."

It's not that I don't understand that he needs to finish what he's working on. It's how quick the shift is and how sharp his tone becomes. Like I've reached the limit of his patience and he's been humoring me this entire time. I give him a tight-lipped smile. "Sorry. I'll get out of your way."

I grab my purse and rush down the stairs, heading for the house and away from Aaron. I don't even know why I'm trying so damn hard to make someone I'm only going to see on very rare occasions like me. He's not worth the effort.

CHAPTER 2
THE FORK IN THIS ROAD IS BENT

Teagan

I let myself into the cottage, and I entertain myself by making use of my brother's kitchen and his cupboard of liquor. In that order. The least I can do when I show up unexpectedly is make him food in the form of his favorite things.

I'm sitting on the front porch on the swing bench, sipping my second martini. Based on the ring marks on the side tables, I'm going to guess Van and Dillion spend a lot of time here in the evenings. They probably cuddle and talk about the life they're building together.

If Troy hadn't cheated on me with my best friend and then dumped me for her, maybe he would have come here and sat on this porch swing with me and talked about our future together. I almost snort into my martini glass at the thought.

Troy would never go to a "cottage" on a lake. Troy is basically allergic to any and all bugs. He blisters when he gets so much as one mosquito bite and then moans about the potential scarring and how itchy it is.

The sound of an engine turning over and the spitting of gravel tells me that Aaron is done for the day. Which I assume means the floor has been installed and I'll be able to sleep comfortably in the garage apartment without imposing on my brother.

Not long after Aaron leaves, the rumble of an old engine and the crunch of gravel under tires alert me to the arrival of either my brother or Dillion. Or possibly both of them, depending. My brother works for an architectural firm in the city, but sometimes he takes on a consulting role for projects on Pearl Lake, which is what he's doing today. He texted a few hours ago to let me know he'd be on-site until about five thirty.

A minute later, Van appears. He's let his hair grow since he moved here permanently, trading in the business cut for something slightly less polished. It looks good on him, as do the T-shirt, khakis, and open plaid button-down.

"Hey, Teag, sorry I couldn't get back sooner to keep you company."

"Don't worry about it. I sort of sprang this on you last minute." I set my martini glass on the table and drag my toes along the deck boards to stop the swing before I stand and accept the welcome hug.

"The drive was okay?" he asks once he releases me.

"Beautiful as always, at least once I left the city. Can I make you a martini? Or get you a beer? I made some maple-bacon muffins and some bacon-and-cheese biscuits this afternoon if you're hungry for a snack."

"I love it when you come to visit. Will you make those bacon-wrapped jalapeños while you're here?"

"Make a list, and I'll make you all the bacony things. Let me get a snack tray ready. Do you know when Dillion is going to be home?" I follow him inside and rush over to the fridge to grab a beer, as well as a couple of apples and some cheese to go with the biscuits and muffins I whipped up. I don't expect my brother to treat me like I'm a guest who needs to be waited on. And I know my showing up out of the blue probably shifted whatever their plans were this week, so I want to show my appreciation.

"Probably not until late. She and her dad have a meeting with one of the families across the lake, and they often like to turn those into dinners."

"Oh, is that something you'd usually have to attend too?" I hunt around in the vegetable crisper and find grape tomatoes, baby carrots, and sugar snap peas to add to the snack tray.

"Yup, but thanks to you I had an excuse to skip this one."

I frown but then try to smooth out my features. "I'm sorry, I wouldn't have come today if I'd known I was interfering with your work schedule."

"You're one hundred and ten percent *not* interfering. These planning meetings are a waste of my time, and they eat up a lot of hours. I mean, don't get me wrong: the food is always good. But there's also the wine, or the cocktails, and I still have to work tomorrow, so avoiding this meeting is a favor, not an interference."

I hope he's not trying to make me feel better about my surprise visit, but I let it go.

Ten minutes later we're back on the front porch and he's on his third muffin.

"So what's the deal with that Aaron guy? He's kind of surly, isn't he?" I nibble on the end of a snap pea.

"You mean Aaron Saunders? The guy working on the garage?" Van asks with a mouthful of muffin.

"I scared the crap out of him when I got here, and he nearly bit my head off for it. He seems . . . like he isn't the friendliest guy in the world." I'm most definitely fishing for information to see if I'm the common denominator for the surliness or if it's his personality.

Van frowns. "Maybe you caught him on a bad day. He's usually a pretty easygoing guy."

"Or maybe he doesn't like me." Which seems to be the case.

"Impossible. Everyone loves you. People gravitate to you like the sun."

"I don't know about that." I pop one of the olives from my martini into my mouth and chew thoughtfully. "Have you talked to Dad recently?"

"Last week, I think? Why, did something happen? Please tell me he hasn't gone back to spending money he doesn't have." I can see my brother doing math in his head already.

"Nothing like that. Everything is fine where finances are concerned. At least they were the last time I checked the credit card and bank statements."

"Okay. That's good. So what's going on?"

"Danielle is moving in with Dad." I figure I might as well spit it out.

"Wow. That's good, I guess? I'd say it's fast, but Dad's been alone for nearly two decades, so maybe not. When is she moving in?"

"The moving truck showed up this morning, so today."

That earns me a furrowed brow. "How long have you known she's moving in?"

"Since the moving van showed up at nine thirty."

"Didn't Dad think to tell you *before* the truck showed up?" Van's eyes look like they're going to pop out of his head. It makes my shock earlier this morning seem reasonable.

"Apparently, the truck wasn't supposed to come until Saturday, but they switched the days or whatever, and Dad wasn't expecting it until noon, so he thought he'd have time to tell me."

"Still, that's not a lot of lead time. You'd think he would have had a conversation with you about it well before it actually happened."

"I should have expected it." I tip back my glass and polish off what's left of my drink. "They've been spending a lot of time together, and I always find a reason to be out when they're having one of their date nights, which have been more and more often."

"How often is often?"

"Three or four times a week." I lean my head back and tip my glass upside down, trying to get the last few olive-flavored drops. "Oh hell. All the signs have been there. Dad always asking what my plans were before she'd come over. Me faking that I had some."

"Aw, Teag. I'm sorry. I didn't know it had gotten so uncomfortable." Van puts his arm around my shoulder.

"It's not bad, though. This is exactly what Dad should be doing, living his best life. I'm glad he has a girlfriend. I'm glad she's moving in. It means he's finally moving on, and he deserves that. And Danielle is nice. Grounded. I can see why they want to take this step."

And now I understand better why Dad mentioned the possibility of going back to his last name a month or so ago. When he and my mom got married, he took the Firestone name, in part because my mom was the last remaining Firestone, and the name would die out with her. To keep it alive, he took on her last name instead of her taking his. I don't think it hurt that the Firestone name had more clout, not to mention the fact that my dad didn't have a good relationship with his side of the family.

"It's good, even if it came out of left field." Van nods, but I can tell he's wondering where I'm going with this.

"I'm twenty-six years old, and I still live with my dad. Which didn't seem so bad this morning, until that moving van showed up." And truly it didn't. I stayed to keep my dad company. "I have to move out, Van. I need to get my own place. I can't stay there and be a wet blanket while they're building a future and a life together. And maybe if we still lived in the old house, it would be fine, because I could move into the pool house like Bradley did, or I could take the nanny suite on the other side of the freaking house, and I'd never see them except maybe in the kitchen if I needed to grab something to eat, or the occasional family dinner. But we are literally on top of each other in this house. I don't want to get in the way of their relationship, and I honestly don't want to subject myself to old-people romance."

"Dad isn't *that* old," my brother says with a sympathetic smile.

"I know, but that isn't the point. The reason I didn't get my own place when we downsized was because Dad convinced me he wanted my company. And now this. I can't help but feel like an afterthought. Maybe that sounds selfish. But I stayed for him, and now I feel like I don't belong there anymore." As I watch a squirrel trying to jump from one tree to the next, I begin to see that it's not just about living with my father; it's more than that. "I work for Smith Financial not because I wanted the job or even love it. I did it because Dad was so thrilled about the prospect of having me work for the same company as him."

"I didn't realize you didn't like the job," Van says quietly.

"I don't *not* like it. It's just not something I find particularly rewarding. I'm decent at it, and Dad loved having me close, so that seemed like it was enough. But now I'm beginning to feel like I've spent most of my life making sure he has someone to support him emotionally, and the decisions I've made weren't about me; they were about making him happy. Which, based on the amount of retail therapy he engaged in over the years, was a complete freaking failure."

Van gives me a stern look. "You aren't responsible for Dad's happiness."

"I know that. And I think that's part of the problem. Logically I'm aware that's true. But I dated Troy because Dad thought he was a good match for me. Not because I was actually in love with Troy. Which is terrible and probably explains why that relationship failed."

"I don't think there are any valid explanations for why Troy did what he did, other than him being an asshole and Portia being a horrible friend."

I don't bother commenting, because the why is irrelevant. "The point is, everything I've been doing I've done to make sure Dad is all right. I don't even know who I am. Or what I like. I have no idea how to take care of myself. I had to learn how to do my own laundry when we moved into the new house, and I shrunk half of my sweaters and turned all of Dad's white shirts a very pale lavender because I accidentally threw a purple bra in with his whites. I didn't even know you were supposed to separate things by color!" I throw my hands in the air and let them fall to my lap. "And that Aaron guy who doesn't even know me doesn't like me!" I don't know why I'm so stuck on that last part, especially since it has literally nothing to do with my current existential crisis.

Van takes me by the shoulders. "Aaron doesn't not like you. He was probably having a bad day. Maybe one of the wives or daughters from across the lake were hounding him to come mow their lawn or something. That always puts him in a mood."

"Mow their lawn? Is that a euphemism?"

"Yes and no. And I'm not entirely sure what to believe. There's a lot of small-town gossip, and I'm unsure what's true and what isn't. Anyway, Aaron aside, not knowing you need to separate your colors is not a crime. I had no idea until I moved out on my own too. What's important is that you're a great person, and you have amazing qualities, one of which is putting other people and their needs ahead of your own."

"Maybe that's something I need to stop doing," I say.

"I would have to agree. I think you need to take some time to focus on yourself and what you want to do with your life. It sucks that Dad didn't tell you about Danielle, but unless it's written in his planner, he tends to forget those important details."

"I need to get my own apartment. And maybe quit my job."

Van's eyebrow lifts. "Are you sure you want to quit Smith Financial?"

"I've been thinking about it for a while. I was considering going back to school or something, but I have no idea what I want to do. I never got to have any of the normal jobs most teenagers have. I never waited tables or worked at a greasy fast-food place. I've only ever worked with Dad, and it feels like it's sucking the life out of me." And now that I say it, I can see that it's true. I get up, do my job, run through the motions, but I have no desire to climb the Smith Financial ladder. "I need to figure out what I like and what I'm good at."

Van's brief silence is filled with the chirping of irritated birds in the trees above us. "Why don't you stay here? See if you can find a local job?"

"Here? In Pearl Lake?"

"You can have the apartment above the garage. It's basically finished."

"I don't want to do that to you and Dillion. You're in your own honeymoon phase. Like you need your little sister crashing your party all the time." But it definitely has allure. And there wouldn't be a ton of pressure when it came to earning a salary, not like there would be in the city.

"You wouldn't be crashing our party, Teag. Dillion adores you, and so do I. We both love having you around. Besides, we'll all have our own privacy with you in the apartment and Dillion and I in the house."

"Don't you think you should ask her first, before you go offering me a place to live?"

"I don't need to. I already know what she'd say because we had this conversation a long time ago."

"You guys talked about me moving here?"

"Yeah. After all the shit went down with Bradley. Honestly, we were both surprised when you didn't jump ship back then."

"I didn't want to leave Dad on his own," I say, realizing how sad that sounds.

"But he's an adult, he can take care of himself, and you can afford to take some time and figure yourself out."

"I'll need to see if anyone in town is hiring." I start biting the skin around my nails, then realize what I'm doing and grab another snap pea instead.

"The garage is rent-free, and I'm guessing you must have some savings, so there really isn't a rush. And you could always ask Dad if you could take a few months off if you don't want to quit right away," Van suggests.

"I don't know if that's the best plan, the taking time off, I mean. It's probably the smarter move, but then I might be leading Dad to believe that I'm coming back, so he'd hire a temp instead of finding someone permanent to fill my position. Regardless, I don't want to go back to the job. If I ask for a few months off, it's like I'm giving myself an out if this doesn't work the way I want it to. If I have a fallback plan, I'm not as likely to stick to my guns."

"Okay. So you quit."

"I quit." Being the secretary to the CFO, while financially stable, is not the most exciting position. "I'd like to have a job lined up before I do that, though."

"It's the busy season, so there's a good chance you'll find something fast. The Stitches could probably use some help."

"I appreciate that, but I'd like to at least try to get a job on my own that isn't connected to your fiancée's family."

"I get it, Teag. Just know in this case you have a potential backup option if you need one."

I hug his arm. "Thanks, Donny. You're the best brother a girl could ask for."

CHAPTER 3

EMPLOYABLE

Teagan

It's late by the time I head out to the garage. I have to use the flashlight on my phone to make my way up the stairs. I'm a little intoxicated thanks to the martinis I consumed over the course of the evening, but it's nothing a tall glass of water and a painkiller won't cure.

Van walks me out, partly because I'm mildly afraid of the possibility that I'll get eaten by a bear, and partly because I need help carrying the bedsheets and the floor fan up to the loft. It's only spring, but I need the ambient noise to be able to sleep, especially since the birds start chirping around here before the sun has even peeked over the horizon.

I'm surprised when we enter the apartment and find that not only has the floor been finished, but an old bed frame has been assembled and tucked into one corner of the room. There's also a mattress leaned up against the wall.

"Did you do this?" I ask Van.

"Aaron must have done it before he left."

I guess I can see why he wasn't all that excited about answering all my questions when he was trying to get this done. "The floors look good."

They're warm, whitewashed wide planks. The dark wood bed frame contrasts perfectly. I'm already planning the palette in my head. Maybe tomorrow I can hit up the local hardware store and pick up paint and wallpaper swatches so I can make this place feel like mine.

"They do. Aaron does nice work. Are you good with the bed where it is, or do you want it on another wall?" Van nods to the empty frame.

"It's good where it is for now. I can move it later if I need to."

Van helps me lay the mattress on the frame, and then I give him a hug and send him on his way. I lock the door behind him and get to work making the bed.

Once that's done, I head to the bathroom and finish unpacking my toiletries. My prescriptions go in the medicine cabinet, and I grab a bottle of water from the fridge, making a mental note to replace it because I have a feeling it might belong to Aaron.

I wash down a painkiller along with my sleep medication to offset the potential for a martini hangover. It takes a good half hour to forty-five minutes for the medication to kick in, so I fire up my laptop and browse the Pearl Lake community website. It's pretty lackluster and not all that easy to navigate. The job board only has two advertisements, both for road construction positions.

There's a note at the bottom citing the community center as the best resource for job postings and that all applicants should apply in person. I guess I'll be making a trip into town first thing in the morning.

I pull up my Pinterest account and key *open concept apartments* into the search bar. I spend the next half hour pinning fun ideas on how to make the most of a small space, jotting down color and layout ideas. After a while I start to yawn, so I shut my laptop, set it on the nightstand, and snuggle under the sheets.

Tomorrow is the beginning of my new life, and I can't wait to start it.

◆ ◆ ◆

I wake up bright and early and determine that the first thing I need to buy is a coffee maker. There's a container of instant coffee on the counter and an ancient kettle that's covered in dust and grime. I've already consumed one of Aaron's waters; I'm not sure I should start drinking his coffee too.

I pull my portable steamer out of my suitcase, wishing I'd unpacked last night so all my clothes wouldn't be quite so wrinkled. I choose an interview-slash-job-application-appropriate outfit—add hangers to the list of items I need—and steam out all the wrinkles. Once I'm dressed and ready for the morning, I pop into Van's cottage.

It's already empty. Dillion and Van must have left for work more than an hour ago, and there's a note on the kitchen counter from my brother.

> Teag,
> You know where the coffee is so make yourself at home. Dillion and I should be back from work around five. If you have the burning desire to make more of those muffins feel free since Dillion and I polished off the rest of them this morning (she ate six and will lie later and tell you it was me). I took a package of bacon out of the freezer and put it in the fridge to thaw, just in case.
>   Have a great day.
>   ~Van

I make myself a carafe of coffee, pour it into a travel mug, and sit outside on the front porch for a few minutes, appreciating the serenity. Birds chirp and squirrels bounce from tree to tree. Hummingbirds flutter nervously, stopping at the feeder for a few seconds before they're off again. Finches fight over the bird feeder hanging from a tree to my left, and one pesky squirrel keeps trying to climb down the metal cone. I have to assume it's been greased with WD-40, because it scrambles madly to keep from falling as it slides down.

I bark out a laugh when the squirrel lands on the ground and two blue jays swoop down and flap around it agitatedly before flying away. The squirrel chatters angrily and bounces off.

I get why Van loves it here so much.

When I'm halfway through my coffee, I top it up and make use of my brother's printer so I have hard copies of my résumé. I don't have my fun résumé paper, but the plain white stuff works in a pinch. I head back up to the apartment to put on makeup.

I'm going for subdued today, because this isn't the city and I don't want to come across as too flashy. I'm wearing a pair of white capris, a pale-pink blouse, and wedge sandals in taupe. I check my reflection, give myself the thumbs-up, grab my purse and keys, and set out on my first ever adventure in Pearl Lake.

My first stop is town hall so I can check out the job board. There are a few requests for farmhands in the next town over. I've never so much as taken care of a fish, let alone livestock—which will eventually be turned into a meal—so I don't know that I'd be very good at that job. There's another advertisement for a childcare helper, but again, I don't have a lot of experience with children, so I don't think that would be a good fit either.

There's also a position at the town hall customer service desk, so I make a stop there before I head for the downtown area, where all the shops are.

An older woman sits behind the desk, typing away on her keyboard. I wait until she drags her gaze away from the screen before I say anything.

"Hi there, my name is Teagan Firestone, and I noticed you're hiring for customer service."

She gives me a once-over, her arched brow denoting her skepticism. "It's not a seasonal position."

"Okay. That's great. I have a résumé." I pull one out of my purse and pass it over.

Her expression grows impatient as she scans the front page. "You need to be a permanent resident in Pearl Lake to apply for a position in town hall."

"Oh, I am. I'm Donovan Firestone's sister. He lives on the lake, and I'm moving here too."

"You'll need to update your résumé, then, and your driver's license before you can apply." She hands me back my résumé, and her gaze returns to her computer screen. Obviously I'm being dismissed.

Undeterred, I leave town hall and head in the direction of the main street. My next stop is Pearl Lake Realty, which is looking for a part-time house stager. I'm greeted by a guy named Tucker Patrick. "How can I help you?" The way he looks me over and his tone are slightly off-putting, but I try not to judge a book by its smarmy cover.

"I was wondering if the position for the house stager has been filled." I point to the window where the sign is displayed.

"Not as far as I know. Do you have a résumé handy? What kind of experience do you have in staging houses?"

I pass over a résumé and try not to fidget. "I've decorated a few houses, and I'm a very quick learner."

"Firestone is your last name? You wouldn't happen to be related to Van?"

"I am. He's my brother."

And just like that his expression shutters. "I appreciate your interest, but we need someone with experience." He passes me back my résumé. "Have a great day."

I stop at two more places, and twice more I'm turned down. Once because they don't think I'm a good fit, and once again because my address is in the city. It's hard not to be discouraged or to let the feeling that I don't belong take root. I don't want to have to go back to Chicago, at least not right now.

I decide to take a break from the disappointment and make a stop at Harry's Hardware, since I need paint supplies and some light fixtures to cover the bare bulbs currently hanging from the ceiling.

I pull into the parking lot and notice that many vehicles are pickup trucks. Normally my car wouldn't stick out, at least not in the city, but here it does.

I shoulder my purse and head for the front entrance. I'm feeling self-conscious at this point. And my outfit is drawing more attention than I'd like, even though I thought I toned it down this morning.

I push through the front door and take a deep breath, inhaling the scent of fresh-cut wood, the chemical odor of paint, and the stinging bite of tire rubber. I don't think I've ever been in a hardware store before, come to think of it. Thankfully, there are signs at the top of each aisle, telling me where everything is.

I grab a shopping cart and wander toward the paint department. For a small town it's a pretty big store with a decent selection, although I'm assuming the mansion-size cottages on the other side of the lake have something to do with that.

I check out their wallpaper selection first, which consists mostly of country themes and floral designs. I stand in the middle of the aisle, tapping my finger against my lip as I browse their selection, looking for colors to complement the furniture I plan to bring back from Chicago.

I stop in front of a very cool geometric pattern in navy and white, which would look great with gray walls and yellow accents. I pick up several paint swatches, including a vibrant mustardy yellow. I can see the pieces coming together, especially with the neutral floors and the white country kitchen.

I bounce a couple of times on my toes and clap my hands once, squealing with excitement. I'll need some fun art eventually, but first the basics. I stop at the paint desk, where a woman who looks like she's fresh out of high school is standing, head down, clearly looking at her phone under the counter.

I wait for her to notice me, but after several seconds I give in and say, "Hi there."

She startles and shoves her phone in her pocket as her cheeks flush. "Oh, hey, hi. Sorry, I didn't see you there. How can I help you?"

I give her my brightest smile. "I'm a beginning painter, and I could use some help figuring out what all I need to paint my apartment."

Her brow furrows as she takes in my outfit, assessing me, maybe. "Apartment?"

"More like a loft." At least that's how I would classify it.

She nods as if she understands. "Like the ones a lot of people put over their detached garage?"

It must be a popular thing to do around here. "Exactly."

"Cool, cool." More nodding. "So you need paint and stuff for the contractors?"

"No contractors. I'm going to paint it myself. I'll need all the stuff: brushes, rollers, trays, and obviously paint." I roll up on my toes, then force my heels to stay on the ground. It's a nervous habit. One I need to get rid of. "Would you be able to help me out with that?" I'm not sure how much experience a high school girl might have with painting, but there's a solid chance she's more knowledgeable than me.

"For sure." She leans on the counter. "Do you have the square footage of the space you're planning to paint? How many rooms, what the dimensions are?"

"Hmm." I tap my lip. I guess I should have realized I'd need that kind of information. "Let me check with my brother. I bet he has the blueprints."

"No problem, I'm here all morning." She smiles and pulls her phone out of her Harry's Hardware apron, keeping it below counter level.

I step aside so I can send Van a message, not that there's a line of customers waiting behind me, but I don't want to be in the way in case someone else needs help before I have the information I need.

Van calls me instead of responding to my text.

"Why do you need the blueprints for the garage? What are you doing?"

"I'm buying paint and decorating supplies. I need the square footage so I know how much paint to buy. I figured blueprints would be easiest, since it will give me all the dimensions. Then I'm not at risk of buying too much or too little."

"Okay. They should be in my email, since I sent them to Aaron. Give me a minute to find them, and I'll send them to you. Sound good?"

"Yup, email or text?"

"Whatever's easier for you."

"Text then, please."

"Awesome. Found it, I'm sending it to you now."

My phone pings, and I check to make sure it's from my brother. "Perfect! Thanks, Donny, you're the best!"

"No problem. Make sure you have drop cloths to cover the floor."

"Will do!" I end the call, pull up the message from Van, and step toward the paint desk, but I stop when I notice a man standing with his back to me.

A very tall, very broad man wearing a black T-shirt and a pair of worn jeans. My gaze drops all the way down to his work boots and slowly climbs back up, pausing to admire his very nice butt, and then up higher, where I can appreciate the defined muscles under his shirt.

"Hey, Chloe, how's your morning going?" His deep voice is familiar.

"Oh, hey. I'm good. How about you?" I glance up to see the girl tucking her hair behind her ear and smiling shyly up at him.

The man with the nice butt leans on the counter. "Can't complain, really. How's Charlie doing these days? He loving college?"

"I think he'd love it more if he could live on campus instead of having to commute," she says with a laugh.

"Not quite as fun when you're still living at home with your parents, huh?" he replies.

She shakes her head and bites her lip. "I'm applying out of state, but I'll need all kinds of scholarships to be able to afford it, so I guess we'll see."

"You're a smart girl, Chloe. I have faith you can make it happen."

The way she ducks her head makes me wonder what his expression must be. "I hope so. I have trig and physics this semester, and I'm managing to keep my average above a 4.0, so cross your fingers for me."

He holds up a giant hand and laps his middle finger over his pointer. "I don't think you need any luck, but I'll keep 'em crossed."

"Thanks. Anyway, enough about boring high school classes. What can I do for you this morning, Aaron?" She's all blushes and nervous lip biting.

I swallow down an annoyed sound when I realize this super-friendly, somewhat flirty guy whose butt I've been ogling is the same guy who was a grump with me. I'd think her reaction to him was cute if he hadn't been so cold. Okay, it's still cute that she's smitten. And I get to see how he is around people he actually seems to like.

He holds up a pair of fingers. "I need two five-gallon buckets of primer."

"Oh, wow. That's a whole lot of primer. Must be a big job."

"It's for one of the places on the other side of the lake." I can almost hear his eye roll. "Someone had the stellar idea to paint their entire living room canary yellow, and obviously they're having remorse about that."

"I remember filling the order for that job!" She leans on the counter, eyes wide. "I thought it was for road painting or something! Did the Haver brothers paint that?"

"That they did."

"What color are they going to paint it now?"

"Decorator's white. I think they burned their retinas with that yellow. I wore antiglare sunglasses, and I still feel like I've been staring directly into a solar eclipse."

"You want me to get a five-gallon bucket of that ready for you too?" Chloe asks.

Aaron gives his head a shake. "Nah, there's a good chance they'll change their mind again. This isn't the first time we've had to repaint rooms for them."

"Must be nice to have all that money to throw around on frivolous things like paint, huh? My mom thought sunset peach would be a great color for the living room and hated it the second it went on the walls, but they've been that color since I was in middle school. After a while you stop seeing it, don'tcha?"

"I'm not sure canary yellow is ever something you can get used to, but I'll take your word for it on the sunset peach."

It's embarrassing to realize I've done that before—had a room painted only to change my mind once it was finished and then had it repainted right away. Maybe that's part of the reason why I haven't been able to secure a job or even an interview today, because I look too much like the people they're talking about.

Chloe glances over Aaron's shoulder at me. "Sorry to keep you waiting, miss. You get the information you need?"

"I sure did!"

At the sound of my voice Aaron's shoulders tense, which makes the muscles under his shirt flex. I'd be able to appreciate the view a heck of a lot more if the reaction I incited weren't a full-body cringe.

I fight the urge to shrink like a wilted flower. I used to do that when I was younger. One of the things I've learned to do when I feel insecure is to smile brighter and stand up straighter. Never let anyone see your weaknesses. It's okay to have them, as long as no one knows what they are; otherwise they can use them against you. Like Troy did. And Portia, and to some extent my younger brother, Bradley.

"Great. Just give me a minute, and I'll help get you set up," Chloe says.

"No rush, thanks."

"For sure." She rounds the counter. "I'll be right back with that primer, Aaron."

"Sure thing," Aaron says with a smile.

Chloe skirts around the counter and walks toward the back of the store, leaving us alone at the paint desk.

I take a step forward until I'm standing next to Aaron. The hairs on his arm rise, and he tucks his thumbs into the pockets of his jeans. I nudge him with my elbow. "Hi, Aaron, fancy meeting you here."

He slowly, oh so slowly looks my way. His expression is remote. He blinks once, twice.

"Teagan, Van's sister."

"Yeah. I remember." His gaze moves over me, another slow sweep. But it's not the kind I associate with someone checking me out or appreciating my excellent fashion sense; it's more the kind someone gives you when they wish you would disappear. "What're you doing here?"

"Getting some paint for the loft so I can start decorating it."

"Why would you be doing that if you're only here for the weekend?"

"To give it some personality." He doesn't need to know about my plan to move here. Which won't happen if I can't get a job.

He glances at the paint swatches and the patterned wallpaper samples. His eyebrow lifts. "Bold choices. Might want to consider picking up some primer in case you have regrets."

"Thanks, but I know what I'm doing."

"You don't look like a professional painter."

I wave a hand around. "Not the painting part, but how hard can it be? It's just rolling paint on walls. I mean the decorating stuff." I was responsible for decorating my dad's house when we moved in, mostly because we couldn't afford an interior designer and a lot of our furniture was too big for the space. We had to sell it and buy new stuff. That was the fun part. Not the selling—that sucked—but the picking stuff that fit the space and a budget.

Aaron glances at my outfit and then back at the paint and wallpaper samples. "I guess we'll see how that works out, won't we?"

"Does that mean you're coming back to put up the light fixtures?" I should not be excited about the prospect, especially with his aloof, surly demeanor, but he sure is nice to look at.

"And the trim, yeah, eventually. Don't worry, I won't interrupt your weekend getaway with all the noise."

"The floors look great. Sorry for making you almost saw off your foot. And thanks for setting up my bed for me. I really appreciate that."

"Can't imagine you've spent much time sleeping on an air mattress. Figured you wouldn't want to start now."

I can't tell if he's being sarcastic or mean or considerate. Probably not the last one.

A woman who looks to be a few years older than me, dressed in worn jean shorts, a white tank, and a plaid shirt tied at the waist, makes a bee-line for Aaron. "A-A. How are you? I haven't seen you in a hot minute." She throws her arms around him, and he gives her a one-armed hug.

"Hey, Tawny. What you been up to? Keeping out of trouble?"

"Absolutely not. What would be the fun in that?" She winks, and he chuckles.

"Up to no good, then?"

"Always. You coming to the beach party next weekend?"

"Depends. You goin'?" He gives her a lopsided grin.

Tawny, who looks vaguely familiar, gives him a playful swat. "Don't you dare use that smile on me, Aaron Leonard Saunders."

"Hey, hey, shhh. Just because you know my middle name doesn't mean I want the rest of the world to."

"Just keeping your head from getting too big for you to fit through doors." She looks my way. I've retreated a few steps from the counter so as not to appear as though I'm either part of the conversation or eavesdropping on it.

She tips her head, and her gaze moves over me, flicking back to Aaron with a smirk that verges on judgmental. "This one of your side projects from the other side of the lake?"

He gives her a disapproving look. "That's not my scene anymore, and she's Van's sister."

I feel like there's an inside story to this that I'm missing.

"Van's sister? Oh, hey! I'm Tawny, I'm tight with Dillion."

"Teagan." I extend a hand and smile brightly.

I could use friends in town, and Tawny seems . . . approachable if nothing else. And very local with her fresh, makeup-free face, casual wear, and Blundstone boots. I'm beginning to see my version of casual and everyone else's may not be the same.

"Oh! We have met. I think maybe over the winter holidays? Van had a New Year's party, and you were there?"

"Oh yes! I don't know if I remember much of that party, though, since there were a lot of martinis."

"Tell me about it. I was drinking vodka cran, light on cran, so that night is pretty much a blur. Dillion and I have been friends forever. Went to high school together. Are you staying with them?"

"I am."

"We girls go to the bar on Wednesday nights for twenty-dollar bottles of wine. It's a step up from drinking vinegar, but it's fun; you should come out if you're around."

"That would be great. If I'm ever around on a Wednesday."

"Awesome." She pulls me in for a quick hug. She turns to Aaron. "I'm sure I'll see you around."

"Hopefully in my dreams."

She looks to me and rolls her eyes. "Man is a relentless flirt. Thank the Lord I'm smart enough not to drink his Kool-Aid." And she's off, shouting hello at someone else two aisles down.

I don't have a chance to say anything else to Aaron because Chloe comes back with his pails of primer on a rolling cart. "I'd ask if you need the cart, but I know you better than that."

"Just means I can get away with one less set of bicep curls." He swipes his credit card, pays for the paint, and grabs one handle in each of his huge, baseball-mitt hands. When he lifts them, the muscles in his arms bulge and the veins pop. They remind me of snaking tree roots with how thick they are.

"Good luck with the paint job." He barely glances in my direction before he's heading toward the front of the store, leaving me staring at his annoyingly perfect butt wrapped in worn denim.

Chloe helps me with the paint; she's far more knowledgeable than I'd expect a high schooler to be, but I find out she's been painting houses as a summer job for the past two years, and she works at Harry's in the morning and takes classes in the afternoon so she can save money for college.

Once my paint and wallpaper supplies are taken care of—she must ask ten times if I'm sure I want the yellow—I head over to lighting and pick out the fixtures. I'll need furniture and kitchen supplies eventually, but this is a solid start.

As I'm waiting my turn in line to check out, I notice the **HELP WANTED** sign posted near the customer service desk. The guy working the cash register looks to be in his seventies, or maybe a bit older based on the way his eyes crinkle in the corners when he smiles.

"Do you know what position they're hiring for?" I ask as I hand over my credit card.

I've been living rent-free all my life, so I should have lots of money saved up, but the reality is I used to spend my paychecks as soon as they hit my account. It wasn't until we had to move that I recognized the lifestyle I'd been living wasn't one I could afford—I was on my way to digging the same hole my father dug for himself.

I took a course on money management, and over the past six months I've been able to squirrel away a decent chunk of change, but I'm going to need a job if I don't want it all to disappear.

The man, whose name tag reads *Chuck*, pushes his glasses up his nose. "Oh, yes ma'am, I surely do. I'm retiring, and they need someone to take my shift. I betcha they'd love to have a pretty face like yours helping out round here."

I smile and thank him, pushing down the insecurities that I'm used to—that people expect me to be just a pretty face. An empty vessel that's nice to look at but can't contribute much to society apart from being pleasing to the eye. And I don't feel like I've done a great job of proving those people wrong so far.

Once I've paid, I take my purchases out to my car, load it all into the trunk, and return the cart. I stand outside the store entrance, debating whether or not I should apply for the position. I'm friendly and can work a cash register. It's worth a shot.

I wish I were dressed more appropriately—say, in a pair of jeans and some kind of plaid or a T-shirt—but I'm not backing down now.

There's a woman around my dad's age standing behind the customer service desk. She turns to address me. "Welcome to Harry's, how can I help you today?"

I point at the **HELP WANTED** sign. "I'd like to apply for the position if it's still available."

She glances up at the sign, then back at me, her expression curious. "Do you happen to have a résumé with you?"

"I sure do." I pull one from my purse and pass it over.

She takes the résumé and scans the front page. Her name badge reads *Noreen S., Assistant Manager.* "Personal assistant to the CFO of Smith Financial? A bachelor's in business administration?" She glances up at me. "You're a little overqualified for a position as a cashier, Teagan Firestone, is it? Would you happen to be related to Van?"

"He's my older brother. I'm hoping to move to Pearl Lake, and I feel that I'd make a great addition to your team. I'm great with people, organized, and I'm very reliable."

She gives me a small, somewhat uncertain smile. "You know, they'd probably love someone like you over at Bernie's."

"Bernie's?" I tip my head.

"The town lawyer. He's been complaining about not having enough help lately."

"I'll keep that in mind, then. I'd still really like the opportunity to work here, though." And I don't know if I can handle another rejection.

She regards me for a few long seconds. "The position is only for one shift a week right now."

"That's fine with me. When can I start?" I cross my fingers and hope like hell this is me getting a job.

The phone rings. "Just hold on a moment." She takes the call, turning her back to me while she has a low, whispered conversation. She hangs up a minute later and turns to me with a smile on her face. "It looks like you're in luck. One of our employees called in sick for her afternoon shift. Can you start now?"

"I absolutely can."

"Why don't you fill out the paperwork, and we'll get you a shirt and I'll show you around the store."

"That sounds great."

She extends her hand over the counter. "I'm Noreen Saunders. Welcome to the team, Teagan."

"Saunders? Does that mean you're related to Aaron? He works for Footprint Construction with my brother's fiancée, Dillion."

"Yup, sure am. I'm his mother."

"Oh, wow. Well, it's nice to meet you, Noreen." The six-degrees-of-separation thing is strong in this town.

CHAPTER 4

MAKING MY OWN WAY

Teagan

As it turns out, the person whose shift I'm working this afternoon happens to work at the paint counter. Chloe gives me the rundown and shows me where to find the contractor accounts and the discount codes before she leaves.

It's not busy, so I spend my time reorganizing the color display, putting this year's most popular colors in their own section before I line up paint chips and wallpaper combinations. My shift is over before I know it, and Noreen, who has come to check on me periodically during the day, stops by to see how things are going.

"Oh, wow." She motions to the wall display. "Did you do all this?"

I worry I've overstepped. "I can put it back the way it was if you don't like it. It got slow there for a while, and I wanted to stay busy."

"Oh no, don't do that. It looks great. Harry keeps talking about getting a professional display organizer to come in, but it's expensive," Noreen says and gives me a warm, reassuring smile. "And now I guess he doesn't have to worry about the expense anymore."

"Harry is the owner?" I ask.

"Yup. He's Harry Junior and took over this place from his dad. I think he'll be real happy with this, Teagan."

"I hope so." I know what an interior decorator costs, so I'm sure a display organizer doesn't do too badly. I'd never considered that it could be someone's job, but I can see how setting up something that's visually appealing can help sales.

"I'm sure he'll want you to do the same thing for our other departments," Noreen says.

"You think so?"

"Oh, definitely. Would you be able to come back in on Wednesday? There's a nine-to-five shift open?"

"That sounds perfect."

Noreen smiles. "I think you're going to be great for Harry's."

I arrive back at Van and Dillion's place in time to help with dinner.

"I can't believe you already have a job." Van sets a cob of corn on a piece of foil, adds a dollop of butter, and wraps it up.

"I'm not surprised at all." Dillion tosses a handful of chopped tomatoes into the salad. "And if you're interested, I can always use help. We're heading into the busy season."

"Thanks, I appreciate the offer." But I'd like to try to get jobs on my own merit and not have them handed to me. "I wasn't sure anyone was going to hire me. I should have changed my address on my résumé." I explain what happened at the first few places I stopped.

Dillion gives me a sympathetic look. "The town can be pretty covetous when it comes to keeping the people who live here employed. They like to give the summer jobs to the kids who go away to college, sort of incentive to keep them coming back, you know?"

"That makes sense. I didn't understand how big the divide was until today." But now that I think about it, I can see why the woman at town hall was so brusque with me. "Oh, and I saw your friend Tawny at the hardware store when I was picking up paint."

Dillion stops chopping peppers. "Oh? I hope she was nice to you."

"She made a comment to Aaron asking if I was a project from the other side of the lake."

"Oh my God! She did not!" Dillion slaps her hand over her mouth. "I'm so sorry."

"He told her I was Van's sister, and she was super nice after that. Invited me out for drinks with you if I'm ever around on a Wednesday."

"Ahhh. Okay. That's good. Tawny isn't a fan of the McMansion ladies."

"I gathered as much. Aaron said something about not being like that anymore. Do you know what that's all about?" I don't know why I care so much about the negative way he seems to react to me, but maybe this has something to do with it.

"Aaron has a reputation for keeping the women on the other side of the lake entertained between the sheets."

"Oh. Is that a bad thing?"

"Not if you're one of the women from the other side of the lake, or at least those are the rumors. I don't know how much of that is true and how much isn't. But there are stories floating around. We joke about him mowing lawns, and we're not referring to their grass, if you know what I mean." Dillion rolls her eyes.

"Huh. Well, that's . . . something."

"Don't be feeding Teagan the town gossip when you don't know if any of it is actually true." Van points a pair of barbecue tongs at Dillion as he grabs the steaks from the fridge.

"He doesn't refute it," Dillion replies with a shrug.

"But does he confirm it? Think about that." Van pushes out the front door, leaving me with more questions than answers about Aaron.

After dinner I leave Dillion and Van and go up to the apartment. They told me at least six times I didn't need to go, but I faked a few yawns and told them I was tired. I'm not, but I want to watch a few DIY painting and wallpapering videos.

My mind is churning. Now that I have this new job, even if it's only part-time, my plan to quit my job in Chicago is that much more real. And I've already said yes to working on Wednesday, so no matter what, I'm committed to being in Pearl Lake.

I don't want to upset my dad, but it's not like this is the first time I've talked about wanting to try something different. I take my mind off the problem I'm going to have to tackle come the end of the weekend by watching a few video tutorials, which turns into two hours of videos, and then, because I don't want to go back to worrying, I grab an energy drink from the fridge and start the arduous and time-consuming job of taping the walls so I can paint them without being concerned about going outside the lines and having to do a million touch-ups.

Of course, once I start something, I'm compelled to finish it, so I lay down several drop cloths, change into a shirt and shorts I don't mind getting dirty, grab the ladder that Aaron left here, and get out the paint supplies.

By the time I'm finished painting two walls a deep, mustardy yellow and I've tidied up after myself—I use the kitchen sink to clean the brushes and rollers—it's closing in on three in the morning. I quickly rinse off in the shower, amazed at how much paint I'm wearing, take my medication, and try to wind down enough that I can go to bed.

I opened all the windows while I was painting even though the stuff I bought says it's low odor. It's chilly with the night breeze blowing through, but at least the paint smell isn't too overwhelming. I wrap myself in a blanket and scroll through Pinterest, looking at the images I've pinned, gathering new ideas for the rest of my space. I'm excited to put up the wallpaper tomorrow and start decorating. And as nervous as I am about telling my dad I'm quitting my job at Smith Financial, I feel good about taking the time to figure out exactly what I want to do with the rest of my life.

I don't wake up until nine, which is late for me. I make the trek to my brother's cottage—which I should probably stop referring to as a *cottage*, since he lives here now—and make myself a coffee.

Travel mug in hand, I head back up to the apartment so I can get started on the wallpaper. The yellow walls look great so far, but I know they're really going to pop once I have the wallpaper on the back wall. I can already imagine where I'm going to put all the furniture and how I'm going to arrange the room so it's cozy and visually appealing.

While I get everything out, I review the wallpaper-DIY video I found last night to make sure I have everything set up properly. I put on some music and start hanging paper. It would be a lot easier with a second set of hands, but it's only one wall, and thankfully everything is straight lines and it's a fairly easy-to-match pattern.

By noon the wallpaper is up. I'm a sticky, gross mess, but the room looks amazing, and that's without any furniture.

I hop into the shower, wash all the glue from my skin, and scrub off any remaining paint from yesterday. I make myself another coffee—this time I try the instant stuff that Aaron must have left here. I must use way too much because it tastes awful, but it's caffeine.

While I cringe-gag-sip my coffee, I make a list of things I'm going to need to avoid always having to use my brother's stuff. I tap my lip and stare at my bed, which I made as soon as my feet hit the floor. There's nothing I dislike more than getting into an unmade bed at night.

The frame is familiar, and it takes me a moment to place why. It's the bed from the spare bedroom, the one that Van and Dillion have taken as theirs. It's smaller than Grammy Bee's room, but he's yet to redecorate that one. He and Grammy Bee were close, and losing her was a lot like losing another parent for him. I wasn't as close to her as he was, and the memories I have of her from my childhood are foggy at best. Indistinct, like an unfocused photograph.

I remember when I slept in that spare bedroom as a little girl, the sounds of wildlife and the tree branches scraping the side of the cottage always scared me. They made it impossible to sleep. Eventually I made excuses to stop coming along, saying I didn't want to be away from Dad. It wasn't entirely untrue. I didn't want to leave my dad alone, but more than that, I didn't want to spend all those hours in that room, staring up at the ceiling, unable to sleep because everything was different and somehow scary.

I shake my head, pushing away the memories, not wanting to think about things that upset me. Which is when I remember that the spare bedroom in the cottage has been completely renovated, and that Van and Dillion bought a brand-new bedroom set. And that means the contents of that bedroom were probably moved to the garage, likely with the thought that some of the furniture would get used up here.

I slip my feet back into my flip-flops and use the inside staircase to check out the contents of the garage.

"Jackpot!" I prop my fists on my hips and grin as I take in the neatly stacked and labeled bins. There are sets of dishes, old pots and pans, and a small kitchen table that's beat up, but a fresh coat of paint and it will work perfectly in the space I have. There's a night table and a dresser and an old mirror that would look great together.

There are all sorts of other amazing treasures that Grammy Bee never got rid of, and Van obviously saw the value in holding on to them, even if only for sentimental reasons. It's looking more and more like I won't have to bring nearly as much stuff back from Chicago as I thought. Some of the pieces I'll have to refinish, but it's a great starting point.

I bring up a few boxes of essentials and get to work washing dishes so I at least have those. I find a small coffee press and old Tupperware that probably dates back to the seventies but is still in good condition.

It's already two in the afternoon by the time I get everything put away. I still want to head to town and stop at the law office so I can drop off a résumé there—I printed new ones with an updated address. But first I need to buy a few groceries so I have more than instant coffee and energy drinks. I love caffeine, but I need other beverage options, and I don't want to drink Aaron's root beer and make him like me any less than he already does.

I create a new grocery list and make sure my outfit is Pearl Lake casual before I leave. I don't have a ton of clothes with me, but I do have a pair of worn jeans and a plain black shirt. My running shoes are metallic pink, but they're the only ones I brought, so they'll have to do.

I drive into town, not even caring that the dirt road is kicking up all kinds of dust and making my black car dirty. I'm in a great mood as I park in a public lot across from the Town Pub. I check my reflection, resist the urge to apply a coat of lipstick—locals don't seem to wear it here—grab my purse, and hop out of my car. I cross the street and notice a piece of paper taped to the inside of the window that reads **BARTENDER NEEDED**.

I can't tell if it's a new or old sign because the windows need a serious wash, but it doesn't hurt to check it out. I know how to make a mean martini, a margarita to die for, and a delicious manhattan. I'm also a self-proclaimed wine aficionado. I'm pretty much an ideal candidate for the job.

I roll my shoulders back and hold my head high as I push through the doors. The first thing I smell is beer. The second is fried food. The third is some kind of cleaner. The interior is dark and the tables are wood, the booths and seats all stained mahogany. It reminds me of an old English pub, which is fitting.

Surprisingly, a good number of tables are occupied this early on a Friday afternoon. Older couples sit in the booths, and several men of various ages occupy the stools, a few sitting next to each other, watching a game on the TV above the bar, sipping pints or bottles of beer.

A man stands behind the bar, a dish towel thrown over his shoulder, pouring pint after pint. There's one server on the floor, loading up her tray and stopping at each table to chat and deliver drinks.

I step up to the bar and wait.

"What can I get for you?" he asks as he sets a beer in front of the man beside me. He smells like metal and cigarette smoke. Not the bartender but the man sitting at the bar.

"Is the bartending position still available?" I ask and then smile brightly.

The bartender arches a brow. "What kind of experience do you have?"

"I brought my résumé if you'd like to see it." I reach into my purse, but he holds up his hand.

"I don't need to see a résumé. Have you ever tended bar before?"

"I'll take another pint, Louis." The guy down the other end of the bar holds up his nearly empty pint glass.

"On it," Louis says.

He moves down to the taps, and I move with him, standing on the other side of the three men lining the bar.

"Can you pour a pint?" he asks.

"Absolutely." I nod vigorously and watch as he tips the glass and pulls the lever, beer pouring out in a golden stream. When it's three-quarters of the way full, he straightens the glass and about half an inch of foam appears, rising to the rim. He delivers it to the customer.

He turns away from me, and for a moment I think I'm being dismissed without so much as *thanks, but no thanks.*

At least until he tosses an apron over the bar when he turns back to me. "Let's see what you got."

"You mean you want me to start now?"

"The afternoon rush is about to start. Consider this your interview."

"Right. Okay." I tie the apron around my waist. "Should I come back there?"

"That's generally the best way to tend bar."

I blow out a breath, muttering, "You can do this. You can serve drinks."

"You can leave your purse there." He motions to a space under the bar. "And you can't wear your hair down." He tosses me an elastic band. The kind you'd find wrapped around a bunch of broccoli.

"I have a hair tie." I rummage around in my bag until I find one and pull my hair into a ponytail, then tuck my purse under the bar.

"I'm Teagan." I hold out my hand.

He gives it one short pump. "Louis. I'll give you a rundown, try to keep up."

He tells me which beer is at each tap, and I do mnemonics to remember what a lager, pale ale, IPA, red ale, wheat beer, and dark ale are. There are only two kinds of wine: red and white. They're both table wines, which I assume means they're cheap and probably not very good. I keep that thought to myself, though.

A pair of men come in and take two seats at the bar. It's just after three thirty in the afternoon.

"You're up. The guy on the left is Mike, and the one on the right is Jerry. They work at the ice cream factory in the next town over. Mike drinks the pale ale, and Jerry drinks the wheat beer. Ask them if they want the special. They usually do."

"Okay. Should I ask them what they want to drink first or—" His arched brow tells me everything I need to know. "I'll pour the beers."

I do exactly what Louis did, tipping the glass so it's at an angle. It's unnerving to have Louis watching me like a hawk while I pour the pale ale first and then the wheat beer. The pale ale has slightly less foam than his and the wheat beer a little more. I don't think I do a bad job, and Louis doesn't comment either way.

Thankfully they're slightly different colors. The pale ale looks like normal pee, and the wheat beer looks like the morning pee after too many drinks and not enough water, possibly of someone suffering from a UTI.

I bring them their beers, thankful when I give the right one to the right man. "I'm Teagan, I'm helping out Louis today. Would either of you be interested in today's special?"

"Sure would, darlin'," Jerry says with a smile. His front tooth is gray.

"Same here. And it's about time Louis hired someone with a nicer mug than his." Mike lifts his beer in my direction and drains half the pint in three long swallows. The foam coats his mustache, and he uses the sleeve of his jacket to wipe it away. "Might as well pour me another one, the first never lasts long."

"Of course, I'll be right back." I meet Louis at the tap. "They both want the special, and Mike wants another pint."

"Pour the pint first, then I'll show you how to put the order in."

I do as Louis says, and he takes me over to the computer. He swipes his card and taps the buttons faster than I can follow. Today's special is the burger. It comes with fries or, for an upcharge, a side salad, onion rings, or waffle fries.

He goes back to the beginning and makes me key everything in on separate orders. I'm very glad I have a decent memory, otherwise this would be a lot more overwhelming.

I spend the next several hours pouring beers, serving wine that smells like it's halfway to vinegar, and placing food orders—mostly people get the special. I mess up a few times along the way, but the customers seem to like me, and when I tell them I'm Van's sister, it wins me some more points.

At seven thirty things start to wind down, the dinner rush long over. I notice that some of the men who were here when I first came in are still sitting at the bar, nursing pints. I want to ask Louis if they're safe to drive, but I don't want to stir up any trouble.

As if he can hear my thoughts, he steps up beside me. "Bob doesn't drive. He lives in one of the apartments above the pub."

I glance up at Louis. I want to ask how often Bob is here and if he always sits at the bar all day long, drinking beers, eating the free peanuts and nothing else as I wipe down the outside of the freshly washed pint glasses and set them in the freezer so they're frosted when I pour a fresh pint. Apart from the Guinness. That's the only beer that gets an unfrosted glass.

"He was a POW in Kuwait." Again, he answers the questions I don't have the courage to ask.

I fumble the glass and he catches it, setting it in the freezer. "Where's his family?"

"Right here." Louis motions to the bar. He pats me on the shoulder. "You're new here. It takes some time to figure it all out."

I nod, although I feel like he's saying a lot more than his words imply.

Five minutes later a man settles on the stool at the end of the bar. The spot has been empty all day. I glance over and my breath catches. Even with the brim of his ball cap covering half of his face, I've come to recognize that set of shoulders. Which should be concerning since I've only seen them a few times. But Aaron Saunders has a presence. Something about him makes the room buzz with new energy. Women sitting at booths cross and uncross their legs. They sip their drinks and whisper to each other.

He touches the brim of his ball cap and says something to the two older ladies who sat down at the bar and shared a special while nursing bottled beers. They do what every woman who seems to be given his positive attention does: giggle like schoolgirls and touch their hair. They throw their heads back and laugh, and he smiles in return, lighting up the entire bar. Based on what I've witnessed so far, Aaron Saunders is a shameless flirt, and the women around here eat it up. They chat for a minute or two, at least until Aaron's phone screen flashes, and his attention shifts to the incoming message.

The women go back to sharing the remains of their cold fries, still stealing starry-eyed glances at Aaron. I find it a little annoying. Especially since he's been anything but flirty with me.

I take a deep breath and make my way down the bar. His phone is in his hands, the corners of his mouth pulled down in a frown. At my approach he sets the device facedown on the bar and lifts his head. His mouth opens and closes, that frown deepening and a furrow appearing between his brows. *Here we go.* I steel myself, ready for his prickly demeanor.

"What the hell are you doing here?" he barks.

Mike and Jerry, who are still sitting at the bar several stools down, food long eaten, beers replaced with coffee, both glance our way.

I smile brightly, not wanting him to see how his sharp tone affects me. "I work here."

"Since when?" His furrow turns into something between shock and annoyance.

"Since today."

"I thought you were here for the weekend."

"Plans change." And mine have changed a lot in forty-eight hours. "What can I get you, Aaron?"

He blinks a couple of times and blows out a breath. "I'll wait for Louis."

I lift one shoulder and let it fall, as if his snub doesn't mean a thing to me. But it drives me bonkers that he has clear disdain for me for no reason I can see. I shouldn't care, and yet it feels a lot like a challenge I want to take on to get him to change his tune. I saunter down the bar, checking on customers, making sure drinks are topped up or bills are handed over and change is made as I go. It's a full five minutes before I reach the other end of the bar, where Louis is.

"Aaron want his usual?"

"I'm not sure. He said he'd wait for you."

Louis raises a single eyebrow. It seems to be his thing. "Do you know how to make a root beer float?"

"Isn't it root beer and vanilla ice cream?"

"Yup, but he likes his topped with whipped cream and a cherry."

I glance over my shoulder to the end of the bar, where Aaron is once again chatting up the two older women, and then back at Louis. "You're kidding, right?"

"Nope. Think you can handle it?"

"It shouldn't be a problem." Ice cream and soda should not be something I can mess up.

"Then go for it. And put in an order for the special, but he likes Caesar salad instead of fries, and one onion ring on his burger. And you don't need to bring him the ketchup and mustard; he takes barbecue sauce instead."

I repeat the order back to him to make sure I got everything, then key it into the system and get to work making the root beer float. I fill a float glass two-thirds of the way with root beer before I disappear into the kitchen.

There's a teenage boy-man working on salads, listening to music. It sounds more like someone is beating the instruments in a tuneless, angry battle and stabbing the singer with pins, but to each his own. He bobs his head to the maniacal beat. When it looks like he's about to break into a drum solo, I interrupt.

"Hi."

He nearly drops the metal bowl full of romaine lettuce, dressing, and imitation bacon bits. He spins around, eyes wide. They skim over me, stopping at my feet for a second before rising back to my face. His cheeks explode with color. "Hi. Uh, who are you?"

"I'm Teagan. I just started working the bar today. Actually, I'm in the middle of my interview. And now I'm supposed to make a root beer float for Aaron Saunders. Do you know him?"

He nods twice. "Sure do."

"Is he particular about his root beer float?"

"He sure is."

"Wanna help a girl out so my interview goes well?" I tip my head to the side and smile.

"Yeah. For sure. I'm more than happy to help. I'm Tanner Freelton." He wipes his hand on his white shirt and holds it out.

I take it, noting his palms are damp, probably because it's hot back here. "We have the same initials. Teagan Firestone."

"Firestone? Are you related to Van? Dillion Stitch's boyfriend?"

"He's her fiancé. They got engaged a while back." I wonder how long it's going to take for me to get used to the way everyone knows everyone else around here. "And I'm Van's sister."

"Right. Yeah. I knew that. That's super cool. I mean, it's cool that you're Van's sister. And that they're engaged or whatever. My older sister is friends with Dillion. Allie. Anyway, let me help you with the root beer float."

"Great. Thanks."

I pass him the glass, and he pours some of the root beer into the sink. "It's gonna foam a lot, so you don't want it to get too messy. It's kind of a science. And I don't use the vanilla ice cream."

"You don't?"

"Nope. I use the caramel-ribbon swirl. Always two scoops." He steps inside the walk-in freezer and returns with a giant container of ice cream. Then he shows me how big the scoops should be and allows me to carefully drop the first one in, then instructs me to set the second one on top, pushing the foam closer to the top of the glass, but it never overflows.

"Nice work," he says. "Now for the whipped cream and the cherry."

I top it with a generous swirl of whipped cream, add a straw, and place a single cherry in the center.

I thank him and return to the bar, placing the float in front of Aaron. He frowns at it. "Did you make this?"

I shake my head.

He narrows his eyes at me.

"I put the order in."

His eyes are still locked on mine as he lowers his lips to the straw and takes a deep haul. His brow furrows, and he makes a face that looks like he's in pain. "Ahhh," he groans and presses his fingers against his temples. It takes me a moment to realize he's given himself brain freeze.

"How is it?"

"It's fine," he grits through clenched teeth, still holding his head.

"Great." I give him one of my bright smiles and move on to the next customer.

A few minutes later I bring the barbecue sauce and silverware over and set them on the bar in front of Aaron, who has managed to polish off his float.

"So it was just fine, then?"

"I was thirsty."

"Do you want another one?"

He purses his lips and looks at the empty glass and then at me. "Yeah," he says on a sigh.

I want to know what it is about me that he finds so irritating. I try to take the glass, but he covers my hand with his. I can't tell if it's the temperature of the glass or the unexpected contact, but it sends a shiver down my spine.

"I'm not finished with it yet. Can I get a spoon for the rest of the ice cream? One of those ones they use for sundaes."

"Sure."

I grab him a spoon, then get to work making another root beer float. This time I don't need Tanner's help.

And this time, when I set it in front of Aaron, he gives me a small, reluctant smile and mutters a barely audible thank-you.

At the end of the night, I help Louis clean the bar—it is not an enjoyable part of the job—and put all the chairs up on the tables.

"So?" I grab my purse from under the bar once everything is done. "What's the verdict?"

"Huh?" Louis asks as he counts out the dollar bills that filled the tip jar.

"Did I pass the test? Do I get the job?" I sure hope so, since I've spent the last nine hours on my feet, serving a lot of stinky beer to a lot of people. And I need to have a discussion with Louis about the wine selection. I had a sip of the red, out of curiosity. I would rather drink an entire bottle of vinegar than try to consume a glass of that stuff.

"Oh. Yeah. Absolutely. You passed with flying colors. You okay with working Thursdays? It's just as busy as it was tonight. I have a couple of people for the weekends, but I could use another set of hands on payday, and customers love you, so yeah, if you're available, you're hired."

"I'm totally available."

"Fantastic. I'll send you home with some paperwork. You get standard server wage plus tips. And did I hear right, you're Van Firestone's sister?"

"I am."

He regards me thoughtfully for a moment. "You mind me asking you a personal question?"

I shrug. "Sure."

"You, uh, don't really look like you need a job tending bar."

"That's more of an observation, not a question," I point out.

"Hmm. You're right. Do you need the job?"

I smile. "I want the job." It's the easiest and most truthful answer. I want to figure out who I am and what I like, and the best way to do that is to try a bunch of new things.

"Fair enough." He pushes a stack of bills toward me. "That's your share for tonight. See you next Thursday."

"See you next Thursday." I head for the door. "And Louis."

"Yeah?"

"Thanks for taking a chance on me."

CHAPTER 5
NEW BEGINNINGS

Teagan

I head back to Chicago on Sunday afternoon. I didn't sleep well last night thanks to my nerves, but with two new jobs secured in Pearl Lake, the move makes sense. I need this. I need to take control of my life and start doing things for me instead of everyone else. This is the mental pep talk I give myself all the way home.

Danielle's red Camry is parked beside my dad's matching white one. I back the ancient truck into the driveway—Van gave me a lesson before I left this afternoon—and park in front of my dad's car.

I don't leave the truck right away. Instead I take a few calming breaths, not that it's particularly effective, considering I stopped and picked up an energy drink on my way here and there are only one or two sips left.

I glance at my purse, debating whether I should go ahead and take one of my antianxiety pills before I go inside and talk to my dad. This move is kind of a major life decision. I give in and grab my purse, find the bottle in the bottom, and pop one of the tiny pills into my mouth.

I give myself a few more minutes to collect myself before I get out of the truck.

When I open the front door, I immediately notice the significant change in decor. Much of the furniture we bought when we moved has been replaced with Danielle's things. It's like walking into a completely different house.

And it makes it that much easier for me to take this next step.

I find my dad and Danielle sitting on a pair of loungers in the backyard, drinking lemonade. I stand at the sliding glass door, watching them for a minute. They look happy and comfortable. And I want him to have that. Happiness and companionship. He deserves it after all these years of loneliness.

I know he blamed himself for my mother's death for a long time, thinking that it was his fault she died on the operating table. That he was the one who pushed her into getting the nips and tucks. But it was her body and ultimately her decision. He loved her with his whole heart, and he never would have wanted her to do something she wasn't comfortable with. At least that's what I choose to believe, despite the fact that it hasn't ever been a conversation we've had in all the years she's been gone.

I'm also her spitting image.

I can't imagine how hard it would be to look at your child and see the wife you lost reflected in her face every single day.

I open the sliding glass door. "Hey, Dad, hey, Danielle, the house looks great! Did you get moved in okay, then?"

"Oh! Hello, Teagan! I was hoping you'd like the changes." Danielle grins nervously and looks to my dad for reassurance.

He squeezes her hand and gives her an it'll-be-fine smile.

I make small talk with them, telling them all about the weekend, trying to figure out how exactly to approach the subject with Danielle sitting there. She makes it easy for me when she announces that she's going to start dinner. And she absolves me of having to offer to help by offering me her chair and making us both a drink so we can have some dad-and-daughter time.

I decline the drink, and my dad holds up his half-full glass and tells her he's fine too.

I wait until the sliding door is closed before I reach over and squeeze his hand. "I'm so glad you two found each other."

"Me too, honey. And I'm so glad you and Danielle get along. I know it's going to be a bit of an adjustment, but it means the world to me that you're trying. I was worried when you decided to take the weekend away that you were upset."

"I'm not upset at all, Dad. You've spent a lot of years alone, and more than anything I want to see you happy, and now you are."

"I really am. Danielle is a good partner. Grounded. Caring. I think your mother would have liked her."

My heart clenches. It makes me sad that he's in his midfifties and still seeking atonement in the form of approval. I hope I'm not like that by the time I'm in my fifties. "Me too, Dad. She would want you to be happy, just like I do."

"I think so too." He gives me a smile that's tinged with sadness.

"I need to talk to you about something." And I need to do it before Danielle comes back.

"Is it about the new living room decor? I know it's different, and you went to all the trouble to make it look perfect—"

"It's not about the living room, Dad. And I honestly think it looks great." I give his hand another squeeze. "I did some thinking over the weekend about what I want for my future and yours, and I've decided I'm going to quit my job at Smith Financial and move up to Pearl Lake for a while."

The smile fades from his face. "I thought you liked Danielle."

"I do, Dad. This isn't about Danielle." I sigh. "Well, it's partly about Danielle, but not in the way you think. I'm twenty-six. I need to move out and learn how to be an independent, self-sufficient adult. And you and Danielle need time to grow as a couple, without another adult in the mix."

"You don't need to move to Pearl Lake to do that, though, or quit your job. We can find you an apartment in the city."

This is the hard part. "I don't want to live in the city, Dad. I want to live in Pearl Lake. Maybe not forever, but at least for a while. I need to figure out my own life. I took the job at Smith Financial because it meant I could be close to my family, and I felt like I needed to be there for you. You seemed so set on me working there, and I didn't want to say no. But I'll be honest: I don't love the job. I don't even know what I love, and I need some time to learn what that is."

"I didn't realize you felt that way. I wouldn't have pushed you to stay on if I'd known." He looks so crestfallen, and part of me wants to backtrack, but I know it's pointless. The truth is already out, and I can't take it back.

"I know that. And it's my fault for not speaking up earlier. And to be honest, I didn't know what I wanted to do. It's not just about the job, though, it's everything else too. As big of a city as Chicago is, there are memories attached to it that I can't escape. Troy is one of those. A lot has changed recently, and I want a fresh start. Van said I can move into the apartment above the garage."

"What will you do while you're out there?" Dad asks.

I shrug. "I've already got two part-time jobs lined up, so it's a good start. I want to try out different things, find out what I'm passionate about, and see if I can find something that's the right fit for me. But obviously I'll give my two weeks' notice, and I can commute back and forth until you find a suitable replacement for me."

"You've already lined up two jobs? How long have you been thinking about this?" He seems shocked.

I don't want to hurt his feelings, but I also don't want to lie. "For a while, but I made the decision this weekend. And I want to reassure you that Danielle moving in isn't the reason I want to make this change, but it is what pushed me to take action. And it's not because I don't like her. It's because I do, and because you have someone in your life who cares about you and is going to stand by your side. And I think I'm ready to go ahead and stand on my own."

"You always put yourself last, don't you, Teagan?"

"I'm trying to learn how to put myself first. At least once in a while."

◆ ◆ ◆

After dinner I pack up my room. I have a lot of clothes. Most of which are not Pearl Lake appropriate. I fill three bags with the outfits that won't be too over the top for small-town living—I'll enlist Dillion's help to vet it all—and box up anything else I think I might need.

Dad tells me I can work remotely to tie up loose ends and that HR has already managed to line up half a dozen interviews within an hour of the job posting. I'm both relieved and a little disheartened by how easy it is to replace me, but I know it's for the best.

In the morning I load up the truck. I'm unsurprised when the musclehead from next door appears, biceps flexing, perfectly straight white teeth flashing as he offers his assistance. I accept it because my dad's weight lifting skill set is limited to dumbbells under twenty pounds, and so is mine.

I decide to take the old living room couch since it's gray and comfortable and will work perfectly in my new living room area. I also take my reading chair from my bedroom. Those two items alone fill the bed of the truck. I don't want to overload it and end up stranded on the side of the road. Besides, I can always bring another truckload back when I visit in a couple of weeks.

Once the furniture is secured, I hug my dad and Danielle and head back to Pearl Lake to start my new life.

CHAPTER 6
MY NEW HOME SWEET HOME

Teagan

I arrive in Pearl Lake just after ten thirty in the morning and bring all the things I can upstairs. I can manage everything apart from the couch and my reading chair, which I'll wait for Van to help me with. I get to work unpacking my clothes, separating them into piles, and then hanging them in the small closet. It doesn't take long before the entire space is filled, and I still have another suitcase left to unpack. I also manage to fill an entire shoe rack, and I only brought my running shoes, flats, and flip-flops.

I clean up and make a trip to the lawyer's office, where I meet Bernie and his daughter-in-law. I show up in a T-shirt that reads SMILES ARE FREE, denim capris, and a pair of sandals. This seems to be one instance in which I could have afforded to dress up a bit more, but neither of them appears put off by my attire. In fact, the second his daughter-in-law looks over my résumé, she demands that he hire me and asks if I would mind working Fridays.

"I'm working Wednesdays at Harry's Hardware and Thursdays at the Town Pub." I'll probably be closing, which means I won't get off until about one in the morning, but business hours at the law office are nine to five, so that shouldn't be a problem. "Fridays are wide open."

"That's fantastic. You're hired." Donna smiles widely. "Can you start this Friday?"

"Absolutely."

And that's how I manage to get my third job in Pearl Lake.

It's only noon, and I still have half a day and nothing constructive to do with it, so I offer to pick up lunch for my brother and whoever else is in the office at Footprint Construction. I'm given a huge list and a bunch of *you're the best* messages.

I can't decide if I want Aaron to be there or not. His frosty demeanor seemed to thaw by the end of the night at the bar. I wouldn't say he was nice to me, but he wasn't a complete jerk either. And I still can't figure out why I care. Maybe because he's a bit of an enigma. Maybe because he's ridiculously hot. Or maybe because he looks like a bad boy and he's got a reputation to match and my most recent ex-boyfriend seemed perfect on paper and was actually a huge, cheating jerk.

I show up just after twelve thirty, laden with bags of food. I'm barely in the door when a familiar voice calls out, "Whoever brought Boones's apple fritters is going to get a big old sloppy kiss!"

I'm nearly bowled over when Aaron comes barging through the doorway and then stops dead when he sees me. His eyes flare and then dip down to the bag I'm holding between two fingers, mostly because it's paper and soaked through with grease. And that's even after the contents have been boxed up.

"Oh, hey, Teagan." His expression shifts to something like irritation or dismay, and I try to coat my feelings in Teflon so the hurt slides off instead of sticking to me.

"Aaron." I give him my sweetest smile, all teeth and eye sparkle.

His gaze bounces from my face to the bag and back up again. "Let me give you a hand."

I tuck the greasy bag behind my back, out of his sight, and pin him with an unimpressed glare. "I see how it is."

"You see how what is?" He takes one step forward, bringing him into my personal space. I'm not short, but he barely clears the top of the doorway, so it's not hard for him to look over my shoulder.

"You're only nice to me when I have something you want."

I try to brush by him, hoping I'll run into Dillion, or my brother, or literally anyone other than Aaron. It irks me beyond belief that he dislikes me so much for no apparent reason when he flirts with every other human being in existence.

He mutters something I don't catch.

I spin to face him, jutting my chin out and tipping my head back so I can meet his storm cloud eyes. "What was that?"

"I was just offering to give you a hand. No need to bite my head off." One side of his mouth tips up in a lopsided smile. As if he knows how much it bothers me and he enjoys getting this kind of reaction.

"I smell Boones!" Van appears in the doorway at the other end of the room, preventing me from saying anything else.

I turn to face him and hold out the bags of food. "These things should probably come with some kind of heart attack warning."

He takes the greasy bags from me and pulls me in for a very brief hug. Then tries to run away with the food, but it's as if a dinner bell went off somewhere, and also as if everyone has turned into some kind of apple-fritter zombie, because several people flood the room, all shouting at Van that he'd better not be sneaking more than his share or he'll be losing a finger.

Dillion gives Van a quick jab on the outside of his thigh, causing him to lose his hold on the greasy bag. She grabs the fritters before they hit the floor and holds the bag to her chest—which is a colossally bad idea.

"Settle down, you're freaking Teagan out!" Dillion yells.

That quiets the group.

Van chuckles and mutters, "Boones are a thing around here." He's still rubbing the outside of his thigh.

"Aaron, get plates. Dad, get silverware. Uncle John, you're in charge of napkins. Van, you're in charge of sitting your ass down. And you get last pick of the fritters, since you were planning to steal one."

"I was just helping, and Aaron was out here first, and for sure he was going to try to lay claim to the fritters before me."

"Fine, you and Aaron get last pick. Everyone, sit your ass down and use some freaking table manners so my poor future sister-in-law doesn't think we're all backwoods hicks who never learned basic etiquette."

"She's making us seem a lot worse than we are," Dillion's dad, Jack, says with a wink.

But a minute later everyone is seated at the table, and Dillion helps me unload the bags, calling out sandwich and meal names. They each raise their hand like kindergartners, and no one starts eating, even after everyone has their lunch.

Van pats the chair between himself and Aaron. "Come on, Teag, have a seat."

"Oh, I wasn't planning to stay." I awkwardly adjust my purse strap. I want to grab my salad and run, and I definitely don't want to sit beside Aaron, who has gone back to ignoring my existence now that I'm no longer holding the bag of Boones's fritters.

"You have somewhere else to be?" Van pushes the chair out. "Sit down. Eat with us."

I give in because I don't want to be rude. Even after I take a seat, no one makes a move to dig into their sandwiches, and everyone is staring at Dillion.

I glance around the table, trying to figure out what exactly is going on. Dillion opens the Boones's bag and removes the box. The table shakes, and I realize that Aaron's leg is bouncing on the floor. Actually, I think there's more than one foot bouncing.

"There's a baker's dozen in here and six people at the table. Everyone gets two, and we'll draw numbers for the last extra, but Van and Aaron are out because they both tried to sneak one before the rest of us came out here," Dillion announces.

"What? That's not fair! I offered to help carry the bags in, not steal the freaking fritters!" Aaron slaps the table with one of his huge hands.

Dillion gives him a look that would make most people wilt like too-hot flowers. "Like hell. How long have I known you, Aaron? You probably tried to smolder-smirk the bag out of Teagan's hand."

He blows out a breath. "It's not even worth the fight. You're not going to believe me anyway."

I raise my hand. I don't know why, other than the fact that I'm sitting at a table with four men who are salivating like a pack of starved wolves over the box Dillion is holding, and I'm in awe of the way Dillion seems to have control over them. I want to know how to do that.

Van nudges me with his elbow. "You don't need to raise your hand, Teag."

"I won't have a fritter, so you can split mine in half so everyone gets two and a half, and then there's just the one full one, so one person will get an extra half." I clasp my hands on the table and grin, pleased with my solution and the fact that everyone gets more than they originally thought they would.

The table goes silent, and four sets of eyes land on me, mouths agape.

"You're not giving up your fritters. You're going to eat them," Dillion says. It sounds a lot like an order.

I purse my lips to keep from frowning. "But I don't want a fritter."

"I can't believe I'm saying this." Aaron turns and props his arm on the back of his chair. His gray eyes meet mine, and his tongue sweeps out to wet his bottom lip. It's full, and it looks soft. Softer than his hands. Soft like a satin pillow and warm like fresh laundry. "You want them, Teagan."

"I don't—"

He gives his head a shake and lifts one finger, touching it to my lip. The contact is brief, but if I had any hair on my arms—I don't because I wax them—it would be standing on end.

"Trust me when I tell you this, Teagan: you absolutely want them. Never, ever forfeit a Boones's fritter."

I nod once, feeling a lot like I'm under some spell. "Okay. I want you. Them. The fritters. I want them." The words are barely a whisper, and I feel my face explode with color at the slip.

Aaron drops his finger, and that infernal lopsided grin appears again. "Yeah, you do."

I swallow down my embarrassment and fight the urge to stare at the table. I try not to make direct eye contact with anyone, but I can feel my brother's eyes on me, so I furtively glance his way. Except he's not looking at me; he's giving Aaron the raised eyebrow.

I have so many burning questions.

Like, what's Aaron's deal? And why has he chosen *now* to be flirty? I'd think it was because he wanted to humiliate or embarrass me, but it doesn't make a whole lot of sense to do that in front of everyone. Maybe it was a slip.

"I want the fritters," I tell Dillion.

She's smirking like she's in on some secret. "Yeah, you definitely don't want to pass these up."

Aaron leans his chair back, balancing on two legs, and pulls the tray free from the printer. He grabs a piece of paper and folds it. He tears it into pieces and slides all but one across the table to me. I take one and pass the rest on. He writes down a number on his paper and passes it to Van, while the rest of us write numbers between one and a hundred on our slips of paper. He and Van sit with their arms crossed, looking dejected about the whole thing.

Whoever is closest to the number Aaron wrote down gets the final fritter. I don't particularly want two fritters, let alone three, so I reluctantly take a pen from the center of the table and curve my free hand around my paper, covering the entire thing with my hair so no one can see what I'm writing down. I bump Aaron's arm and mutter an apology.

I give him a furtive glance as I flip my paper over and cover it with my hand.

"You're a lefty?" He nods to the pen still poised in my hand.

"Yup."

"Okay, show me what you got!" Dillion says.

Dillion, Jack, Uncle John, and I flip our papers over. Dillion has number thirty-three, her dad has fifty, Uncle John has seventy-five, and I have one. Van flips the one Aaron passed him and reveals ninety-nine. I sigh in relief, because I did not want the extra one, but I didn't think I'd be able to get out of participating.

I expect everyone to finally dig in, but instead, Dillion uses a pair of tongs to dole out the fritters, setting two on each plate except for the one for Uncle John, who gets three.

When they're all plated, the guys lunge across the table for them, snatching them up like unfed hyenas. The room is suddenly filled with groans and chewing.

I sit there, looking around the table as these men and Dillion devour the fritters. I can't help myself. I glance at Aaron and nearly choke on a laugh. He's melted into his chair, head lolling back, cheeks puffed out because his mouth is full, groaning every time he chews.

"Jeez. You look like you just had a freaking orgasm," I say without thinking.

His head lolls in my direction, and he lifts his hand in front of his mouth, since he's still chewing and apparently he does have some manners. "It's like an orgasm for your taste buds."

Van nudges my arm and pushes the paper plate toward me. "You have to at least try one."

I've spent my entire life telling people that I don't like sweets or dessert. It's untrue. I love sweets and dessert. I make them all the time. For other people. But I don't eat them, because sugar is very addictive, and I already have enough vices, so I try to avoid it unless it's in the form of an energy drink.

But everyone looks so happy.

And the fritters smell so good.

One little bite won't hurt.

Unlike the others, who are busy stuffing them into their mouths with their fingers, I cut mine with a knife and spear the chunk with my fork. I pop it into my mouth and let the flavors hit my tongue.

First is the sugar and cinnamon, followed by the sour tang of lemon. Then the crunch of the fried dough, delicious and savory, followed by the soft, hot apple ring that fills the center. "Oh, wow. This is really good."

"It's better than good. It's the best damn thing in the world."

"Heaven better have Boones's fritters, or I'm going to haunt that place for the rest of eternity," says Uncle John.

I finish one of the fritters in the time that the others eat both of theirs and polish off their lunch. I pick at my salad for a few minutes, then pack it up so I can take it back to the apartment. Then I offer my second fritter to the rest of the table. Dillion has to cut it into five pieces so everyone gets their fair share.

I already spoke to Van last night, so he knows how the discussion went with our dad, but I haven't talked to him about the furniture that's currently sitting in the bed of the truck. I'm crossing my fingers that I'm right and no one will steal it while I happen to be out.

"I'm going to need some help getting a couple of pieces of furniture up to the loft when you get home," I tell Van as I help clean up the table.

"Big stuff or small stuff?"

"A couch and a chair. But that's it."

"Aaron, you think you can give me a hand with those at the end of the day?"

"Oh, you don't need to do that. I can probably help you get them up there."

Aaron acts like I haven't said a word. "I can do that. I need to take a few measurements for the trim."

"See, we've got it all sorted out. You'll have a couch to hang out on before the end of the day."

Everyone goes back to work after lunch, leaving me on my own to explore the downtown area, and eventually I make my way to the south side beach. Dillion and Van have taken on the project of cleaning up the town beach. There are two beaches on the lake, the other one on the side with all the big mansions. It's beautiful and pristine, with white sand, lifeguards, and a marina.

On the south side of the lake, where the townspeople live, it's different. The beach isn't as well maintained; the sand is coarser and the beach not as carefully groomed. At least it wasn't the last time I was here, but I can see they've already made significant improvements since they petitioned the town back in the fall.

Over the winter they couldn't do much physical work to the beach, but they made a plan, and as soon as the ice thawed and the snow melted, a cleanup crew came in to fix the place up.

The formerly derelict and falling-apart docks have been replaced. The sand is groomed regularly, and the seaweed that washes up on shore has been cleared away. A little surf shop and an ice cream store in mini-cottage-style huts have been built at one end of the beach. I can see, with time and effort, more of those shacks going up, catering to the beachgoers.

I can imagine how amazing it would be if there were a miniature Boones shop down here and how much business they would get if they were here on the weekends and during the summer, serving those delicious apple fritters. The smell wafting across the beach, mixing with the fresh water, the scent of sunscreen, the sound of kids playing and families laughing.

I close my eyes and tip my chin up, letting the sun warm my skin, daydreaming about what it would be like if Pearl Lake could be my forever home. I could build a life here. I could fall in love with this town, exactly like my brother did.

CHAPTER 7

MAKE IT WHAT YOU WANT

Teagan

I head back to the loft around three thirty, wanting to freshen up before my brother and Dillion get home from work.

Okay. That's a lie. My brother has seen me at my worst plenty of times. I don't care if my hair and makeup look decent when he's around. Or Dillion for that matter.

But Aaron is a different story.

He shouldn't be. At all. I should not care one iota how I look, but old habits die hard. And I'm still trying to figure out what the heck happened at that lunchroom table.

I swear there was flirting and smolder, which is very, very different from his reluctant politeness at the bar and his grumpy disdain prior to that.

The first thing I do when I get home is grab an energy drink from the fridge and head to the bathroom to fix my makeup.

I probably spend a good half hour in the bathroom, applying makeup in such a way that it looks like I'm not wearing makeup at all. I even go so far as to remove the mascara I put on this morning and replace it with a coat of lighter brown, followed by a coat of clear. My hair is pale; my eyelashes are also light. Black mascara is obvious, but brown mascara isn't, and a coat of clear makes them look longer while also still natural.

I get a message from Van that they're leaving the office in about half an hour.

I loathe idle time. It gives me an opportunity to fret. So I do something that will keep my hands busy and my mind occupied until my brother comes home: bake muffins.

It doesn't hurt to start small here, considering the oven is new and needs to be tested out to make sure it cooks evenly.

I pull out all the ingredients—which I purchased on my recent trip to the grocery store. There are certain things I need an abundant supply of at all times—almond milk, peanut butter powder, frozen bananas, and basic baking essentials. The baking essentials are stored in the small pantry beside the fridge.

I quickly measure out the ingredients, wipe the muffin tin down with oil so they won't stick to the pan, and grab the strawberry jam. Muffins that taste like doughnuts filled with jam are the best, but Van likes them jam-free, so I leave a few without.

It only takes about ten minutes to whip them up and put them in the oven. While I wait for them to bake, I melt butter and prepare the cinnamon-sugar topping.

The muffins have just come out of the oven when I hear the crunch and pop of gravel under tires. I quickly pop them out of the tin, but I don't have time to let them cool. I grab a pair of tongs and dip the first muffin in the butter, then allow it to drip for a few seconds before I roll it in the cinnamon-and-sugar mix.

I manage to get four done before there's a knock at the door. The one that opens into the garage, rather than the one that opens to the landing outside.

I wipe my hands on my apron and rush to open the door, moving aside as Van backs into the loft carrying my reading chair. Aaron appears at the other end. It's a bit loud, being hot pink with gray polka dots, but it will go well with the yellow walls and the navy-and-white wallpaper I picked out.

"Where's this thing going?" Aaron grunts.

"You can set it over there for now. I'll figure out placement later." I motion to the corner.

Dillion appears a few seconds later, holding the seat cushion and the gray lumbar pillow that says **I LOVE BOOKS MORE THAN BOYS**. It's not untrue. Good books very rarely let you down.

"Oh, wow. Why does it smell so good in here?" Dillion tosses the pillow on my bed and looks around the space, her eyes widening when she notices the fresh paint and the new wallpaper.

"Right? What is that? Some kind of candle?" Van asks.

Aaron and Van carry my chair across the room and tuck it into a corner, out of the way. I'll move it later so it has a better position in the room and acts as functional art.

"Wow. When the heck did you have time to paint and hang wallpaper?" Van asks, but he's not looking at me; he's looking at Aaron.

"He didn't. I did." I clasp my hands behind my back, waiting to see what they're going to say and if Aaron will make a snide remark about the color.

"When did you have time to do this?" Van asks. "And since when do you know how to paint? Or wallpaper?"

"Last week. And I watched a couple of DIY videos." I'd like to say it wasn't that hard, but it sure was a lot of work. Still, I think it came out decent for a first-timer.

"The color looks great. I would never have the balls to paint a room that shade of yellow, but it works," Dillion says.

"Thanks. I looked at a bunch of Pinterest pictures and thought it would complement the space, especially with the east-facing windows."

"I'm glad you didn't paint the entire place that color, or we'd all have burned-out retinas."

And there's the comment I was waiting for.

"You wanna grab the couch now, Van?" Aaron starts heading for the stairs.

"Sure, sounds good. The place looks great, Teag." Van gives me the thumbs-up and disappears back downstairs with Aaron.

Dillion starts to follow, so I assume I should probably come down and help with the cushions, even though I'd prefer to finish dipping and rolling the muffins while they're still warm.

Dillion spins around, though, and nearly crashes into me. "Shit. Sorry." She grabs me by the shoulders to steady me and herself. "Okay, so what the heck is going on with you and Aaron?"

"Nothing?" It's more question than anything else, because I honestly have no idea.

She shakes her head. "Not buying it. He's being super weird around you."

"If by *weird* you mean mostly grumpy and jerkish, I would have to agree."

"He wasn't jerkish at lunch."

"I had something he wanted."

"He can get Boones's literally anytime he wants. It's on his way home from work, so I don't think that's it."

"What's his story, anyway?" I glance toward the open door, the sound of Aaron's and Van's voices carrying up the stairs.

"I'll tell you later, after he leaves," she whispers. "What in the world is that glorious smell?"

"Muffins that taste like doughnuts."

"Is that a candle scent? I swear those companies thrive on masochism, making something inedible smell that good."

"No, I made muffins that taste like doughnuts. I was finishing them off when you guys showed up." I motion to the stove, where most of the muffins are still naked. "Do you want one?"

"Do bears eat garbage?"

I smile. "Yes. Yes, they do."

I love Dillion. She's not like any of the women I used to hang out with back in Chicago. She's down to earth and generally doesn't give a crap about things like style and makeup. I think I've seen her wear lip gloss once. And her hair is mostly in a ponytail because it's curly and unruly.

She follows me to the stove, and I hand her a plate with one of the dipped, jam-filled muffins. She takes a generous bite, cinnamon sugar falling on the plate and sticking to her lips. "Oh my gosh," she mumbles through a mouthful of muffin. "These are the best muffins in the history of the universe."

"Thanks, they're super easy to make. I can give you the recipe if you want." The muffins have cooled enough that I don't need to use tongs to dip or roll them anymore. I make quick work of those and set the last one on the plate as Van appears at the top of the stairs, carrying one end of the couch. It's wide for the doorway, so they rotate it on its side and do some maneuvering to get it up the final stairs and into the loft.

The guys set the couch down once they're inside the loft, and Aaron lifts the hem of his shirt, swiping away beads of sweat from his forehead and exposing his delicious, rippling abs.

"So yummy," Dillion mumbles.

"I know."

"I'm talking about the muffins, not Aaron," she whispers.

"Oh." I tear my eyes away from him and shoot my soon-to-be sister-in-law a warning look.

"Where do you want this?" Van asks, still out of breath.

"With the back of the couch facing the wallpapered wall, please."

Dillion shoves the last of the muffin into her mouth and wipes her hands on her jeans, then decides that's not going to work and washes them in the sink. While Van and Aaron move the couch into position, Dillion and I grab the cushions from the truck.

When we return, Aaron is standing by the fridge, drinking a root beer, and Van is holding a mostly empty glass of water while drooling over the muffins.

"The ones on the small plate are jamless; the rest have strawberry jam in them. Feel free to help yourself," I tell them as I put the cushions back on the couch.

"I love you more than words, sis." Van shoves an entire muffin into his mouth.

I cringe and look away, not wanting to see the sugar and cinnamon sprinkling the floor because he's failed to use a plate.

"You need to try one of these, man, they're the best," Van says to Aaron through a garbled mouthful of food.

"I'm good, thanks."

I keep my eyes averted, telling myself that I shouldn't be hurt because he doesn't want to try my muffins. Feeding people has always been part of my love language. I started not long after my mom passed away, maybe because I remember her always making treats for us. Every day we'd come home from school and there would be some kind of baked goodies: fresh bread, healthy muffins, and on Fridays there would be cookies or what she called "treat muffins." I stopped eating them when she passed away and started making them instead.

"Seriously, have one." Van holds the plate in front of Aaron, and he caves, probably because he doesn't want to be rude.

Two seconds later a low groan comes from the other side of the room.

"I told you. Teag makes the best muffins. And cookies. And biscuits. And bread. If there's flour involved, she's basically a wizard."

I laugh at that. "It's a hobby." But I feel a tinge of pride as they both reach for seconds. I might not know what I want to do with the rest of my life, but at least I know I'm good at a few things that make people happy.

I add the throw pillows and take a step back. I still need end tables, a coffee table, and some art, but it's coming together.

Dillion stands next to me, her hands on her hips. "This really brightens it up."

"Thanks. I wanted to delineate the space since it's all one big room, and the best way to break it up is with some color and pattern." I'm planning to paint the wall behind the bed, too, to give it some dimension, and I'd like to get one of those room dividers to make the bed feel separate from the rest of the living space.

"What are you doing tomorrow?"

"I don't have anything planned."

"I have a meeting with a homeowner on the other side of the lake. They're renovating their pool house. Maybe you want to come along and see if you have any ideas on how to make the most of the space?"

"Sure." I shrug. "I can do that."

"Great." Dillion beams. "I can tell them what kind of wood to use and what cabinet styles would work, but I don't have the eye for color that you do."

I wave the compliment away. "I spend a lot of time on Pinterest."

"Pinterest terrifies me. I'll start looking at cabinet ideas, and three hours later I'm staring at bare-chested guys."

"Ahh, yes, it can be a rabbit hole for sure."

The ping of a phone has us all checking our own.

"I should head out." Aaron shoves his phone back in his pocket.

"Thanks for your help today." I motion to the couch.

"No problem. Thanks for the muffins." He kneads his neck. "Sorry I ate so many of them."

There are only two left on the plate.

"Don't worry about it. I can always make more, and they're best when they're right out of the oven."

"Not gonna argue with that. I'll come by tomorrow morning and get the baseboards up so I'm not in your way." His gaze shifts to Dillion. "Then I'll head over to the Winslows' and work on finishing up the landscaping there since it's supposed to be a nice day."

"Works for me," Dillion says.

"See y'all later." And with that he's out the door.

"Is it me, or has Aaron been throwing out the vibes?" Van points at me, but he's looking at Dillion.

"I wasn't paying attention to anything but the muffins." Dillion nudges me with her foot, as if to say, *See, I'm not the only one who's noticed.*

CHAPTER 8
GIVE ME THE DIRT

Teagan

I get up extra early the following morning and make a fresh batch of muffins, then leave them on the counter with a note for Aaron to help himself to as many as he'd like.

Dillion drops Van at the office since he is in the middle of consulting on a project for Footprint, and we drive around to the other side of the lake for our meeting with the homeowner. "Okay, so what's Aaron's story?"

"I was wondering how long it would take you to bring him up." Dillion grins as she taps the steering wheel to the beat of the music coming through the speakers. "We grew up together, and he hung out with my brother, Billy, in high school, but he got a scholarship and went to Indiana for college."

"Really? What college?" He doesn't strike me as a city boy.

"Notre Dame."

"Oh, wow! For what?"

"Structural engineering. And he played for their football team, at least for the first couple of years. He never finished his degree as far as I know. Dropped out in his last semester."

"Why? Was he struggling to keep up or something?"

"I don't know. I was in Chicago at the time, going to school and then working, but when he dropped out and came back to Pearl Lake, my dad hired him, and he's been working for him ever since."

"Wow, that's an expensive education to walk away from in the last semester of your degree."

"Agreed. I don't know what happened, and I've never asked. And no one seems to know. It's a bit of a closed subject. He's always happy to give his input on project designs and layouts, but his résumé doesn't even have his education on it." Dillion chews her bottom lip for a second. "I always wondered if maybe it had something to do with his mom."

"She works at Harry's. She's the one who hired me. Does she live in town?" I don't know why I'm so intrigued by these little facts about him.

"Just outside, actually. She moved when Aaron went to college. And she raised him on her own."

I'm trying to paint a picture of the man I've met so far. Went to school out of state but never finished. Has most of a structural engineering degree but chooses to work with his hands for the only contractor in town. Loves apple fritters and muffins and apparently has an epic smolder that he uses to get things he wants—like apple fritters. "What happened to his dad?"

Dillion shrugs. "From what I know, his mom got pregnant and decided she wanted to keep the baby. I think there was a scandal there."

"Scandal how?"

"The town's gossip is that Aaron's father was renting one of the houses on the nice side of the lake and Aaron's mom got involved with him. Like a fling maybe? Apparently he was married, though, so that's where the scandal is. Like I said, it's all rumors. I don't have the whole story, so don't take anything I'm telling you as gospel." Dillion isn't big on gossip, which makes sense, seeing what her family and Van have been through. "Anyway, Aaron's been known to ride more than the lawn mower on the other side of the lake. He's a compulsive flirt. Charming, always has the right line. Except with you, anyway. He was all flirty at the office when you brought the fritters and then awkward when he helped move the furniture."

"He was probably only flirty because of the fritters." I run my finger along the edge of the window, gathering dust on the tip.

"I guess it's possible, but why would he have agreed to come help move the furniture? He easily could have said he was busy."

We arrive at the house, which is pretty much a mansion on a lake, putting an end to the Aaron inquisition.

I tamp down the envy as we make our way up the front steps of the lake house. It's beyond beautiful. It's a tough pill to swallow, being this close to a way of life that used to be mine and is no longer. I remind myself that it was all an illusion. None of it was ever truly ours. We were cash poor, lines of credit stretched thin, a facade of wealth when we were scraping the bottom of the barrel.

And even when I didn't know that it was all a farce, I was never actually happy. Always trying to meet the expectations people laid out for me. Wanting to be perfect, be the ideal. It was never enough; no matter how hard I tried, I could never achieve the perfection I was desperate for.

The homeowner, who is the wife of an NHL player, is a woman named Stevie. She's incredibly gracious, showing us around the house, offering us refreshments. We walk through the pool house, which is half the size of the house my dad currently lives in, and as I take in the space—huge windows looking out onto the lake, white walls and unfinished surfaces, a beautiful blank canvas—I can see it all coming together.

"Why don't we start with flooring and favorite colors, and we can go from there?" I ask.

"Sure, we can definitely do that." Stevie points to her pale-pink hair. "As you can see, I'm a fan of pastels."

"All pastels, or just pink?" I ask.

"Almost all. Except for peach."

"No peach." I make a note in my tablet, and we talk everything from wall color to fabrics, flooring, and furniture. Dillion weighs in on things like cabinetry and flooring, but I'm the one they both look to when it comes to everything else.

It's well past noon by the time the meeting wraps up. We plan to meet again next week, when I'll have a floor plan, layout, and design ready.

"You're incredible, Teagan! I had no idea you were so amazing at interior design," Dillion says once we're back in the truck.

"I'm not. I told you, I look at a lot of Pinterest pages."

She shakes her head. "Stop downplaying your talents. You've been in the loft for less than a week, and it's still under construction, and it already looks homey. It's more than just looking at Pinterest pages; you have an eye for what works to bring a room together. I know you've already picked up a shift at Harry's and the Town Pub, but maybe you want to come on as a design consultant? We could start with one day a week? I have to talk to my dad first, but honestly, what you just did would take me several meetings instead of one, so I can't see him putting up a fight."

"Sure. I can do that. But I'm also working Fridays at Bernie's, so it'll have to be Mondays or Tuesdays. Or a day on the weekend if that works better."

"Bernie the town lawyer?" Dillion asks.

"Yup."

Dillion's eyebrows pop. "When did you get that job?"

"Yesterday." I tap my lip, trying to remember when I stopped in there. "Or maybe the day before?"

"Wow. You're really filling your dance card, aren't you?"

"I'm trying a bit of everything so I can find out what I'm good at." Most of the jobs are minimum wage, apart from Bernie's and the pub, but for now it's about the experience.

"If Tuesday works for you, it's probably a good day for us, but we might need you on the occasional Saturday, if that's okay. And we can pay you a consulting fee? I can look into what interior designers usually charge per project."

"Sure. That works."

Dillion pulls into the driveway and grins when she sees the Footprint Construction truck that belongs to Aaron parked in front of the garage. "Ooh, have a fun afternoon."

I roll my eyes. "We'll see how nice he is to me when no one else is around." I hop out of the truck. "Thanks for letting me tag along this morning. It was fun."

"Thank you for making my life a million times easier. See you at dinner!"

I climb the stairs to the apartment, already humming with nervous energy. I pause halfway up to take a few deep breaths, then rummage around in my purse for a pack of mints. I pop one in my mouth and climb the rest of the way. The door is propped open, and the low bass of guitar riffs filters through to greet me.

I peek through the door and am greeted by the glorious sight of Aaron's bare back. He's kneeling on a pad on the floor, shooting nails into baseboards. A few long white planks lie in the middle of the room on a sheet of plastic. It's obvious that he's trying his best not to make a mess or disturb any of my things.

I glance at the counter and smile when I notice several muffins are missing from the plate. I made banana-chocolate-chip ones this morning. Somewhat healthy, but still delicious.

I clear my throat so as not to scare the crap out of him again. When he doesn't react, I wait until he's finished nailing the board before I call out, "Hey there!"

He glances over his shoulder. Most of his face is obscured by the brim of his ball cap. "Oh, hey." He unfurls from his crouched position on the floor. "I thought I'd be done before you got back. What time is it?"

"Just after noon."

"I didn't realize it was that late." His gaze moves from my face down to my feet and then darts to the side, toward the kitchen counter. "Thanks for the muffins."

"You're welcome."

"I shouldn't be much longer, and then I'll be out of your hair."

"You don't need to rush. If you'd rather, I can go up to the cottage and leave you to it." I thumb over my shoulder, then cross my fingers behind my back, hoping he won't take me up on that offer.

"You don't need to do that on my account, but it's pretty noisy work, so it's up to you. I've got a few more boards to nail, and then I'll fill the holes. Once that's finished, I'll get started on the door hardware so you have a bathroom door that closes properly."

"I could help fill the nail holes?" I offer. I don't know what all that entails, but it doesn't sound too difficult.

"If you want, sure." He shrugs. "It's tedious but not hard."

"I can deal with tedious. I'll change, and then you can show me what I need to do."

"Sounds good." He grabs another board, and I head to my closet.

I grab a pair of yoga shorts and a tank top—which seem like a reasonable outfit to wear for filling nail holes. I can't imagine it being an exceptionally dirty job. Not like painting walls.

I shove a towel in the hole where the doorknob will be so I can change. I check my reflection, apply extra deodorant, and resist the urge to dab perfume behind my ears; otherwise it means the bugs will eat me alive later. I learned that the hard way the first time I came to visit Van.

I wait until Aaron has finished nailing the board he's working on before I interrupt again. "Okay. Ready to be put to work." I clasp my hands behind my back so I'm not tempted to fidget.

He sets his nail gun down facing the wall and heads for his tool-box. He produces a small container, what looks like a metal spatula, and a rag.

"Come on over, and I'll show you what you need to do." He pats the floor beside him, and I drop down and cross my legs.

He rests one knee on the pad and opens the container, explains how to fill the hole, and lets me try a few times, giving me pointers and explaining that we'll give it a light sand after it's dry, followed by a finish coat of paint.

He nails the final baseboards and starts filling holes on the other end of the wall. Now that he's no longer using a nail gun, I don't have to shout to ask him questions.

"How did you get into this?" I ask.

"Construction?"

"Mmm, and working with the Stitches."

"I always had jobs working with my hands growing up. I'm not big on sitting behind a desk." He shifts his knee pad over and moves a couple of feet in my direction.

"Did you go to school for it? Is that how you knew it was what you wanted to do?" I'm fishing for information. Trying to fill in the missing pieces from what I've learned this morning.

"I went to college, but not for this."

"Oh? What did you go for? Did you realize it wasn't for you?" I ask, thinking I'm going to find out why he dropped out in his final semester.

"I got in over my head. What about you? Did you go to college?"

I'm not surprised he's deflecting and decide not to push, since this is the first time we've had a conversation where he hasn't seemed put out by the fact that he has to talk to me. "Yup. Sure did. I took business administration and public relations."

"You have two degrees?" He seems mildly surprised by this.

"I double majored."

"Seems like a lot of work."

"I have insomnia, so I don't sleep much. It kept me occupied instead of staring at the ceiling all night, wishing my brain would shut off." That and I couldn't decide which degree would be the better option, so I did both at the same time.

He looks my way, and for a few seconds his expression is pensive. "So why are you here working all these odd jobs at random places?"

"The abridged version is that I didn't like my job and I wanted a fresh start, and to figure out what I want to do with the rest of my life."

"Seems a bit like an existential crisis. What's the unabridged version of that story?"

"You don't want to hear it. That's what therapists get paid for." I haven't been to see one since I was a little girl. My dad took me a few times after Mom died, but I didn't like it, and he didn't want to force me to go.

"I'll listen to your woes for muffins," Aaron offers with a grin.

I chuckle and shuffle across the floor. I'm close enough to Aaron that I can smell his deodorant and the faint salty scent of sweat. His jaw is covered in a dusting of scruff, as if he couldn't be bothered to shave over the last couple of days.

"I don't know that muffins would be adequate payment."

"Why not? You seem like you've got it pretty together. What made you decide to leave the city and live here?"

"My dad's girlfriend moved in with him last week, and until Sunday, I lived with him."

He stops filling holes to look at me. "You two don't get along, you and this girlfriend?"

"It's not that. She's nice, and I think she's great for my dad. He's been alone for a long time, ever since my mom died. I can't even remember him trying to date or get over her. I don't know how much you know about my family or our situation, but he spent a lot of years burying his grief and putting our family in a lot of debt."

He shifts his knee pad over so he's only a few feet away. "Yeah, Van talked about that a little. Your younger brother is in jail for fraud."

"He tried to frame Van. It was awful. And I'm not justifying what he did, but I think a lot of it stems from not having stable, active, involved parents around growing up. At least I hope that's it and he's not some narcissistic douche hole who will never be a better person."

"That had to be hard on your family," Aaron says quietly.

"It was. But it was also the wake-up call my dad needed. I think he finally recognized he wasn't even present in his life. That he was just . . . existing. Van helped him consolidate his debt, and we moved into a house he could afford. I couldn't see what a pampered brat I was until we had to sell pretty much everything and start over. And I didn't want to leave my dad on his own, not after what happened with Bradley and with all the changes, so I moved with him rather than get my own place."

Aaron flips his ball cap around so the brim is backward. "That seems like a pretty selfless thing to do."

"I don't know if I would consider it selfless. I did it as much for myself as I did for him. It gave me a sense of purpose, a reason to hold on to something familiar in a sea of change."

"You still put him before yourself. That's a selfless act."

"I needed to be needed, at least by someone." I wave the metal spatula around, not sure if I should be embarrassed that I'm sharing my sob story with a man I find hopelessly attractive, who might only be listening to me ramble because he likes my muffins. Still, I keep talking. "Anyway, while all that was happening, my dad went for grief counseling and met Danielle, his girlfriend. He absolutely deserves to be happy, and that's what she makes him. But last week when she moved in, I saw that everything I've been doing—working for the same company as my dad, as his assistant, living in the house with him—none of it was for me. I don't even know what I like, or what I'm good at, or if there are things I'd like to be good at that I'm not."

"You're good at a lot of things as far as I can tell." Aaron motions to the loft.

"I'm good at talking, that's for sure." Filling people's ears with my nonsense is one thing I excel at. "Anyway, I need to figure out what I want because I honestly have no idea, so here I am."

I force a bright smile and look up.

I don't expect Aaron to be right beside me, his storm cloud eyes fixed on me. And for once he's not looking at me with annoyance or pity.

"That's my story." I focus on filling holes again.

"It's quite the story."

"Everyone has one."

"This is true." He's quiet for a moment before he continues. "And I mean it, Teagan: I think you're probably good at more things than you know. You already know you can fill holes like a pro."

I give him the side-eye and roll my eyes at his grin. "I've heard that's your specialty."

"Is that right? Already jumping on the small-town-gossip train?" He's still smiling, but there's an edge to his tone.

"You flirt with literally everyone," I point out.

"That doesn't mean I sleep with everyone."

"Just the ladies whose lawns you mow?" I know I've taken it a step too far when his expression shutters.

"You don't know shit about me, Teagan."

"I didn't before, but I do now." I don't know why I'm needling him like this. It's obvious I've hit a nerve. But I feel like I'm finally figuring him out, and I like the reaction I'm getting.

"And what exactly do you think you know?" He pushes to a stand, and his abs, all eleven million of them, ripple as he rolls his shoulders back and glares down at me.

"That you don't like the reputation you seem to have earned." I push to my feet too. "I also know that you flirt with everyone *except* me.

87

Why is that, Aaron? Why are you only nice when I have something you want? What's so off-putting about me?"

"That's not true. What's off-putting are rumors and gossip. I hadn't pegged you for someone who fed into that garbage, especially with your history." He starts toward the door, so I jump in front of him, blocking his way. Which is essentially pointless since there are two doors to choose from.

"I was kidding about the lawn mowing. I didn't realize you were going to take such offense to it. And less than a minute ago you basically agreed with me about you flirting with everyone. Why are you so angry all of a sudden?"

"I'm not angry." He tries to step around me again, but I'm right in his face.

"Yes you are! Your face is beet red, and your nostrils are flaring, and your hands are balled into fists." I tap one of them with my finger, then fling my own in the air. "I was trying to flirt with you, and now you're pissed off!"

"By referencing all the 'lawns' I've mowed." He unfurls his fists and makes air quotes around the word *lawns*, then crosses his arms. "That's your version of flirting?" he asks incredulously.

"Okay," I concede. "That probably wasn't my best attempt, but you fluster me! And I can't get a read on you. One second you're nice and complimentary, and the next you're angry. What is the deal?"

His jaw cracks. "What are you going to do? Hold me hostage until you get the answer you want?"

"If I have to, yes."

"Why can't you let it go?"

"Not my style." Actually, it's totally my style. Or it was. But something about Aaron makes me want to push buttons and figure him out. Especially with how up and down and all over the place he is with me.

"You're not the way I thought you'd be," he snaps.

"What's that supposed to mean?"

"You show up here with a freaking metallic-pink zebra-print suitcase—"

"It's cheetah print."

His eyebrow rises. "Excuse me, a metallic-pink *cheetah*-print suitcase, looking like you stepped off the goddamn runway, all wounded bird—"

"Wounded bird?" I hate that it took him all of ten seconds to pick that up about me. Troy always told me I wore my emotions on my sleeve. I didn't want him to be right, but maybe he is.

"You were on the verge of tears," he points out.

"You practically bit my head off two seconds after I walked in the damn door!" I fling a hand toward said door.

He mirrors the movement. "Because you scared the shit out of me!"

"Why are you so agitated?"

"Because I don't need complications in my life, and you're becoming one!"

I feel like a sad balloon that's been pricked with a pin.

Your family situation is too complicated.

I can't be with someone who attracts this much negative attention.

You're dragging me down with you.

All the excuses Troy gave me as to why he was breaking it off with me and why he'd started sleeping with my best friend. She had been the one to comfort him, to agree that he was right: I was too much of a complication for his family. They didn't need my drama.

I step aside. "That's enough. I don't need to hear any more. You can go."

"Shit. Teagan—"

"Leave. Please." I lift a hand but keep my eyes on the floor. On his scuffed work boots. On my bare toes. I need a pedicure.

He sighs but does as I ask, pulling the door closed behind him with a quiet click.

I inhale to the count of four and exhale to the count of eight. "Way to go, Teag. Good job embarrassing yourself."

My fingers and toes start to go numb. I head for the bathroom and open the medicine cabinet, scanning until I find my antianxiety medicine. I take a few deep breaths, warring with myself before I finally give in. I'm on the verge of losing it, and I would prefer for that not to happen.

Not when Van and Dillion will be home from work soon, probably asking all kinds of questions. Ones I'm going to have to dodge or lie about.

Whatever Dillion thought was going on with Aaron was very wrong, because he definitely doesn't want anything to do with me.

CHAPTER 9
NICE WORK, DONKEY

Aaron

I stand outside her door for five minutes. Because I'm a donkey. A giant, stupid donkey.

So fucking stupid.

Stupid. Stupid. Stupid.

"You're twenty-seven years old, dipshit. How hard is it to tell a woman you actually like her?" Pretty fucking hard, I would guess, considering I insulted the hell out of her. Like this is some high school–level crush.

And after she basically bared her soul to me.

Okay. She didn't bare her soul, but she told me some personal stuff.

And I shat all over that sharing by being a dick.

Because she called me out. And she was right.

I have a reputation in town for getting into bed with the women on the other side of the lake. For a while I got nice and familiar with those entitled women and the sounds of their orgasms. Past tense. At least since last summer, when shit hit the fan. And the cost outweighed the benefit, which was no-strings sex with women who seemed to think I was a shiny toy they could play with, consequence-free.

When that changed, I stopped providing orgasms to the sad, lonely women in their huge, empty lake houses.

But that kind of thing follows a person around for a long time, like the stench of garbage that's been baking in the sun too long; it burns itself into people's memories until that's all they can see or remember.

And I've done a terrible job of trying to dispel those rumors.

I haven't done *anything* to dispel them.

I've been happy to let them fester like wounds. It allows me to avoid relationships with substance. And the local women who I've known my entire life have zero interest in becoming notches on my bedpost. So it served its purpose. Until now.

There's something about Teagan. Under the metallic-pink ridiculousness and that bright, sunshine smile and her bubbly personality is a layered and complex human being. One I sincerely want to get to know better. Because I feel like behind all that sunshine is some darkness. The kind of murky shadows that might match mine.

It's been years since I've felt any kind of real draw to a woman, and now that I do, I can't seem to manage it without being a giant donkey.

I bang my head against the door and grip the knob. Then twist. Just to see if she locked it behind me.

She didn't.

I push it open and call her name, but no one answers.

Maybe she went out the other door.

I should leave. I can come back tomorrow and apologize. But instead of doing that, I take another step inside and close the door behind me.

The loft is one big open space, so the only places she can hide are the bathroom or the closet. The sound of running water tells me which location she's in. I still haven't installed the doorknobs yet, so there's a three-inch hole where the knob should be, a sliver of pale-green fabric belonging to Teagan's shorts visible through the gap.

Her fingers, with perfectly filed nails, appear in that hole, and a moment later the door opens. She startles. "What are you still doing here?"

"I don't think you're a wounded bird. That's not what I wanted to tell you. At first that's what I thought. You reminded me of the women across the lake." I cringe at the look of disbelief on her face and rush on to explain. "You're too perfect, too put together, and then you almost started crying, and I decided you must be like them, and I'd sworn off getting involved with anyone like that again. Because you're right, I did mow a lot of lawns on the other side of the lake for a couple of years—literally and figuratively. I figured why not, right? They were using me because . . ." I motion to my abs. I don't even remember where I left my damn shirt. "And I was using them because I didn't want to get involved with anyone who wanted more from me than orgasms."

She crosses her arms. "Why?"

"Why what?" I actually have no idea what I said to her. Mostly it was a pile of word vomit I'd like to flush down a toilet.

"Why didn't you want to get involved with anyone who wanted more from you than orgasms?"

I would like to hear the word *orgasm* come out of Teagan's mouth without it being related to the women I *used* to sleep with. "Because I wasn't in the headspace for it. I needed uncomplicated."

But it got *really* complicated because one of those women, who'd told me she was in the middle of a divorce, hadn't been quite honest.

Teagan's staring at me like I have two heads. "I only flirt with women I'm not interested in."

Her brow furrows. It's so fucking cute. She has this little button nose that scrunches up when something doesn't make a lot of sense.

Based on the amount of nose scrunching she's done, not much of what I've said so far has made sense.

I want to be honest with her, but the difficult part is letting someone see enough of you without showing them all your ugly truths. I have secrets, the kind I keep buried. Stuff even my mother doesn't know. But for some reason, I want to know Teagan more than I want to keep her at arm's length.

"My first impression of you was wrong. I thought you were a pampered, entitled rich girl, but you're not. I realized that the day I saw you working at the Town Pub, and then again when you managed to do all of this with no help." I motion to the yellow walls and the wallpaper, which I thought was hella ugly in the hardware store but looks awesome in here. "And you make really fucking amazing muffins. I think you're incredibly talented and selfless, and I wanted a reason not to like you, but I don't have any, and I didn't know what to do with that, so I acted like a donkey."

"A donkey?"

"An ass. I was an ass." I adjust the brim of my hat. "I think you're gorgeous, inside and out."

Both of her brows are arched. "Okay," she says slowly, drawing out the word.

"I like you." I close my eyes and blow out a breath. I don't think I've ever fumbled this much with a woman in my life. It's a lot easier to get naked and use my mouth for things that don't include a lot of words. "I'm such an idiot. Why can't I shut up?"

"Want some help with that?" Her voice is soft and low and very, very close.

My eyes pop open, and Teagan is standing right in front of me, chin tipped up. Her eyes are the color of a cloudless summer sky. She's not short. I'd guess that she's close to the same height as Dillion. Maybe even taller. But I'm pushing six feet five, so even the tall women don't seem all that tall to me. Her long hair is pulled up in a ponytail, wisps of it having come loose, skimming her cheek. Her tongue sweeps out, dragging across her bottom lip. It's fuller than her top lip, making it look like she's halfway to pouting when she's not smiling. And most of the time she's smiling. Except when I say something asinine. Because I'm a donkey.

"What?" I blink down at her, feeling like the awkward, gangly teen I once was. I don't know what exactly it is about her that makes me impossibly stupid. Usually I'm disgustingly smooth with women. But with Teagan, I'm a hormonally paralyzed idiot.

She crooks a finger, beckoning me closer. But there's only six inches separating us. If I take a step forward, my boots will touch her toes. So I bend instead, until my ear is next to her lips, like I'm waiting for her to tell me a secret.

For a moment I consider the fact that I've been up and down the stairs to the loft at least a dozen times. The only air circulation in here is from a portable fan, so I've been sweating and shirtless for several hours. I might not smell all that fresh.

But that thought disappears when her fingertips drag along my collarbone and I feel the warmth of her breath at the edge of my jaw.

"Aaron."

Her palm wraps around the back of my neck. So soft. So warm.

I swallow and grind out, "I'm listening."

Her thumb finds that spot between my ear and my jaw, and she presses, gently at first and then more firmly. Her lips brush the shell of my ear, and she whispers, "Look at me."

I feel like a marionette, and she's pulling all my strings. I turn my head toward her, and her lips brush across my cheek, sending a hot shiver down my spine, lighting me up like a pinball machine.

Teagan Firestone is a dangerous woman. Sweet, beautiful, broken, and yet . . . bold and resilient. She's a lethal combination, and it's all compounded when those soft lips meet mine.

I don't even know what's happening. Well, I know. I'm kissing her. Or she's kissing me. She definitely started it.

It's like an explosion. Like an entire warehouse of firecrackers igniting at the same time. I groan into her mouth and wrap an arm around her waist, pulling her flush against me.

Our tongues tangle, and her other hand grips my biceps, sliding up and over my shoulder. She knocks my hat off my head, and it drops to the floor behind me. And then both of her hands are in my hair, sliding through the damp strands, gripping at the crown, angling my head farther to the side. Deepening the kiss.

Dragging it out.

Our tongues battle and then soften, find a rhythm that's slightly less frantic. She sighs and moans, hips starting to roll, like she's dancing to a song only she can hear.

In a moment of clarity, I feel around behind me and flick the lock on the door. She startles and bites my tongue. With our mouths still connected, she walks me backward across the room, toward her bed.

I feel the mattress against my calves.

She pushes on my chest, breaking the kiss. She's not physically strong enough to knock me over. Maybe with a roundhouse kick or a knee to the balls, she could bring me to my knees. But I fall back on the bed, propping myself up on my elbows, legs spread wide, erection making itself known against the fly of my jeans.

Her bottom lip is caught between her teeth, and her eyes roam over me on a hungry sweep.

"What're we doing here, Teagan?" I don't know why I ask. It's pretty fucking obvious what the plan is. And my body is totally on board. Normally I wouldn't even think twice about it. Not when a woman I find attractive is very clearly showing me what she wants.

But Teagan is nothing like the women I typically end up in bed with.

"Whatever we want." She pulls her tank over her head and tosses it on the floor. And then she hooks her thumbs into the waistband of her shorts and tugs them down her long, toned thighs, leaving her in nothing but a pink satin bra and matching panties. Clearly it's her favorite color.

She reaches behind her and flicks open the clasp of her bra. The straps slide down her arms, freeing her breasts. They're high and full, perfect handfuls. She takes two steps toward me, until she's standing between my spread knees.

I let my eyes drop, taking in all that bare skin. The dip in her waist, the curve of her hips, soft in all the right places. She's fucking perfect. I lift my gaze back to hers. "You seem pretty clear on what *you* want."

She hooks her thumbs into her panties and pushes them over her hips. They slide down her legs, and she steps out of them. I sit up and drag my fingertips from the outside of her knee all the way to her hip. Gripping gently, I lean in and circle her navel with my nose, pressing my lips against her soft, warm skin.

She hums and runs her hands through my hair, nails scraping gently across my scalp, sending another hot shiver down my spine, making goose bumps rise along my skin. Before I can go any lower, she tugs on my hair, pulling my head back as she climbs onto the bed and straddles my lap.

"Don't you—"

She settles a palm on my chest and brushes her lips over mine, cutting off my question. "Sometimes it's better not to think too much. Sometimes all we need to do is feel."

That's a loaded statement. One I'd like to learn more about, later. When we're not about to have sex.

Her hands slide down my chest until she finds my belt buckle. She undoes the clasp, pops the button, and drags the zipper down. She sucks my bottom lip between hers while her hand dips into the waistband of my boxer briefs. She sighs and I groan as her fingers explore. Freeing me from the fabric, she wraps her fingers around me.

I work with my hands all day long. They're calloused from manual labor, and it doesn't matter how often I moisturize and use a pumice stone; half the time it feels like they're made of sandpaper. So Teagan's hand is damn well bliss.

My hips lift on their own, seeking her touch, and I make a sound that's somewhere between a growl and a grunt. She smiles against my lips and slides forward, her chest coming flush with mine.

At first all I can focus on is how good it all feels. And I almost lose my damn mind when she rises up and skims her sex with my erection.

But then I realize that her plan is to jump right on in, no foreplay, no lead-up. Just get naked and get right to it. Which defeats the entire purpose of sex, as far as I'm concerned.

I grab her around the waist and flip her over. She shrieks and clutches my shoulders. I quickly tuck myself back into my boxer briefs, because too much stimulation is going to make this end a lot more quickly than I'd like. At the same time, I adjust my position so one of my knees is between hers and the other is pressed up against the outside of her left thigh. That way she can't rub all that softness and warmth on me and threaten to scramble my brain again.

"What're you doing?" Her bottom lip juts out, all pouty and inviting.

I dip down and suck it between mine, biting lightly before I pull back. "What're *you* doing?"

"Well, I was about to ride you like my personal roller coaster, but now I'm not."

If she had room to cross her arms, I bet she would.

I grin and brush my nose against hers. "Why you trying to rush through all the good stuff?"

She wiggles a hand between our bodies and cups me. "This is the good stuff."

I give my head a slow shake. "That's the endgame. The fourth quarter. We're not even close to halftime yet."

"Are you comparing sex to football?"

I ignore the question since it seems rhetorical, based on her smirk. "I'm just getting started here, Teagan, so don't rush me." I drop my head and take her mouth again, slowing things right down.

Every time my lips leave hers to explore more of her skin, she grips my hair and tries to strong-arm me back up to her mouth. She also keeps trying to free her leg from between mine, but I drop my hips, making it impossible.

As it is, she can only wrap one leg around my waist. I keep up with the slow exploration, devoting attention to her pert nipples, before revisiting her mouth. When I start to make the trip south to the promised land, she grips my hair and yanks my head up, eyes wide with panic. "What're you doing?"

"What does it look like I'm doing?" I run my hand down her side and over her hip, trying to unhook her leg. Her heel is pressing into the center of my back, right on top of a knotted muscle.

"You can't go down on me." She looks horrified by the prospect.

That gives me pause. "You don't like oral?" The only reason I can see that being a possibility is if her previous partners didn't know what they were doing.

"I haven't showered since this morning." Her cheeks burst with color. It's freaking adorable. As is the way her eyes keep darting away and her bottom lip gets caught between her teeth. Even as she says it, her hips shift the tiniest bit so she's rubbing up on my thigh. "If you give me a minute—"

I cut her off before she can finish that thought. "I haven't showered since last night, so unless you ran a half marathon this morning, I'm going to go ahead and say you're a hell of a lot fresher than me, and you haven't been complaining. Take your own advice, Teagan—stop thinking and just feel. Unless you want to stop. Because we can absolutely hit the pause button and do this another day."

"What? No! I don't want to stop."

"Good, me either."

I kiss my way down her stomach and shift so I can settle between her thighs. I take my time, teasing, nipping, lapping at her, figuring out how much pressure she likes based on her moans and sighs. Being with her feels different. It's not just about us both getting off, which I obviously want, but with Teagan it's about getting her there. She isn't here because she's looking for a distraction. I'm not something to pass the time. A fun toy to enjoy and discard. We have chemistry, and as much as I didn't want to acknowledge it at first, it's the unspoken connection we share that I want to explore. And not just while we're naked.

But when she tells me she's getting close and grips my hair with her fingers and breathily murmurs how good I make her feel, I refocus my attention and make her come. When she's sated and boneless, I pull my wallet from my back pocket, shuck off my jeans and boxers, and flip us over so she's once again straddling my hips.

I fish a condom out of my wallet, and she plucks it from my fingers. Teagan tears it open and rolls it down my length. Rising up, she angles my erection and sinks down, taking me inside.

I grip her hips, keeping her still for a moment as I absorb the sensation. It's been a lot of months since I've been with anyone. And years since I've been with someone for reasons other than physical release.

Teagan's ponytail slips over her shoulder as she rests her palms on my chest. I reach up and pull the tie free. It falls in soft waves around her face, and I slip my hand behind her neck, pulling her closer. Her hair tickles my chest as I bring her lips to mine.

She rolls her hips, sweet moans humming across my lips. We move together, a push and pull, slow at first, but it feels too damn good, and eventually need and instinct take over. I sit up so we're chest to chest again, and I cup her ass, lifting and lowering.

We can't kiss anymore, the pace too frantic, so I bury my face in her neck, breathing in the salty-sweet scent of her skin. It's only when she moans my name, body quaking, that I let go and let my own release drag me down into that sweet euphoria where all thoughts are muted and only sensation exists.

CHAPTER 10

DECADENT

Teagan

Aaron wraps his arm around my waist and flops back on the bed, head landing on a pillow. I turn mine and rest my cheek on his chest. The wiry hairs tickle and prick my skin, but I don't move. The sound of his heartbeat is a rhythmic, powerful thump in his chest.

We're both sweaty and sticky. It's glorious. And nothing that I'm used to. I'm not forward like this or used to acting on attraction without a whole bunch of dates first. His hand smooths up my back. It's rough—not the action but his hand. It's like someone stroking your back with a loofah.

After a minute of just breathing and letting the orgasm aftershocks settle like ripples on the water, I lift my head and rest my chin on his pec. Strands of hair stick to my face and my lips. Damp and unruly. I try to blow them out of the way, but I'm unsuccessful.

Aaron brushes my hair out of my eyes and over my shoulder. It slips back down, fanning out across his broad chest. He tucks his arm behind his head and grins. "You're full of surprises, aren't you?"

I shrug. "How do you mean?"

"Dunno, just didn't expect you to be quite so . . . take charge. I like it."

"I'm all about turning over new leaves."

He grins. "I'm happy to help you out with any new leaves you want to turn over that also include nudity."

I snicker and push up on his chest, lifting off him.

He tries to grab me by the hips, but I roll off the bed and spring to my feet. For a second my legs threaten to give out, but I regain my balance.

He props himself up on one elbow. "Hey, where are you going? What happened to pillow talk?"

"Pillow talk?" I can't tell if he's serious or not. I slide the closet door open and search for my bathrobe.

"Yeah. Pillow talk. You know, you tell me how huge I am and how you can't believe how amazing I am in bed, and I agree, and then you spill all your deep, dark secrets and make me promise never to tell a soul."

I bark out a laugh and glance over my shoulder. "That's not pillow talk, Aaron, that's ego stroking. And I'm not telling you all my deep, dark secrets because you gave me an orgasm. You're going to have to work a hell of a lot harder than that if you want those."

"I gave you two orgasms, not one."

"You better not start keeping a running tally." I finally find my bathrobe, in the very back of the closet, and free it from the hanger.

"It sounds like there's a threat attached to that statement. And also like you're not opposed to getting naked with me again, which I'm completely on board with, in case you were wondering."

"I wasn't wondering, actually." I slip my arm into one sleeve.

"Hey! Stop doing that. Stay naked. Come back to bed." He pats the mattress.

As enticing as it sounds, I ignore the request. I want to stay in bed and do exactly what he suggests, but I don't know what it is we're doing yet, and pillow talk is a level of intimacy I'm not ready for. Personal conversations are different when you're naked—and they make me feel more vulnerable than I'd like. "I'm jumping in the shower. You're welcome to join me."

"You're killing my afterglow." I hear his feet hit the floor and smile as I pad across the room.

I manage to get the shower turned on before his arm wraps around my waist and he pulls me back into him. He tosses the spent condom in the wastebasket and burrows through my hair, one hand slipping under my robe to cup my breast as his lips find my neck.

"I'm sweaty." I still tip my head to the side, transfixed as I watch our reflections in the mirror. I'm tall, but he has more than a head on me, and he's so broad. It makes me feel delicate.

"You're delicious, every inch of you," he murmurs, his eyes lifting to meet mine in our reflection. The mirror steams, turning us into an indistinct blur as my robe drops to the floor and I pull him into the shower with me.

Half an hour later I'm clean and my legs feel a lot like they're made of Jell-O, not that I'd tell Aaron that. His ego does not need any inflating. He leans against my counter, wearing his jeans and his T-shirt, which was hanging over the arm of my pink polka-dot chair.

Apparently, he likes to work shirtless not because he's looking for attention but because it's nice to put a clean shirt on at the end of the day, especially if he leaves work and goes straight to the local pub for dinner.

"Do you want a root beer?" I ask as I open the fridge, enjoying the blast of cold air.

"Sure, thanks."

I grab a bottle of root beer for him and an energy drink for me. He nabs it from my hand before I can pop the tab. He makes a face. "Now I know why you're like the Energizer Bunny in bed. How can you stand the taste of this stuff?"

"How can you stand the taste of that stuff?" I point to the jar of instant coffee.

"Fair." He hands the can back to me.

"It's best when it's ice cold." It hisses as I open it and gulp down a few mouthfuls to wet my parched mouth.

"You got anything to eat in here? I skipped lunch." Aaron pats his flat, six-pack stomach.

"I think I have some lunch meat? I could make you a sandwich. Or if you can hang on for"—I glance at the clock, and it's already four in the afternoon—"an hour, we're having steak for dinner. You're welcome to join us. I made fresh buns."

"I like your buns." Aaron waggles his brows.

I give him a look. "That was the worst."

"You're still smiling, so it couldn't have been that bad."

"The *worst*."

"I've got more lines. I'm gonna drop my best ones on you when you least expect it, and you're gonna swoon so hard."

"Or laugh so hard that I pass out is more likely." I like this version of Aaron. He's fun, playful even. "Can you wait for dinner, or do you need food immediately?"

"I can wait. What else are we having besides steak? And are you sure there'll be enough?"

"Why don't we go to the house, and we can check it out. If it looks like we're short, we can always make a trip downtown and pick up extra."

"Okay. Sounds good."

We leave the garage and head to the house. It's slowly transitioning in my head from cottage to permanent home. We have more than enough steak, and we also have shrimp. I start pulling things out of the fridge and decide I might as well make biscuits too.

"Can I do anything to help?"

"You can spin the lettuce." I point out the spinner and push the field greens toward him.

He makes a face, as though I've asked him to clean up dog crap.

"Do you have a problem with lettuce?"

"The only vegetables I eat are corn and potatoes, and they have to have lots of butter on them, and salt."

"You have the palate of a five-year-old."

"Lettuce tastes like dirt."

"It tastes healthy."

"Exactly. Like dirt."

I'm shaking my head, ready to fire off a joke about how he probably likes to eat canned spaghetti, when I hear the sound of gravel crunching on the driveway. "Um, question."

Aaron stops dumping lettuce in the spinner. "Fire away."

"We're gonna play it cool, right?" I feel stupid the moment I ask it.

"As opposed to not playing it cool?" He sets the lettuce down and grabs me by the hips, lifting me until my butt rests on the countertop, and steps in between my legs.

"What're you doing?"

"Demonstrating not playing it cool." He takes my face in his hands, tips his head to the side, and presses his lips to mine.

I start to protest, which means he can slip his tongue into my mouth for a stroke before he breaks the kiss. He sets me back on the floor and moves out of my personal space. "Just clarifying that you don't want me to do that in front of your brother and Dillion."

I don't have a chance to answer because the door flies open. "How much you want to bet Aaron and Teag—oh, hey!" Dillion stops in the doorway, and Van nearly knocks her over.

"Hey," Aaron and I say at the same time.

Dillion's eyes bounce between us and all the food laid out on the counter. "Does this mean we need more steak? Because I'm not sharing mine."

"I bought four," Van tells her. "I'm glad you're here, Aaron. I need to pick your brain about that new monster of a home the Strykers want to build."

"Sure. You know I'm always up for a challenge. You got drawings?"

Aaron and Van take the steaks out to the barbecue, leaving me and Dillion on our own. "You look like the cat who ate the canary."

"Don't start," I mutter, then add, "I need a better poker face."

"You've got a royal flush going on." She steps in and takes over where Aaron left off with the lettuce.

I roll my eyes and huff a laugh.

"Guess he likes you after all."

"Just stop." I elbow her in the side.

"I have a million questions, which I'll save for later."

We finish making dinner and eat outside at the picnic table. "How soon do you think you can have preliminary ideas for the Winslows?" Dillion asks me.

"Probably by the weekend. I'm going to get started tonight with an idea board since it's all fresh in my head."

"I think it's great that you're helping out with the design side of things," Van says before he takes another bite of steak.

"Seems like a good fit, considering the way you transformed the apartment in the garage in less than a week," Aaron agrees.

I duck my head. "It's something I do for fun."

"Well, you do a damn good job," Dillion says. "If you're interested, we have a meeting with the Palmerstons on Saturday morning. It's all the preliminary planning, but it might not hurt to have you sit in on it anyway. And the guys just finished laying the interlocking stone for their outdoor kitchen. You could give them some ideas, maybe?"

"Oh, sure. I can definitely do that."

"Don't take advantage of my sister. Teagan can't say no to anyone," Van says teasingly.

"Unless you're busy," Dillion adds. "I don't want to overload you or anything."

I roll my eyes. "I can say no." I turn my attention to Dillion. "Don't listen to Van. I can totally handle it. Do you have pictures of the outdoor kitchen? That way I can go into the meeting with ideas."

"You have some, don't you, Aaron?" Van asks.

"Yup. Sure do. If you give me your number, I'll text them to you." A slight smirk tips one corner of his mouth.

"I'll share Teagan's contact with you," Dillion offers.

"That'd be great." Aaron's smile is wry as Dillion pulls out her phone and taps at the screen. A moment later Aaron's phone pings.

He pulls it out of his back pocket, and a few seconds later my phone pings too.

Van glances between us and gives his head a shake.

After dinner Aaron makes an excuse about needing to take a couple more measurements in the loft before he takes off, so I leave with him. The measurements are clearly a ruse, because the second we're inside and the door is closed, his mouth slants over mine. A minute later he breaks the kiss.

"What're you doing tomorrow?"

It takes me a few seconds to switch gears from kissing to answering questions. "Um, I work at Harry's from nine until five."

"And after that?" His gaze is on my mouth.

"I'll probably work on the Winslow idea board and maybe paint the wall behind my bed. Or put a decal up or something."

He scratches the back of his neck. "I have a McMansion project I need to work on during the day, but I should be done before five."

"McMansion project?"

"That's what we call the houses on the other side of the lake."

"Oh, right. Is it a lawn-mowing kind of project?" I squeeze my eyes shut and make a face that I'm sure isn't the least bit attractive. *Way to be too needy after sleeping together once, Teagan. Okay, twice, but still.* "You don't have to answer that. It's not my business."

"I haven't mowed any of those kinds of lawn in the figurative sense in a long time."

I crack a lid. "We're talking about sex, right, and not the literal act of cutting someone's grass with a lawn tractor?"

Aaron smiles. "Yes, we're talking about sex. I don't get involved with those women anymore, but if you're interested, I could come over *after* work and finish up the trim, and we could do this again." He motions between the two of us.

"I would like that."

"Me too." He tugs me forward by my belt loop and wraps his arm around me, bending until our lips connect. And we start all over again.

CHAPTER 11

INTO THE SWING

Teagan

As promised, Aaron shows up just after five the next evening, carrying a backpack and a bag of takeout from the diner where Dillion's mom works.

"What's this?" I motion to the backpack.

"A change of clothes for after I'm done with the trim. And I brought my shower stuff, because as nice as you smell, I'm not partial to *me* smelling like roses and chamomile."

"Lavender and rosemary."

"Pretty much the same thing."

"Not even close, but okay." I step aside so he can come in, which he does before he drops the backpack and the takeout on the floor, takes my face in his calloused hands, and kisses me until my toes curl.

Everything else is forgotten: the food, the things he came over to do—other than me. He kisses along the edge of my jaw, hands sliding under my shirt. "This okay?"

"More than okay."

"How was your day?" he asks as he lifts the fabric over my head and drops it on the floor.

"Good. Yours?" I get to work unfastening his belt.

"I couldn't stop thinking about you. And every time that happened, I got a really inconvenient hard-on I couldn't do anything about. It was a good thing that I was working alone, on a roof, otherwise it would have been embarrassing as hell."

"I guess it's also good we can do something about it now."

"So good." He yanks my pants down my thighs and takes my panties right along with them. Then he spins me around and pins my back against the door. "All day, Teagan." He drops to his knees and hikes one of my legs over his shoulder. "You were all I could think about."

An hour later we're seated at the kitchen table, me with a martini and Aaron with a bottle of root beer, eating takeout from the diner.

Aaron picked up three different meals, and one included a side salad. I'm in awe of the way he shovels in food, barely tasting it.

"I already took care of the trim, so you don't have to worry about that." I pop a cherry tomato in my mouth.

He pauses with a forkful of pasta halfway to his mouth. "When did you have time to do that? I thought you were at work all day."

"I woke up early and couldn't fall back to sleep because my brain went straight into high gear. Anyway, I bought a bunch of light fixtures, and I thought maybe you could show me how to install them."

"I can install them for you no problem."

I spear a piece of grilled chicken and dip it in my salad dressing. "I know *you* can, but if it's not too much trouble, maybe you could show me, so I know how in the future."

Aaron tips his head, a small smile playing on his delicious lips. "Oh yeah, sure. I can definitely do that."

"Thanks." I return the smile and pop the piece of chicken in my mouth.

There are no leftovers because Aaron polishes everything off. Apart from what was left of my salad. He wasn't lying about hating vegetables.

His phone rings as I'm washing up the dishes. "I gotta take this. I'll just be a minute." He presses a kiss to my temple and disappears outside for a few minutes.

When he returns, the dishes are done, and he sets everything up so we can install the light fixtures. He adjusts the ladder, turning it into what looks like one of those old climbers kids used to hang off in the playground at school. Except it's silvery metal and not painted red. He lays a thick plank over the top and secures it, then helps me up onto it. I have to sit down, feeling unsteady. "I'm only a few feet off the ground. Why does this feel so much higher?"

"Because you're not used to it. You're not going to fall, babe, I promise." He gives my calf a squeeze. "I'm going to pass you the chandelier, and then I'll climb up after you."

I don't know if *babe* is a common term of endearment for him or not. Troy used to call me *doll*, and it drove me up the wall, but for some reason I don't mind *babe* coming from Aaron. "Okay. Then what?"

"All you have to do is hold the chandelier for now."

He climbs up beside me and hops to his feet, then holds out his hand. When I give him a skeptical look, he quirks a brow. "What are you worried about?"

"Losing my balance and falling."

"You won't. You've got thighs of steel. I would know since I've had them wrapped around my head and my waist recently." He winks. "Now come on, babe, there's an orgasm waiting for you after we install this."

"Well, in that case." I slip my hand in his, letting him help me to my feet.

I like this, having him teach me things. Practical things. Stuff I'd have to watch videos to learn otherwise. And it gives me reasons to touch him and have him touch me. It feels a lot like another form of foreplay. Especially when he moves to stand behind me, a foot bracketing the outside of mine, and drops a kiss on the side of my neck.

Every time I do something correctly, I get another kiss and more words of praise. By the time we're done with the chandelier in the main living area and the ceiling fan over the bed, I'm ramped right up, like I've consumed a four-pack of energy drinks after a pot of coffee.

"You did good, babe." Aaron's arm wraps around my waist, and he drops his head, lips moving against my neck. "And you were sexy as hell doing it."

That term of endearment is growing on me. "Thanks for being so patient." I tip my head to the side.

"No thanks needed. You're boss-level sexy when you're handling my tools."

"Such a bad line." I laugh and then sigh as his lips part and I feel the warm, wet swipe of his tongue on my skin. I reach up and wrap my arm around the back of his neck, back arching with the stretch until I can feel the nudge against my butt, telling me exactly how sexy he thinks I am. "Is it time for that orgasm now?"

"Absolutely. Maybe even more than one if we're both lucky."

Over the weeks that follow, I begin to settle into life in Pearl Lake. Sometimes I find it hard to toe the line between the locals and the McMansion owners. I used to be them, but now I'm working all these very different jobs, and I feel as though I'm learning new things about myself every day. I see now that I took my comfortable life for granted, and I try to appreciate the little things more than I used to.

What makes the transition easier is the fact that I have a very gorgeous, very talented man showing me his skill set in the bedroom several times a week. We haven't put a label on it, but whatever it is we're doing, it's fun and I enjoy his company.

At first Aaron's visits are planned around finishing up stuff in the loft. It truly is the small things that need taking care of. He shows me how to install door hardware and teaches me tricks about screwing on plate covers, like that I need to use a flathead screwdriver, and that I want the slot to be vertical on both screws to give it a neat, finished look.

But even the final touches don't take long, so I keep trying to find things that I need help with, and Aaron keeps on coming over to give me a hand. I don't want it to stop, but I also don't want to turn this into something bigger than it is. It feels like more than just sleeping together, but I don't know if I'd go so far as to consider it dating, since we generally hang out at my place, work on projects, and have sex.

After about two weeks I've exhausted all the interior projects, and still Aaron finds reasons to stop by. He needs to check the electrical panel. There's a squeaky floorboard; he wants to tighten the screws on my bed frame. Usually whatever it is takes all of five minutes, and then we're tearing each other's clothes off.

He doesn't stay the night, but he always makes time for pillow talk. Mostly it's about the projects across the lake and funny stories about the families over there. At ten he gets dressed, gives me a long, lingering kiss, and tells me he'll see me again soon.

It makes me anxious that I don't know if *soon* is going to be a couple of days or the next night. But we're having fun and I don't want that to change, so I try to go with the flow, which I'm admittedly not very good at.

I realize fairly quickly that I need to find things to do with my time other than ogle Aaron and have mind-blowing sex with him. So a few weeks into our arrangement, I make myself unavailable and agree to go out with Dillion and her friends for drinks at the pub after my Wednesday shift at Harry's.

As I'm getting ready, which looks very different from my old routine—I'm not used to leaving the house with a naked face, but I've toned it way down—my phone rings as I'm applying a coat of clear mascara. I automatically assume it's Aaron. He favors phone calls over any other type of messaging, even if they're only thirty seconds long. I hit the answer button without checking the number and nearly poke myself in the eye when I get a woman's voice rather than Aaron's telling me I have a collect call from Chicago Penitentiary and to press one if I'd like to accept the charges.

I take a deep breath, waiting for the call to connect.

"Hey, sis." Bradley's voice comes through the line.

"Hey, how are you hanging in there? You doing okay?" Bradley has reached out to me a number of times since his incarceration, but his calls always catch me off guard, since they're unpredictable.

From what my dad has said, he talks to Bradley almost every week, and when I'm around, I'll jump on the call too. Van is still struggling to get over what Bradley did and having a much harder time forgiving him, which I can understand.

"It's boring as hell here and their library sucks the D, but I've made a friend named Moose in the kitchen, and he sneaks me extra bacon on Saturdays, so that's a plus, right?"

"Can you get in trouble for that?" I ask, putting my mascara wand back in the holder.

"Only if someone finds out."

I roll my eyes. Leave it to Bradley to try to game the system while in jail.

"How are things going for you? Any new gossip on your ex-asshole? Give me the dirt."

"Um, there isn't any dirt to dish, to be honest. Or if there is, I don't know about it."

Bradley sighs. "Well, that's too bad. You know I'm living vicariously through you, since the only drama around here involves dudes shanking each other over dessert."

"Are you serious?"

"The chocolate cake is pretty decent."

I can't tell if he's joking or not. He's always had a bit of a morbid sense of humor. And jail certainly isn't going to make it better. "But shanking someone over dessert? How crazy are these guys? What if I call the lawyer and see if we can't get you transferred to a different facility? One that's safer."

"It's prison, Teagan, it's never going to be safe. You don't need to worry about me, though. I've got it under control."

"Are you sure?"

"Yeah, I'm sure. Look, I'm dying for something decent to read, and I've already gone through everything you sent last time. Do you think you can restock me? I can give you a list, and you can mail them."

The first time I sent him anything, I included nail clippers, thinking they'd be useful, only to have the entire package mailed back for having contraband. "I can do that. Give me a list, and I'll hook you up with whatever you need. Have the restrictions changed at all?"

"I don't think so, but you can check the website. They get the newspaper here, but never the *Wall Street Journal*, so if you can pick up a few of those, that'd be great."

I take down the information and Bradley's long list of books and magazines he'd like.

"Thanks, Teag, it means a lot that you'd do this for me. I know you and Van are close and it puts you in a weird position."

"You're still my brother, and I still love you," I reassure him. And I do; even if I don't love what he did to our family, I still care about him. It's hard because I feel partly responsible for helping put him there, despite the fact that he broke the law and has to face the consequences. Bradley isn't exactly built for prison life.

"Can I call you next week? Around the same time?"

"Yeah. Of course. You can call me every week."

"Okay. Great. I gotta go: there's a guy waiting behind me, and he's getting impatient."

"Okay. I love you, Bradley. Stay safe, okay?"

"I'll do my best. Talk to you next week." He ends the call, and I set my phone on the vanity. I plant my palms on the cool surface and drop my head, taking a few deep breaths, trying to curb the mounting panic. It happens every time I talk to Bradley. He's said before that he'd call again the next week, but more often than not he doesn't. And the timing and day are never the same.

I don't want Van to think I'm taking Bradley's side, but I also don't want to leave my younger brother with no one and nothing. Sending him books at least shows I care.

I open the medicine cabinet and pull out my prescription, rolling the bottle between my fingers, trying to decide if I can deal with everything tonight or not. I haven't had to take my anxiety medication all that much since moving here. Although the last couple of days I've been stressed about the Footprint Construction design consultations because I had to go back to the drawing board with one of the rooms in the Winslows' pool house. I forgot to take my sleep meds and spent most of the night on my laptop. It meant I was exhausted the next day for my shift at Harry's and basically mainlined energy drinks to get through the day.

And now, after the call with Bradley, I don't feel like going out at all. I can't talk to Dillion about this. Her loyalty lies with Van, as it should. But if I bail on her tonight, Van might come up here to find out why I didn't go, or worse, I'll call Aaron and ask him to come over.

And while seeing Aaron would be a great way to take my mind off things and relieve some stress, I worry that I'll do something stupid, like tell him about the call from Bradley and that I feel guilty about hiding it from Van. I like what we have. It's fun and easy and mostly light. I don't want to start bogging things down with my insecurities and my fears. If I get clingy, he's going to stop coming over, and I'd like this to continue for as long as possible.

So I do what I need to in order to avoid disappointing Dillion and potentially messing up this thing with Aaron. I pop the cap on the bottle and shake my medication into my palm. But I break one in half instead of taking the full pill, hoping it will be enough. I set it underneath my tongue and let the bittersweet pill dissolve. This stuff tends to make me tired, so I crack an energy drink to offset the effects.

By the time Dillion comes knocking on my door, I'm calm again, and all my worries are softened. The edges like Sherpa blankets, fuzzy and comfortable. The fears all tucked away. I just wish they would stay that way.

CHAPTER 12
MR. MYSTERIOUS

Teagan

"Okay, so I've kept my mouth shut so far, but I need to know: What the hell is going on with you and Aaron?" Dillion asks as soon as we're on the dirt road, heading toward town.

"We're hanging out. He's teaching me all kinds of stuff, and he's fun to be around."

"What kind of stuff is he teaching you? How to have multiple orgasms?"

I can feel my cheeks heat. When I was in college, I briefly went out with a guy who was amazing at giving multiples. Unfortunately, it was pretty much the only thing he was good at. As much as I appreciated having three orgasms in a row, when it was always followed by several hours of him playing video games, I stopped answering his calls. I haven't been with another guy whose sexual prowess matched his, until now. Aaron is the whole package, giving in bed and great at conversation.

"Oh my God!" She slaps my arm. "Are you sleeping with Aaron? You totally are!"

"We're having fun."

"The naked kind of fun?" Dillion is practically bouncing in her seat. I've never seen her this excited about anything. Not even her engagement ring. And that's saying something, because she was pretty excited about that.

"Yes, the naked kind of fun. Can we not make a big deal of this, though? I don't know what we're doing, and it's pretty casual, so I'd like to keep it low key." As long as I keep telling myself that the butterflies in my stomach are just anticipation and I continue to do what I'm doing now—make sure I'm not always available and don't call on him when I need emotional support—then I can keep a nice, clean line between fun and feelings.

Dillion taps on the steering wheel. "Sure, sure. Not making a big deal at all. But now I want to know if the rumors are true."

"What rumors?" I do not like the spike of jealousy that comes with that question.

"That he's got it going on." She motions below the waist. "And that he's an animal in bed."

I twist a lock of hair around my finger. "Well, he's definitely got it going on, and I don't know about an animal, but he has a high drive and excellent stamina." He's very attentive and seems to derive an immense amount of pleasure from giving me orgasms. "Please don't tell my brother any of this. Or say anything to Aaron. I don't really know what this is, and like I said, I don't want to make a thing of it."

Dillion raises a brow. "Van already knows."

"How?" I sincerely hope he didn't come knocking on my door when Aaron was over and hear things he shouldn't have.

"Aaron's truck is parked in the driveway four nights a week. After work. And he's here for hours. He was almost finished with the loft when you moved in, so it's pretty obvious what's going on. But it's cool. I'll keep it to myself. I can't speak for Van, though. I'm sure he's already done the protective-bro thing."

"I seriously hope not."

We pull into the parking lot of the Town Pub, and Dillion backs the truck into one of the only available parking spots. As soon as we step inside, I'm surrounded by familiar faces and smells. The comforting scent of fried food and the pungent aroma of fresh beer mix with the sound of happy chatter. Some of the patrons recognize me and wave as I pass, calling me over to say hi.

"I didn't know you were working Wednesdays now, too," Mike, one of my Thursday regulars, says.

"I'm here as a customer tonight, but I'll be behind the bar tomorrow."

"Good, you pour a better pint than Louis." He winks and we move on, stopping a couple more times before we reach the booth in the back corner where Dillion's friends are already seated.

Dillion introduces me to Allie, as well as Tawny, who I've already met.

"Hey! I'm so glad you finally came out." Tawny's smile is genuine, if somewhat chagrined. "Next time we can go to my place, though, if it's weird to hang out where you work."

"Oh, I'm fine. I don't mind," I tell her.

It only takes a minute before Aubrey, one of the regular servers, comes over to take our order. Tawny passes me a glass, since she and Allie ordered a bottle of wine, and I also order a Coke for the caffeine.

When I lived in the city, I used to go out for cocktail night with my girlfriends. We'd also go to clubs and order bottle service. I'd spend hours getting ready, picking out the dress I wanted to wear, getting waxed and plucked and my hair and makeup done. I hated the clubs. They were loud, with bad music and too many people. Troy would always get drunk and gropey.

This is so much nicer. The faces are familiar, and I find that I'm glad I didn't bail, even though I considered it earlier.

"You've been here for, what? Less than a month? And you already know pretty much everyone in town," Tawny says.

"It's because I'm a new face."

"Maybe, but I was at Boones's last week and so was Harry, and he was going on and on about his new hire and how you were redoing all the displays and if they needed someone to help them out, they should look at hiring you."

"Really? I had no idea." I tamp down a sudden spike of panic. "I don't know if I can take on any more jobs, though, since I picked up a shift at the diner on Mondays."

"You mean the one where my mom works?" Dillion asks.

"I must have forgotten to mention it. It was when I picked up lunch on Monday. She was running herself ragged trying to keep up with the lunch rush, so I said I'd be happy to help out."

"Oh my God, I thought Van was joking when he said you can't say no to anyone. How many jobs is that now?"

"I can say no. I just didn't want to. And five. This is a good way to find out what I'm good at and what I like doing. Plus I'll only be there for a few hours, so it's not a big deal. Oh, I was wondering if you all have one of those farmers' markets on the weekends around here."

"We used to, back when we were kids. I'm not sure what happened to it, but I'm guessing maybe not enough interest or whatever," Dillion replies.

"Really? I would have thought a farmers' market would do well here. It's such a great way for local businesses to connect with the summer folk. I wonder what it would take to get it up and running again."

A shadow passes over the table, and I look up as a body drops down on the bench seat beside me, with it the scent of Aaron's cologne. I startle, sucking in a shocked breath.

"I thought when you said you were having a girls' night you'd all be sitting at your place painting your nails and watching cheesy romcoms." He stretches his arm across the back of the bench seat, his fingertips brushing along my shoulder.

Tawny and Allie look from me to him and back again, mouths agape.

I tip my head up so I can look at him. It's clear he's been working late; he's still wearing his work clothes, and he smells like a combination of sawdust, gas, and fresh-cut grass. His shirt is clean, though, because he always keeps an extra in his truck or his backpack, which he brings with him everywhere he goes.

His storm cloud gaze meets mine, roving over my face, a half smile tipping up the right side of his mouth.

"The night's still young, you never know where we might end up," I say with a wink at the girls.

I have no idea what the protocol is here. He's naturally flirty. That's just the way he is. So him sliding into the booth and putting his arm around me is par for the course. I should definitely not read into it.

"Like the next town over at the Steel Sword!" Tawny slaps the table, eyes alight with excitement. She's already on her second glass of wine since Allie is the designated driver of their pair.

"The Steel Sword? Is that the name of a bar?" I wrinkle my nose. It does not sound like a place I want to go.

"Oh, it's a bar, all right." Dillion grins widely.

Aaron's playful smile drops, and he looks over my head at her. "You're not taking Teagan there."

"Why not? What's wrong with the Steel Sword?" Troy used to monitor where I went and with who, but I realize now it was so he could sneak around behind my back with Portia. I don't think this is anything close to the same, but I don't like that my head goes there at all.

"Yeah, what's wrong with the Steel Sword?" Allie props her chin on her fist.

"Didn't they get shut down for violating the health code?" Aaron's eyes swing her way and narrow. "And Teagan doesn't need to see a bunch of second-rate strippers fumble their way out of their clothes when she has me around." He turns his hot gaze on me. He's close, his sweet breath washing over my face. He's been drinking root beer. His fingers sweep up the side of my neck. There's a hint of vulnerability and maybe the tiniest bit of worry lurking behind his eyes, as though he's not fond of the idea of me going there. "Listen, babe, you don't need the Steel Sword. You want a lap dance, you come to me."

"Hey, Saunders, stop hitting on the locals. They know better than to let you into their beds!" Billy, Dillion's younger brother, calls out from the pool tables across the room.

Aaron flinches, and his brow pulls into a furrow. He turns his head slowly in the direction of the heckling. "I'm having a conversation!"

"I'm gonna let Tommy take your shot if you're not over here in thirty seconds." Billy sets his nonalcoholic beer on the table and starts chalking up his cue.

Aaron rolls his eyes and turns back to me. "I gotta show them what real pool looks like." He pushes up off the bench and unfurls to his full height. "Don't leave without saying goodbye." He takes a step toward the pool tables but stops and turns back to us, narrowed eyes on Allie and Tawny. "And I mean it: don't take her to the Steel Sword." He braces one hand on the back of the bench and leans down, the fingers on his free hand settling under my chin, and he tips my head up. "By the way, you look fucking delicious tonight. If I lose this game, it's your fault for being such a distraction." He brushes his lips over mine.

It's all too brief. He winks and saunters across the room, toward the pool table.

My table suddenly feels like there's an earthquake happening under it. Allie and Tawny both look like their eyeballs are going to pop out of their heads.

"Oh my gosh, oh my gosh, oh my gosh," they both whisper-shriek.

Tawny leans forward and looks around the bar. I do the same and notice there are quite a few people looking at our table. "I guess now we know who Aaron's mystery woman is!"

"Mystery woman?" I echo.

"I saw Billy in town, and he was complaining last week about Aaron not being around to help him with something. I guess he kept blowing him off because he was busy with you, but he wouldn't give him a straight answer. Billy figured it had to be a woman, because Aaron has been in a great mood lately," Tawny says.

"Aaron is usually pretty upbeat, though," Allie says.

"Yeah, but he's been whistling, with a hop in his step and a twinkle in his eyes," Dillion adds.

I give her a look. "What is this? A Hallmark movie?"

She laughs. "Seriously, though, Aaron is a fun guy, but there's always been an edge to him, like there's something dark hiding behind that smile of his. He's different than he was in high school, which I guess is to be expected. I don't know. I can't put my finger on it, but what I do know is that he's been in a ridiculously good mood lately and he hasn't been flirting with everyone."

"He was just flirting with me," I point out.

Dillion rolls her eyes. "That's my point. He's only flirting with you, from what I can see. On Monday we were at one of the jobs across the lake, and they have a college-aged daughter. She was flouncing around in her bikini at nine in the morning, full makeup, following Aaron around like a lost puppy, and he wouldn't give her the time of day. Eventually he told her she had to find something else to do because she didn't have on the appropriate footwear to be around power tools."

"Ouch." Tawny makes a face.

Dillion shrugs. "He wasn't wrong, but before you arrived, he would've at least flirted back."

I glance over at the pool tables as Aaron heads toward the door with his phone at his ear.

"He's kind of, like . . . mysterious," Allie says.

He does disappear outside to take phone calls pretty often when we're together. I just assume he needs the privacy.

"He dropped out of college in his final semester; do you know what happened?" I ask Tawny and Allie, since they're local and Dillion lived in Chicago for almost a decade until she moved back to Pearl Lake last year. I haven't tried to bring it up again since the last time we talked about it.

Tawny looks over her shoulder, checking to make sure no one is eavesdropping. She lowers her voice and shakes her head. "Not really. He came back a couple months after Christmas break in his final semester. He went through a rough patch. Had that little piece of land, and I think he lived in a trailer for a while. No one saw much of him. Got shit-faced drunk a few times here. Once I think he ended up in the hospital."

"Is that why I always see him with root beer?" I ask.

Tawny shrugs. "Maybe? It was pretty bad. Something must have happened at college, but none of us know what it was. After the hospital thing, I think he stopped drinking altogether."

"And then he started working for the Stitches," Allie adds.

"And sleeping with the McMansion women," I mutter.

"Yeah, but it's been a long time since we've heard anything about that," Tawny says.

"I think last summer was when he put a stop to things. Remember when he was at Harry's and one of those women showed up and made a big scene right in the middle of the lumberyard?" Allie says to Tawny.

"Oh yeah, that was something else." Tawny looks over her shoulder at the pool table, but the guys aren't paying attention to us.

I lean in and lower my voice anyway. "What kind of scene?"

"She was day drunk," Tawny says. "She started freaking out on him, saying she knew she wasn't the only one and how dare he. Aaron's mom works there, so that was . . . not the best."

"What happened?" I ask.

"He told her she wasn't making sense, and she needed to stop making a spectacle of herself," Allie tells us. "I guess she wasn't in any kind of state to drive, and he didn't want her to keep making a scene, so he took her home. He was livid. I don't think it was long after that he stopped whatever he was doing. But there are other stories. I don't know if I'd believe them all, though."

"He goes away for a weekend every month, too," Tawny says.

"That's right. He always disappears once a month, but I don't know where he goes, apart from out of town." Allie turns her attention to Dillion. "Do you know what he does?"

Dillion shrugs. "Beats me. He's been doing it for as long as I've been working for my dad. Once he said something about going to see some friends, but I wouldn't think that'd be every month."

"See, this is what makes him such a mystery." Allie gives me what looks like a reassuring smile. "Anyway, I don't think it's anything you need to worry about. It's pretty clear Aaron is into you. I've never seen him kiss anyone in public. Unless you count when he gives his mom a peck on the cheek, which is super swoony."

I glance over at the pool table again and find him leaning up against the wall, watching me, not the game he's involved in, and I have to admit it seems that way. Which is good, because I feel a whole lot the same.

At ten we pay the bill because Dillion and Tawny both work early. I stop by the pool table on our way out to say good night to Aaron.

He leans on his pool cue, his expression holding a hint of nervousness. "I'm almost done here. I could give you a ride home if you want to wait."

"It's kind of out of your way, isn't it?"

He shrugs. "I don't mind."

I glance over at Dillion, who's chatting with her brother, Billy. The smart thing to do would probably be to go home with Dillion and take this night for myself. Not because I don't want Aaron to drive me home. It's honestly the opposite.

It's only been a month, and I already like him more than I want to admit. My tendency is to jump in with both feet and look after I've taken the plunge. I fall hard and fast. I like being needed and wanted. But Van has a point: I do have a hard time saying no, even when I should. Only this time I don't want to say no; I just think I should because I'm worried that if I stay, I'm somehow giving up the independence I'm working on. Or maybe I'm overthinking it.

"Unless you don't want to hang around." Aaron chalks his pool cue.

"I'll stay."

He smiles, almost shyly. "I need to finish kicking Billy's ass, then we can go." Aaron pats the stool beside him. "Have a seat, babe. This shouldn't take long."

"You stayin' for a bit, then, Teag?" Dillion tips her chin toward Aaron.

I nod, and she comes over to give me a one-armed hug. "We'll talk tomorrow. Have fun, you smitten kitten."

Aaron offers to buy me a drink, but I decline. I had one drink, and my medication amplifies the effect. I'm already tipsy; I don't need another drink or I risk getting emotional, and today has been kind of intense.

Aaron stands beside me between shots, explaining how the game is played and what the rules are. I'm a distraction, apparently, because it takes nearly twenty minutes for them to finish, and Aaron loses because he sinks the eight ball without calling it. He doesn't seem to care all that much. He slides a twenty into the front pocket of Billy's shirt and gives him a pat on the chest, telling him to enjoy the victory while it lasts.

Billy tries to push him to play another game, and I don't need to be up early, since I don't have to work until four in the afternoon, but it's only the middle of the week, and Aaron has early mornings. His job is often dependent on weather and daylight, so he starts with the sun most days.

His fingertips rest against my lower back as we cross the parking lot to where his truck is parked. "You have fun with the girls tonight?"

"I did. Tawny and Allie are nice, and I really like Dillion, which is good since she's going to be my sister-in-law eventually. What about you? Did you have a good time with the guys?"

"Yeah, they've been hounding me to come out, and I've been pretty busy lately. They gave me a good razzing when they put two and two together and figured out the reason I hadn't been around all that much was you." He unlocks the door and helps me up into the passenger seat.

Once I'm settled, he rounds the hood and hops into the driver's seat. I haven't been inside his truck before. The one Dillion drives is new, with leather interior. It's clean and smells like pine air freshener.

Aaron's truck is older and obviously used for work purposes. There's a layer of dust on the dash and a surfboard air freshener that, judging by the smell of sawdust and nails, probably hasn't been changed in a while. The back seats are pushed up, making room for a toolbox and various tools that line the floor. It's organized and tidy but dusty. The cup holder has an empty Dad's root beer bottle in it. The same kind that's still sitting in my fridge.

"Sorry 'bout the mess."

"It's not messy."

"It's not entirely clean either." He stretches his arm across the back of the seat, fingers sliding under my hair until his palm rests against the back of my neck.

I shiver at the touch.

"You cold? You want me to roll the windows up?"

"The windows are fine."

He pulls out of the lot and heads toward Van's place, which I guess is my place now too.

"You gotta work tomorrow night, right?" His thumb sweeps back and forth along the edge of my jaw, by my ear.

"Yup, at the pub. You going to stop by and let me make you a root beer float?"

"Maybe." He grins. "What's your weekend looking like? You have to go to the city, or you sticking around here?"

"I'm sticking around this weekend. How about you?"

"I'm around this weekend, but next weekend I gotta head out of town. I'm always back on Sunday night, though." He pulls into the driveway and parks the truck in front of the garage. He gives the back of my neck a squeeze and tips his chin toward the garage. "You thinking about inviting me up?"

Of course I am. I've been thinking about it the entire ride home, whether I should ask, how I should frame it. Obviously, I'm hoping he wants to come up and get naked with me, but he usually leaves my place at ten, and it's already close to eleven. "It's kind of late for you, isn't it?"

"Is that your way of saying I should take my ass home, or are you legitimately worried about me not getting enough sleep?"

I laugh and shake my head. "You can come up, but don't call me tomorrow complaining about your lack of sleep."

"Deal." He turns off the engine and hops out of the driver's seat, meeting me around the passenger side. He threads his fingers through mine, and I follow him up the steps to the loft. We barely make it through the door before our mouths collide. We fumble our way across the dark space, banging into furniture. Clothes drop to the floor and we fall onto the bed, groping and caressing.

We're desperate and needy, frenzied and feral. Aaron rolls a condom on and enters me on one quick stroke, but once he's inside me, the urgency seems to wane.

The kisses slow and he rolls his hips, grinding against me, pulling me higher and higher until we both tip over the edge.

He rolls us over so I'm sprawled across his chest. I trace patterns on his chest. Most of his tattoos are on his back, apart from the hourglass on his triceps.

"You keep that up and I'm going to pass out on you."

"I don't mind."

"I gotta be up at the ass crack of dawn. I don't want to ruin your sleep." He runs his fingers through my hair.

"You won't."

"You're sure?" His lips brush my temple.

"I'm sure."

"Good, 'cause your bed is warm and I don't want to drive home," he mutters, already slipping into semiconsciousness.

I rest my cheek on his chest, smiling as I listen to his heartbeat settle, slow and steady. I nod off, too, and wake up at two in the morning, still tucked into Aaron's side. I lie there for a while, willing my brain to shut back down, but my bladder is screaming, and I know if I don't take my medication, there's no way I'll be able to fall back asleep.

I carefully extract myself and tiptoe across the room. Not that I need to be quiet. Apparently, Aaron sleeps like the dead. I have confirmation of that when I knock my flat iron off the vanity and he doesn't stir at all. Once I'm done in the bathroom, I climb back into bed and curl into Aaron's side. It takes me almost two hours to fall back to sleep, but at least I'm comfortable, and for the first time in forever, I feel grounded. And I want it to last.

CHAPTER 13

THE BALANCING ACT

Teagan

I wake up the next morning to an empty bed. It's not a surprise, considering it's after ten and Aaron has to be at work early. There's a piece of paper on the pillow beside my head. I expect messy, rushed scrawl, but it's the opposite. And it's not one line but several, in neat cursive.

> Teagan,
> Thanks for letting me crash at your place. I probably would have passed out in my truck and slept in the driveway if you hadn't. And I have a feeling I missed the pillow talk because I was so wiped out. I promise I'll make it up to you next time.
> I'll be honest, I tried to wake you up before I left for work, but you weren't having it. You're adorable when you talk in your sleep.
> Have a great day and I'll see you later at the pub.
> ~Aaron

I hug the paper to my chest, smiling at the ceiling. I'm not sure whether I believe he tried to wake me up, but it's possible. Sometimes I can sleep like the dead, especially when I'm late taking my medication, like I was last night.

Early in the afternoon I head downtown so I can stop by town hall and talk to one of the councilors about the possibility of setting up a farmers' market and what that would entail. The great thing about small towns is that someone is always around and wanting to talk.

I introduce myself to Bernadette, one of the town councilors, who also happens to be Bernie's wife.

"You're Donovan Firestone's sister, aren't you?" she says as she shakes my hand.

"I am." I return her smile with one of my own.

"I'm so pleased to meet you! Bernie has said such wonderful things about you! And so has Donna. She's so happy to have Fridays off! She's been wanting to take some recreational courses the next town over, and now she can."

"She told me about that! I've seen some of her stained glass projects, and they're beautiful."

"They are, aren't they? It's so lovely that she finally has the opportunity to pursue some of her own interests. Not that she hasn't been a big help for Bernie, but I'm sure you know how it is. It's nice to be able to focus on the things we love more as we get older."

"Absolutely. I think it's great that she's taking time to try new things."

"Exactly! You're never too old to find a new hobby. And she's even sold a couple of pieces, so her hobby is paying for itself. She's been invited to a craft fair in the fall, so she's planning on making all kinds of fall-inspired stained glass to sell."

"That's great! And it's actually part of the reason I'm here today."

She offers me a seat in her office, and I share my idea with her. The main street in downtown Pearl Lake is short, and often busy in the summer with all the vacationers. The street leading to South Beach isn't as high traffic, since it's mostly locals who use that beach, but it could be the perfect place for a farmers' market.

"We used to have one years ago, but they can be expensive to run, and not everyone can afford the table fees. They started letting out-of-towners participate, and it stopped being about the community, so the locals didn't want to be part of it anymore. Plus, there's cleanup after the event, and you'd need to have enough vendor interest for it to be worthwhile."

"I agree. I'm thinking twenty or so vendors, and maybe we could poll the community at the next town council meeting to gauge interest? I can write up a proposal and present it. I'd also be more than happy to organize everything. I think it would be a great way to help bolster the small businesses. We could start with an end-of-summer event and see how it goes?"

"I don't think it hurts to see if people would be interested. It's a big project, though; are you sure you want to take it on all by yourself?"

"I used to do some event organization when I worked in the city, so this isn't too outside the realm of what I'm used to."

"Well, if you're up for it, then I say go for it. The next town council meeting is a week from Monday."

"That's perfect. I'll have a proposal ready, and if it's okay, I'll send it to you first?"

"Of course. You can bring it in, and we can talk it over and make any necessary tweaks before the council meets."

She walks me out and shakes my hand. "Your grandmother would be proud of you and your brother."

My heart squeezes at the compliment. I didn't get to spend as much time with Grammy Bee as Van did, but I know she was an active and well-loved member of this community. "Thank you, that means a lot."

My shift at the Town Pub starts in an hour, so I jump back in my car and head in that direction. I fish around in my purse for the energy drink I tossed in there. Despite waking up late, I'm still tired from the broken sleep. I crack the tab and gulp down half of it in the parking lot.

It doesn't hurt to show up early, and if I sit around in my car, waiting for four, I'm liable to fall asleep. Louis calls me behind the bar as soon as I walk through the door, the afternoon rush having already started, and tosses me an apron.

The usual suspects begin filtering in. By four thirty the bar is lined with locals, chatting about the weather, weekend plans, and how they can't wait for the buggy season to be over. At seven thirty, Aaron takes his seat at the bar, and I make him a root beer float and order him the special.

I don't expect him to hang around, since he was up late last night and still has to work tomorrow, but like last night, he hangs out with a few of the local guys, playing pool and alternating between soda water and root beer. I don't think I've ever seen him order a beer that didn't have *root* attached to it, and the story Allie told me last night sort of explains why.

The crowd starts to dissipate around eleven, and instead of keeping me until close tonight, Louis has Audrey stay, since there are still at least half a dozen tables open and the bar has quieted.

Aaron is still hanging around when I cash out, so he walks me to my car. I can't decide if I want to invite him back to my place again or if I should wait to see if he brings it up. I frown when I notice one side of my car sits lower than the other.

"That doesn't look right," I mutter.

"Oh shit. You've got a flat." Aaron rounds the side of my car and bends to look at the driver's side tire. He has to use the flashlight on his phone since the lights in the parking lot aren't that bright. "That tire is going to need replacing."

"Do you think someone did this on purpose?" I bite my fingernail. My car stands out in this lot. Mostly it's work trucks and older cars. There aren't a lot of BMW convertibles on this side of the lake.

Aaron arches a brow. "Not likely. It's probably a nail or something. That kinda thing happens all the time around here."

"You're sure? You don't think I made someone mad? Maybe I need to trade in my car for something less"—I motion to the convertible—"pretentious."

"You're literally the friendliest person on the face of the earth. Everyone here loves you," Aaron says.

"Right. Okay." I blow out a breath and drop it. This isn't the city, where people slash tires because they don't like the make of your car. Or the fact that your younger brother is a convicted felon. "I have a spare. It's in the trunk. Should we put it on?"

"I can do that for you," Aaron offers.

"Maybe you could show me how?" I'd like to be able to change my own tires.

"Yeah, for sure I can, but it'd probably be better in the morning, when we can see what we're doing."

"That makes sense." I'll either have to call a cab in the morning or have Dillion drop me off, and walk here after my shift at Bernie's to pick up my car.

"You wanna stay at my place tonight? It's real close by. We could come back before I go to work, and I'll show you how to change the tire. You'll still have plenty of time to go home and shower before you need to be at Bernie's, if we get up early enough."

"Are you sure?" This is the first time Aaron has invited me back to his place in the weeks that we've been seeing each other. I don't want to pass up the opportunity, but I also don't want to make this his problem.

"Yup. It's right on my way to work."

"Let me check to make sure I have what I need." I pull the rolled-up pants and shirt I always carry around in my purse out and hand them to Aaron.

"Not sure pink is my color," he jokes.

"Ha ha. I always bring an extra set of clothes, especially after a night at the pub, since there's a solid chance I smell like stale beer and french fries."

He steps in close and drops his head, nose skimming my throat as I rummage around in the side pocket of my purse, checking to make sure I have my extra medication with me. I fumble around and tip my head to the side as he inhales and murmurs, "Nope, you don't smell like beer and fries, you smell like dessert, and I can't wait to devour you when we get back to my place."

I lean back into him, body already warming. "Is that one of your cheesy pickup lines?"

"It's not cheesy, it's true." He nibbles my earlobe.

I elbow him playfully in the side. "We're in a parking lot, not your bedroom. Cool it."

"We'd be in my bedroom a hell of a lot sooner if you stopped searching for the closet to Narnia in your bag."

"I need to make sure I have one more thing."

"I have extra toothbrushes, so you should be good there."

"I need to make sure I have my prescription."

"You can't skip it for one night?"

I shake my head. "I have to take it at the same time every night, or it throws me off."

"Right. Okay. We don't want that," Aaron says.

I typically carry enough for a couple of days in my purse, in case of unexpected situations like this. I finally snag the little case and give it a shake. It makes a rattling sound, which tells me I'm right: I have what I need. "Yup! Looks like we're all set. I can stay at your place tonight."

"Great." He grins and laces our fingers together, leading me down the next row, where his truck is parked.

He wasn't lying when he said his place was close. It's only a short drive from the pub. Aaron turns down a bumpy side road and then down an even narrower driveway. It widens after about fifteen feet, opening up to a circular driveway. A small log cabin sits in the middle of the clearing, and to the right is a garage, or maybe it's more of a shed. It doesn't look big enough to house the truck, but I imagine it's where he keeps his tools. The moon hangs low in the sky, reflecting off the water in the distance.

It's too dark for me to see where exactly we are on the lake, but we're a fair distance from Van's place. Which reminds me: I should send him a message so he doesn't worry when my car isn't in the driveway in the morning. I let him know that I won't be home until tomorrow after work. He gives me a thumbs-up in response and follows with a message:

If Aaron is tired tomorrow I'm blaming it on you. Play safe.

"Everything okay?" Aaron asks as he turns off the engine and pulls the key from the ignition.

"Yup. Just letting Van know I won't be home until tomorrow."

Aaron flips his keys around his finger and motions between us. "He cool with this?"

"He's my brother, not my dad, Aaron. And I'm a grown-ass woman. I can do what I want."

He chuckles. "I'm aware that you're a grown-ass woman, and I'm also aware that you can, and do, do what you want. I just mean, he's not giving you grief or anything? It's not like he doesn't know about my reputation around here."

"Van doesn't pay much attention to gossip, and if he had a problem with it, he would have said something already. He's not in the habit of getting involved in my personal life."

"Just making sure."

I feel like he wants to say more, but instead he unbuckles his seat belt and opens his door. I do the same, then jump down from the passenger side. I close the door and meet him around the front of the truck, falling into step beside him as we make our way down the stone path and up onto a platform deck that seems to wrap around the entire cottage.

He unlocks the front door and ushers me inside, hitting the light to the right of the door, illuminating the space. It looks a lot bigger on the inside than it does from the outside. The kitchen is to my left; one wall of upper and lower cabinets, a wall oven, a fridge, and a dishwasher take up the space. The other side has a gas cooktop and sink built into an island.

A small table with sides that flip up is tucked against the far wall. Next to that is a set of sliding glass doors leading to the deck. A couch, with its back facing us, is set in front of a wood-burning fireplace. To the right is a TV hung from the wall. Three doors line the right side of the cottage, one of which presumably contains Aaron's bedroom. Where I'm going to sleep tonight. With him.

"It's not much, but it's comfortable," he mutters.

"I love it. It's cozy." I tip my head up and turn to look at him. "And it smells like you."

He grins. "What do I smell like?"

"Like cedar and cologne."

"Hmm. Interesting." He heads for the fridge and opens the door. "Can I get you something to drink? I have root beer, milk, chocolate milk, water, and that's about it. Oh, and"—he picks up a mostly empty container of orange juice—"expired OJ."

"The root beer is such a surprise."

He gives me a chagrined smile. "It's my drink of choice."

"I sort of figured that. I'll have water, please."

"Are you hungry? I don't have much in the fridge, but I've got lots of snacks. Chips, pretzels, granola bars, nuts, that kind of thing. You can check out my stash, see if there's something you want." He motions to the pantry cupboard.

"Your cupboards sound like a convenience store." I take him up on his offer to have a peek inside, not because I'm hungry but because I'm curious.

"That would be a fairly accurate assessment. I'm not home for meals very often."

"And cooking for one isn't all that satisfying," I finish for him.

"Exactly."

I poke around in his cupboard while he pours us glasses of water. It really does resemble a convenience store shelf. The bags of chips and pretzels are stacked three or four deep, by flavor. "Wow. You weren't kidding about the nuts." There are hickory-smoked almonds, sriracha-and-honey almonds, salted almonds, unsalted raw almonds, almond trail mix, and several other cans of nuts to choose from.

I spot a bag in the back and pull it out. "Goldfish crackers?"

"They're good in soup. Which I eat a lot of in the winter."

"Let me guess: canned tomato soup and grilled cheese is your favorite."

"Less my favorite and more my go-to since it's fast and easy. You wanna keep looking so you can poke some more fun at my juvenile eating habits? There's probably a few boxes of mac and cheese in there somewhere."

"And boxed scalloped potatoes?" I arch a brow.

"Don't start knocking boxed scalloped potatoes, or you can get right back into the truck and I'll drive that sweet ass of yours home." He points to the door.

I roll my eyes. "You're not driving my sweet ass anywhere, except maybe into your mattress later."

"Now who's throwing around the cheesy lines?" His gaze moves down my body on a hot sweep, though.

"Accurate, not cheesy."

"Not accurate if you keep making fun of my eating habits." He crosses his arms, but he's smirking.

"I happen to love boxed scalloped potatoes. I always cook them in a super-shallow pan, and take them out like five minutes early."

"So the potatoes are still a little crunchy," he finishes for me.

"Exactly. Me and my younger brother, Bradley, loved them that way. Van used to get so annoyed that they weren't fully cooked." My smile wavers at the memory.

"It must be hard to have all those memories and try to reconcile them with who he's become."

"He's still my brother; he did something terrible, but it doesn't mean I'm not going to love him. I hate what he did but not him as a person, if that makes sense."

He moves closer; his fingers drift along my cheek. "Your heart is too pure for someone like me."

"What?" I must have heard that wrong.

"Sorry." He gives his head a shake. "Do you wanna sit? We can talk?" He thumbs over his shoulder to the couch.

It's alluring, the idea of opening up to him. But even if I misheard him, I have a feeling too much talking tonight is going to make him hazardous to my heart. Right now I don't want to think, I just want to feel. "It's pretty late. Maybe you should show me your bedroom instead?"

"Yeah. I can definitely do that."

Half an hour later I'm tucked into his side, both of us sweaty and sated. His bedroom is 100 percent him. The frame is rough-hewn wood, and the dresser matches. There isn't much in the way of furniture, the room being built for function instead of style. But the comforter is gray-and-navy plaid, the sheets the same shade of navy. There are only two pillows and no extra blankets. It's a bachelor bedroom through and through.

"So I've been thinking." His fingers sweep up and down my spine.

"Oh? What about?" I settle my hand on his chest and prop my chin on the back of it so it's not digging into his pec. My stomach flips at his expression. He looks nervous.

"You and me." He sounds uncertain.

"Okay."

"I don't really know how to do this." He scratches above his eyebrow.

"Do what?" The panic is instant and makes my stomach somersault.

"I've never had a woman in this bed."

"Because you usually sleep with women at their houses?" I'm trying to figure out where he's going with this.

"Yeah. No. Shit. I'm not very good at this." He blows out a breath. "Look. I don't do relationships. It's just not . . . something I have much experience with, and it seems like something I'd be likely to fuck up. I don't let a lot of people into my personal space and definitely not my bed."

"Do you not want me to sleep over?" My throat feels like it's starting to close up, and my heart squeezes painfully. At least if I have to do the walk of shame, it'll be dark.

"No. I mean yes, I want you to sleep over. I like you. I want you here. What I'm trying to say and really sucking at it is that I like spending time with you."

"And you'd like to spend time with me in your bed?" I try to make a joke, because he seems pretty stressed out, and for a second I thought he was kicking me out after sex.

"Yeah." He smiles. "Exactly."

I smile back but swallow down the stupid lump that's formed. I remind myself that he's literally just told me he doesn't do relationships, so any romantic notions I've started concocting need to be tossed out with the trash.

"Wait. No."

"You don't like spending time with me?"

"I do. A lot. And not just in bed. I was thinking maybe I could take you out for dinner or something. We could go to Lake Geneva. They have nice restaurants. The kind where you can wear a dress and get all fancy. If you want. I mean, I don't mind going to places around here either."

"You mean like a date?"

"Yeah. Like a date. Unless you don't want to call it a date. Then it can just be dinner." His eyes dart around.

"I'd like to go out for dinner with you."

"Yeah?" He sighs in relief and grins.

"Yeah." I smile back.

"Great. How about Saturday night?"

"It sounds perfect."

"I'll set it up, then." He kisses me softly and reaches over to turn out the bedside light. "Night, Teagan."

"Night, Aaron."

Three seconds later he's breathing deeply. I honestly have no clue how anyone can fall asleep that fast. I lift my head from his chest and check to make sure he's not faking it. He's not. He's completely out.

I think I can count on one finger the number of times I've fallen asleep that quickly, and that was because I had to be sedated to have my wisdom teeth pulled and they were impacted. The black eye and the swelling were the worst. I refused to go to school for two weeks until the bruising went away.

I move his arm so I can get to my purse and take my medication. I don't want a repeat of last night, when I accidentally fell asleep and then woke up in the wee hours of the morning. It took forever for my mind to settle again. I also take the opportunity to use the bathroom before I climb back into Aaron's bed and snuggle into his warm, solid body.

The thing about sleeping in a bed that isn't mine is that I wake up a lot. For the first couple of weeks after I moved to Pearl Lake, I would wake up at four in the morning. Sometimes I could go back to sleep for a couple of hours, but sometimes I couldn't.

I wake up at four thirty and lie there for a while, listening to Aaron breathe, trying to match mine to his and shut my mind off. But I can't.

So eventually I roll out of bed, grab his shirt from the floor, and slip it over my head, reveling in his scent as I pad out of the room, closing the door behind me so I don't wake him up. He gets up early enough as it is; I don't want to rob him of precious hours of sleep.

I make a stop in the bathroom and check my reflection in the mirror. There are terrible bags under my eyes because my sleep hasn't been great the past few days. The call from Bradley weighs heavy on my mind. I don't want him to feel alone, but every time I talk to him, it brings up all kinds of memories. Like the day our mom didn't come home after she had surgery and I had to comfort him when he was asking where she was. I shut down those thoughts. They're not helpful, and all they're going to do is make me more anxious.

I grab my purse, take my morning medication so I'll be able to focus today, and spend a few minutes covering my bags with concealer so I don't look quite so unrested before I head for the kitchen.

The coffee maker is sitting on the counter, so I go in search of filters and grounds. I've never heard of the brand, so all I can do is cross my fingers and hope it's good.

Once the coffee is brewing, I look through his cupboards. I don't expect to find anything to bake with, but I'm pleasantly surprised when I discover a box of biscuit mix and a bag of flour. I have no idea what Aaron would need it for, but I'm grateful for it. He also has baking soda. It's probably meant for the fridge to keep odors down, but I can make do.

He does happen to have bacon, eggs, and milk in the fridge. As well as butter. I have everything I need to make breakfast, which, based on the boxes of cereal more suited for young children, I'm guessing isn't something he makes much time for.

I'm on my fourth cup of coffee and have just pulled a tray of biscuits out of the oven when an arm wraps around my waist. Aaron's sleep-warm lips find my neck. "What's all this? It smells amazing."

"I made breakfast."

"I see that. How long have you been awake?" He grabs a biscuit from the cookie sheet.

"Those are probably still too—"

He bites into it, and steam pours out, almost reminding me of a witch's cauldron brewing. "Ow! Ow. Shit!" He chews quickly, head tipping from side to side, crumbs falling to the floor.

"Spit it out!" I point to the sink.

"No. Ow. Man, that's hot." He swallows the mouthful, or what managed to stay in. Half of it looks like it's on the floor. He sets the rest of the biscuit on the counter and grabs the water from the fridge, chugging straight from the bottle. "I think the roof of my mouth is going to peel from that."

"I don't understand why you didn't spit it out."

"Because it's delicious. What the heck is that? And how did you make it with Goldfish crackers and chips?" He takes another long swig of water.

"You had flour and baking soda and the rest of the things I needed. Although you're almost out of butter now. Let me make you a plate."

"Can I do anything to help?"

"If you have jam, you can put that on the table? And maybe the salt and pepper? You take your coffee with cream and sugar, right?"

"Yeah. How'd you know that?"

"Dillion had me pick one up for you a while back."

"Oh. Right. Okay." He grabs the jam from the fridge and sets the table for two.

I make him up a plate and set it in front of him, then fill the other plate with the leftover biscuits in case he wants more. Lastly I pour him a coffee and freshen up mine.

He shovels in mouthfuls of cheesy eggs between bites of buttered biscuits. He's halfway through his plate when he looks up. "Aren't you going to have anything?"

I wave a hand around in the air. "I've been nibbling all morning, testing everything."

"You didn't have one of these, though." He points at the biscuit. "You gotta eat one. They're amazing."

I take one from the plate and cut it in half, then slather one side in strawberry jam. I break it apart, checking to see how flaky they are. I didn't have a pastry blender, so I had to make do with forks, but they still turned out delicious.

"You sleep okay?" he asks between bites of food.

"I woke up a little early. You?"

"Like the dead."

"You were out literally two seconds after you said good night."

"Yeah. It's a blessing and a curse. I can fall asleep whenever and wherever, and it pretty much takes a bulldozer to wake me up." His gaze shifts away, and he looks out the window, toward the lake.

The sun is rising above the tree line, pink and yellow rays reflecting on the water.

"You have a beautiful view." I prop my chin on my fist and watch as the sun slowly rises over the treetops in the distance. "Does it ever stop being magical?"

"I don't think so. I've lived here most of my life, and I never stop thinking it's stunning."

"Where did you go to college again?"

"Indiana."

"Right. And you studied structural engineering?"

"Yeah, but I prefer working with my hands than sitting behind a desk."

He said that last time I brought it up, and I have to wonder if it's his script when someone asks him these things. "So that's why you didn't finish your degree? Because it wasn't what you wanted to do?"

"Something like that. Yeah." He jams another forkful of eggs into his mouth and pushes away from the table, and his chair scrapes shrilly across the floor. "I should probably get ready and take you back to your car. It won't take long to change out the tire, but I know you still need to head home and get changed for work."

"Yeah. Yes. Of course." I push back my chair, trying to understand what I did or said to shift his mood so abruptly. He opens the cupboard under the sink and scrapes what little is left on his plate into the garbage.

As if he can read my thoughts, he grabs me by the wrist and pulls me into him. "Thank you for making breakfast. I don't think anyone has cooked for me like that since . . . I don't know. It was amazing, and it's gonna make me want you to sleep over all the damn time now." He plants a chaste, lingering kiss on my lips. "And I like you in my shirt. I also wish I had time to get you out of it before we have to leave."

I look at the clock over the stove. It's six thirty. "How long will it take to change the tire?"

"Maybe twenty minutes or so."

"And when do you have to be at work?"

"Usually I'm there around seven thirty, but I'm not officially on the clock until eight."

"That should be lots of time, don't you think?" I grab the hem of his shirt and pull it over my head, tossing it on the floor.

Apparently, that's all it takes to convince Aaron that we do indeed have enough time.

CHAPTER 14

DATE NIGHT

Teagan

On Saturday evening Aaron comes knocking on my door at six for our dinner date. I check my reflection in the mirror one last time and glance over my shoulder to make sure my dress looks good from all angles before I open the door.

"Oh, wow." I exhale on a low whistle. "You clean up nice."

He's wearing a pair of black dress pants, a light-gray button-down, and a slate-gray tie. His hair, which is often covered with a baseball cap, is styled neatly, and if I had to guess, I'd say it's been cut recently.

"You look damn well amazing." Aaron's gaze moves over me in a hot sweep.

"Do you want to come in for a minute?" I step back to make room for him to enter.

"I do, but I don't think it's a good idea." He brings his finger to his lips and taps it twice.

I frown. "Why not?"

"Because if I come inside, I'm going to find a reason not to leave again, and I want to take you out for dinner, especially with you looking like my favorite dessert."

"Oh my gosh." I swat his chest. "That was a terrible line!"

"That wasn't a line, that was the truth and a promise." He grabs my hand and pulls me up against him. "I'm going to treat you like an all-you-can-eat buffet later. You got an overnight bag with you, right?"

"I do."

"Go get it, and let's get out of here before I get inside you."

"The worst lines ever, Aaron."

"It's not a line if it's the truth." He raises both hands and takes a step backward so he's on the landing rather than inside the loft.

I grab my clutch and my overnight bag and lock the door behind me before following Aaron down the stairs. He gives me his arm as we cross the pebbled driveway. I hesitate a step when I realize it's not his work truck in the driveway but a white sports car.

"Is this yours?"

"Uh . . ." He rubs the back of his neck. "It's not."

"You know, you didn't have to commit a felony for our date. My car is sitting right there."

Aaron laughs. "I borrowed it from my neighbor. He's in his early eighties and only drives to the grocery store and back. I take his car to the garage when it needs servicing, so when I asked if I could borrow it, he agreed. It smells like old man, but it's pretty nice otherwise."

"I can't believe your eighty-year-old neighbor drives this, or that he lent it to you."

"I'm a good driver."

"I know that. I just mean, that's a sweet ride. Bradley would never let me drive his Porsche, and I'm family."

"Oh, well, that's kind of the way it is around here. And don't look too closely because Chuck has hit a lot of things while driving that car."

"Chuck is your neighbor? And he's eighty?"

"How do you know Chuck?"

"He's the one retiring from Harry's Hardware."

Aaron laughs. "He says that every single year, and then he retires for a month and comes back. I think he likes the party they throw him, and he's been working there since he was twelve, so they don't mind celebrating him like that. He's been a fixture in that place for as long as I can remember."

"This town is something special, isn't it?"

"It has its moments, that's for sure."

We chat as we head toward Lake Geneva, talking about work. "I'm going to attend the next town council meeting and propose a farmers' market."

"We haven't had one of those in years. Who wants to take on that job?" Aaron asks.

"I thought it would be a good way to connect the community. But maybe it's too much. I don't know if people will trust me enough to want to be part of it." And maybe I'm biting off more than I can chew.

"I think it's a great idea. Lots of people talk about putting things like that together, but there hasn't been follow-through. You'll have tons of interest, and the town loves you, Teagan. If you need suggestions or someone to bounce ideas off, I'm here."

"Okay. Thanks, I appreciate that. I've run events for Smith Financial before, so it's not outside of my wheelhouse, but being a new face might be a deterrent."

"Not if you have some old faces backing you up," he says with a wink and a smile.

Twenty minutes later we arrive in Lake Geneva, which is much busier than Pearl Lake. The whole vibe is different, almost like the city has been transplanted here in some ways. Upscale restaurants line the main street, which is well maintained. The nightlife here is different as well. While my dress tonight would make me stand out in Pearl Lake, here I blend right in. In fact, I feel underdressed and like I should have tried harder, but surprisingly I don't care what anyone but Aaron thinks.

We arrive at Fresco's, a seafood and steak house. It's the kind of place I used to go to all the time. Upscale everything, pretty drinks, and tiny appetizers, the food as much art as it is a meal. For years I didn't appreciate what I had. How this kind of dinner out should be an occasional splurge and not a weekly occurrence.

And I feel bad that until now I've never truly appreciated how hard people work to be able to afford this kind of treat. I would have to save most of my paychecks this week to cover the cost of a single meal here.

"Hey, everything okay?" Aaron squeezes my hand.

"Oh yeah, everything's fine."

"Are you sure? Your face kind of says something different."

"Really. I'm fine. It's been a while since I've been somewhere as nice as this, and it got me thinking about how I didn't appreciate it when I had it."

Aaron brushes a tendril of hair away from my face and places his finger under my chin, tipping my head back. "Then I'm glad I get to be the one to take you out for a fancy dinner, and we can appreciate it together."

I smile up at him, and he dips down, lips pressing softly against mine.

The host greets us, and a server takes us to our table, which is outside on the patio overlooking Lake Geneva. It's different from Pearl Lake, the lake bigger and busier. Even from here I can see that most of the lake boasts the same huge homes that take up the north side of our lake. Beaches break up the green swaths along the coast, lit up and lined with restaurants and bars. The water is dotted with party barges, the sound of laughter and music floating across the lake.

I check out the wine list, cringing internally as I note the prices beside each of them. It's embarrassing that I never used to consider the cost of things until we suddenly found ourselves up to our eyeballs in debt. What's even more humbling is the fact that some of these bottles cost what I collectively earn in a week. Minus tips from the pub and the diner, anyway. And what I make in tips during one shift at the Town Pub is almost the same as my regular wages at the diner, the pub, and Harry's Hardware in a week all rolled together.

"What are you going to have to drink?" I ask Aaron.

He grins. "The usual."

"You mean root beer? Do they even have that here?"

"They better, or I'm going to ask to speak to the manager." His summer-storm eyes twinkle with mirth. "But you should order whatever you like. And stop looking at the prices, which I know you're doing."

"How could you possibly know that?"

"Because it looks like you're doing math in your head. And you're biting your lip. It's distracting and making me think about all the ways I plan to put those lips to good use later. Stop beating yourself up for your upbringing and enjoy a night out with me, Teagan. This is the first time in a lot of years that I've taken a woman out to a place as nice as this one, so don't rain on my parade."

"When was the last time you went on a date like this?"

"Back in college." His gaze returns to the menu.

"Who was the lucky girl?"

"Why does it matter?"

"It doesn't. I'm just curious."

"Her name was Alexis."

"Was she your girlfriend at the time?"

"We dated for a while."

"What's a while?"

"A couple of months maybe. She didn't have a lot of depth. She was book smart, but it was as if all her intellectual capacity was channeled into her courses and there was nothing left over for the rest of the people she involved herself with. All she wanted to talk about was how much weight her roommate had gained and how annoying it was that her dad wouldn't put a grand in her account every time she needed a new pair of shoes. The entitlement was a lot to handle. Anyway, it probably should have ended a lot sooner, but she had a few redeeming qualities, none that I would be inclined to talk about for fear of seeming shallow and like a giant douche."

I laugh. "I don't think you need to elaborate on those special skills."

He scratches the back of his neck. "Please don't judge me too harshly."

"I'm pretty sure I was probably that girl at some point, which is embarrassing. But I can also admit to having dated someone with the depth of a puddle back in college."

"This is a story I think I need to hear."

We're interrupted briefly when the server comes to take our drink order. I'm impressed when he doesn't so much as bat an eyelid at Aaron's request for root beer. I order a glass of prosecco, and Aaron suggests calamari as an appetizer, and I agree.

Once the server has left, he makes a go-on motion and props his chin on his fist. "Tell me about this guy you dated in college."

"It was brief."

"But long enough that you brought him up, and obviously there are some interesting memories attached to him, based on the way your cheeks are on fire. Give me the dirt, Teagan. Don't forget that I know how much of a firecracker you are between the sheets."

"Shh. You don't need to tell the entire restaurant."

"No one is listening to us." He motions to the tables around us. "They're all in their own little bubbles, just like us."

He has a point. "His name was Andy, and he didn't go to my college."

"Okay. So how did you meet him?"

"At a bar. Anyway, I gave him my number, and we ended up going out on a date. It was a struggle to find things to talk about, but eventually we ended up back at his place, and, well . . ." I wave a hand around in the air, not feeling like I need to finish that story. "Anyway, the, uh, between-the-sheets part was a lot of fun, but I found out that he had a criminal record, so I lost his number really fast after that. It was fun while it lasted, though."

"Wait, you went out with a felon?"

"It was very, very brief, almost too brief to count."

"Were you a bit of a bad girl in college?"

I shrug. "Not really, apart from that one time. I never went away to school, but I had friends in the dorms, and I stayed there sometimes. I spent a lot of time trying to meet expectations that weren't always reasonable or attainable. Sometimes I still do. It's a hard habit to unlearn."

"Can I be honest?"

"Of course." I tuck my hands under the table so I don't give in to the urge to bite my fingernails. I shouldn't have told him that story.

"I love that you're this closet badass and that you don't let everyone see that side of you. I also kind of want to hunt down this Andy guy and beat the hell out of him, which isn't rational and definitely doesn't speak to my feminist side, but there you go."

"If it makes you feel better, you are far better at other things than he could ever hope to be."

Aaron shakes his head. "It doesn't, actually—wait, yeah, it does make me feel better." He holds his fingers a hair's breadth apart. "But not so much that I don't still want to kick his ass."

The server brings our drinks, and we order our main course. Portion sizes here are so much smaller than they are at the pub, which is good, because most of the time I have leftovers for days when I get a meal from there.

I order the salmon and Aaron gets the steak. The conversation shifts away from our former dating habits and back to the farmers' market.

"Do you want it to be locals, or will you see if some of the McMansion families want to participate?"

"I thought local would probably be best to start. Do you agree?" It's nice to pick the brain of someone who knows both sides of the lake like Aaron does.

"Maybe for the first one? I think over time, though, it could be a good way to bring both sides of the lake together. Plus the McMansion folk have lots of green to throw around, and there are a group of hockey wives who do fundraising. They could be great to have on your team."

"Do you mean the Winslows and their friends?"

"Yeah, exactly. There's a whole group of them who bought on the lake. There are a few over here too." He motions to the lake visible through the window. "This is where they came to retire. Not that any of them are truly retired. I think they could be a great resource for you moving forward. And they're all good people, real grounded."

"It would be great to see the lake community come together as a whole. I know it's kind of a utopian idea, but working together would be more effective." I take a sip of my drink, then switch to water because it's going down fast.

"If anyone can make people see the benefit of working together, it's you, Teagan."

I duck my head. "I don't know about that."

"I do," he says with conviction. "Everyone in Pearl Lake loves you. My mom talks about how amazing you are every time you have a shift at Harry's and how creative and friendly you are."

"You know your mom is the one who hired me, right?"

"She might have mentioned that." He rubs the back of his neck. "It's weird that you've already met my mom and probably talk to her about me."

"We try to keep it professional at work, but sometimes she mentions that you've been busy lately."

Aaron rolls his eyes. "That's her hinting at wanting me to invite you both over for dinner. I figured I should take you on a few dates first before I start making you hang out with my mom."

"I like her. She's nice." I genuinely mean that.

"She likes you too. And so do I. And pretty much everyone in this town." He shifts the conversation away from his mom. "You're approachable, and you have the benefit of being in with both sides of the lake. I think you can do amazing things that are going to be good for everyone on the lake. Just make sure you ask for help when you need it, since I know you're not the best at saying no."

"Don't you jump on that train too."

He raises an eyebrow, one side of his mouth turning up in a smirk. "How many times have you said no to getting naked with me?"

"That's not even remotely the same thing and absolutely not something we're talking about right now." I set my napkin on the table. "And on that note, I'll be back."

"Where are you going?"

"Ladies' room."

When I return to the table, there's a woman standing with her back to me. She's blocking my view of Aaron, and I assume that also means she's blocking his view of me. "It's been almost a year; I swear he doesn't suspect anything. He's going back to the city this weekend. Why don't you come by, and you can fix those lights in the kitchen for me?" Her fingers skim the edge of the table, and I hear the creak of Aaron's chair as he shifts away from her.

"That's not gonna happen."

"Oh, come on, Aaron, tell me what you need, and I'll get it for you. What about a new four-wheeler? I didn't hear you complaining about the Sea-Doo when it showed up at your place."

"Don't try to hold that over my head. You're more than welcome to take it back."

"I don't want it back. Come on, Aaron. I miss you. I can make it worth your while."

I would like to say I can't believe what I'm hearing, but I absolutely can. Portia's mother had a slew of pool boys who came and went over the years. "Gifts" were always exchanged for favors. I shift enough that I can see Aaron and he can see me.

His expression changes from annoyance to disquiet. He pushes back his chair and stands, as he did when I left the table. The woman must realize she doesn't have his full attention anymore and looks over her shoulder, as if she's prepared to chastise the server. At least until her eyes land on me.

She's not unfamiliar. Although she looks like every single woman in her midfifties who's desperate to stop the aging process. But I have a feeling I've met her before in passing.

"Oh, hello." She gives me an appraising once-over.

"Teagan, this is Katrina. I've done some work on her house in the past. Katrina, this is my girlfriend, Teagan."

I struggle to contain my shock over the sudden g-bomb.

I extend my hand, as I've been taught to do. "It's so lovely to meet you, ma'am."

She blinks at me twice before she slips her hand into mine and gives me a dead-fish handshake, which is not unexpected, since I purposely called her *ma'am* to remind her that she could be Aaron's mother.

Which raises all kinds of other questions. Ones I'm not planning to ask.

Katrina is about as warm as a week-old corpse, but the insult does the trick, and she leaves us, heading across the room to a table full of women. I have to wonder how many of them have experienced Aaron's skill set as well. Not that it matters. I'm here with him on a date, and that tells me she and I aren't even remotely in the same league. We're not even playing the same game.

I'm not a secret he's keeping locked behind a bedroom door.

I take my seat across from him. His expression has shifted, those summer-storm eyes taking on shadows. "Are you okay?" I ask.

"I'm sorry about that. If you want to go, I understand."

"Go where?"

"Home. If you want to skip out on the rest of dinner, I can take you home." He stares at his half-empty glass of root beer.

"Do you want to take me home? And by *home* do you mean your place or mine?"

His gaze lifts. "I don't want you to be uncomfortable."

"I'm not uncomfortable. Curious maybe, but not uncomfortable. Are *you* uncomfortable?"

"It's awkward. I can't go anywhere within a half-hour drive without running into someone I know. And shit like this happens. It's one thing to hear about my reputation; it's another to witness it firsthand."

I wonder if this has happened to him before, in the past. If he's tried to take someone out and one of the women from the other side of the lake has ruined the evening by approaching him. Or worse, propositioning him like Katrina did, in a public restaurant, of all places. "You live in a small town, Aaron; you can't escape your past or your actions in a place like this. I knew that before I agreed to go out with you. And that"—I incline my head in the direction of Katrina's table; she and another woman have their heads bent together, and they're looking in this direction, so I smile brightly and wave—"isn't exactly unfamiliar. I mean, my boyfriend slept with my best friend, and everyone knew. Except me. I can't tell you how many times someone would come up to me in the middle of a public place and tell me how sorry they were. And how bad they felt for me. And two minutes later they'd be off in the corner, whispering with each other about my family scandal. Just like those women seem to be doing."

"If I could go back in time, I would change a lot of things," Aaron mutters.

"I think we'd all do that if we could see the future before it happened. Can I ask you why you slept with those women?"

Aaron rubs his bottom lip. "Convenience, I guess. I knew I was just something to pass the time. They were lonely, neglected, with husbands who traveled a lot. Although"—he raises one finger—"I never slept with the hockey wives."

"Because their husbands are huge and could kill you?"

"That's one reason, but mostly because those women are super devoted to their husbands. The women I slept with had already filed for divorce. Or said they were about to." He shakes his head and pokes at his cheek with his tongue.

"That sounds like a story."

"You sure you want to hear it?"

"If you don't mind telling it." Now that I've met Katrina, it doesn't bother me that he's slept with all these women as much as it did before. Maybe because they were serving a purpose and there weren't any feelings involved.

"Last year Katrina told me she was in the middle of a divorce, but that wasn't true. She threatened to divorce her husband, but she hadn't gone through with it. She was never going to bail on her gynecologist husband, who apparently can't find a clitoris with a map and a microscope. The man looks at vaginas all day every day. If anyone should know what he's doing, it's that guy."

I nearly choke on a sip of my prosecco. As it is, I suppress a cough-laugh.

"You all right?" Aaron asks.

"I'm fine. Please, I need to know what happened."

"She's going to live in misery forever because she doesn't want to lose the life of leisure. Which was fine. I didn't want to be her boyfriend. But I thought they were separated, and I found out they weren't when her husband showed up early one Friday afternoon. I had to jump two stories into the rosebushes or risk losing my balls. That was the last time I mowed lawns on that side of the lake. The Sea-Doo was an apology gift."

"Wow. That's quite the apology."

"Rosebushes cause a lot of damage." Aaron shrugs, but he looks like he's waiting for me to get up and walk out on him.

I glance over at the table where Katrina is with her friends. "It's sad that those women are so miserable and they're willing to stay trapped in it because they don't want to lose their comfort. I was the same way. I used to spend ridiculous amounts of money getting my hair and nails and whatever else done. I needed the brand names and the status that came with all those things. I'm embarrassed by the way I used to act and the things I put value on. It took losing it all for me to finally see that all of it was an illusion. A mask to hide all the discontent." I blow out a breath. "Sorry, that was a tangent you didn't need. What I'm trying to say is that if anyone should be uncomfortable, it should be that woman, not you. I don't want her to put a damper on our date, so if you want to go, we can go, but I don't need you to take me home unless that's what you want to do."

"I don't want her to ruin our evening either."

"Okay. So we don't let her." I slide my hand across the table and touch the tips of his fingers.

His shoulders relax, and he curls his fingers around mine. I see something vulnerable lurking behind his eyes. "You're a dangerous woman, Teagan."

"Why do you say that?"

"Because you make me want to believe in the future."

I want to ask more questions, but our dinner arrives.

I've learned something new and important about Aaron, though—there are layers to this man, secrets and vulnerabilities. I want to uncover all of them and teach him that he can and should be loved, not in spite of them but because of them.

CHAPTER 15
TWO LIVES

Aaron

The week after our date night passes in a blur of sleepovers and late nights. As much as I want to stay at Teagan's Friday night, I don't. I have to be up early on Saturday morning, and she seems preoccupied with the farmers' market proposal. I already know she has a hard time sleeping, and I don't want to make that worse by keeping her up late and making too much noise when my alarm goes off at an ungodly hour. I've noticed she has to take medication daily. At first I thought it was birth control, but those typically come in those perforated packages, and the prescriptions I've seen in her medicine cabinet are in regular bottles. I don't want to snoop, but I'm assuming one of them must help her sleep.

So I leave her place around eleven, feeling like crap over the disappointment on her face. But we both could use a decent night's sleep, and I need a night on my own so I can shift mental gears.

I get up Saturday morning, pack an overnight bag, and hop in my truck, leaving Pearl Lake behind. I need the two-hour drive to clear my head. I don't know how long I can reasonably keep this from Teagan.

Or if I should. Hell, I've been keeping it from my mom ever since I dropped out of college. So keeping it from Teagan is kind of a given, seeing as they work together, and how unfair would it be for me to put my secret on her like that? It's another layer of complication and one of the reasons I haven't allowed myself to get close to anyone in a long time.

As soon as I pull into the driveway, the front door flies open and a little body comes flying down the front steps, skipping the last two. He nearly falls over and jump-hops around while he waits for me to park the truck. Jamie's mother rushes out after him, yelling for him to stay put so he doesn't end up under my tires.

Jamie has his mother's eyes and hair, but I can see so many similarities to me in him too. We have the same smile, same nose. I step out of the truck, round the hood, and crouch down as he comes barreling toward me, nearly tripping over his own feet.

"Yay! You're here!" He throws his arms around me, and I wrap him in a hug, dropping my head and breathing him in. The more time that passes, the less he looks like his mom, and the harder it gets.

"I missed you, kiddo. How you doing?" I set him back down on the ground. "You're getting so big! I think you must have grown a whole foot since I was here last month."

"I lost a toof!" He pokes his tongue in the space where one of his front teeth should be.

I look up at Lydia and arch a brow. "Seems kind of early for that."

"He lost it playing hockey with the kid down the street. About a year earlier than it was supposed to, so he's going to have toothless school pictures for a while." She ruffles his hair and accepts a hug from me.

"You doing okay? You need me to take him to an orthodontist or anything? If it's not covered by your plan, I can take care of it."

"It's fine. I took him to the dentist, and she said it's not a big deal, he's just going to be minus a tooth for longer than usual."

"Okay. But honestly, Lydia, if you need anything, you need to tell me."

"You already do more than enough." She threads her arm through mine and rests her cheek on my biceps, giving it a squeeze. "We missed you."

"I missed you guys too." I drop a quick kiss on the crown of her head and let her guide me into the house.

"Grampy's coming for dinner, and we're having burgers and corn and tater salad. I got a new LEGO set! Will you help me build it?" Jamie grabs my hand and pulls me away from his mother, guiding me toward the living room, where a box sits on the table.

"Of course I'll help." I have a present for him in the truck, and I'll have to go back and get it for him once we're done with this project.

"He's been so excited. He's had it for a week and refused to open it until you got here."

"That's a whole lot of patience."

"I wanted to make it with you, and Mommy doesn't understand the struct-tons like you."

Lydia leans against the doorjamb, watching for a moment as Jamie tears into the box, freeing the instruction manual and the bags of pieces. "Can I get you anything to drink? Coffee? Root beer?"

"I want a root beer!" Jamie's eyes light up.

"What's the magic word?" I ask him.

"Please can I have a root beer, Mommy."

"Two root beers, coming right up." Lydia tosses a wink my way and heads to the kitchen, leaving me and Jamie with our LEGO project.

◆ ◆ ◆

I don't get back to Pearl Lake until Sunday night. Spending time with Jamie is fun but also mentally and emotionally exhausting. I wish I lived closer so I could see him more often than I do, but Lydia's family lives in Chesterton, so she won't move this way.

I brush off Teagan for the next couple of days, not because I don't want to see her but because I do. I want to forget where I've been all weekend and lose myself in her.

So instead of being forthcoming about where I've been and who I've been with, I tell her I'm tired and need to work late on some projects across the lake. I also don't respond to a lot of her texts, or I give one-word answers. I know I can't keep this from her forever, but I don't want this to change what we have. I feel like we're in a good place, and this could mess things up.

On Wednesday, when the guys invite me out to play pool, I drive by the pub and notice Dillion's truck and Allie's car and bail.

But by Thursday night I feel like I'm in withdrawal. I wonder if this is what drug dependency is like. And I also feel like shit because I haven't heard from Teagan since Tuesday. I'm guessing I hurt her feelings by avoiding her. Which is reasonable. I told her I wanted to date her, then went away for the weekend and snubbed her. I'm mixed-message central over here.

So after work on Thursday, I head home, shower, shave, change into fresh jeans and a T-shirt, and head over to the pub, where she's working. I know I'm in trouble by the way my heart beats double time as soon as I lay eyes on her. And I feel even worse for keeping things from her, like the reason I was gone all weekend.

I slide into my seat at the end of the bar and murmur hello to the two women sharing a meal on the stools to my right. Fran and Gertie are locals and have been friends their entire lives. Their husbands are best friends and long retired, and every Thursday night they play cribbage and Fran and Gertie come to the pub for beers and dinner.

Teagan's steps falter when she notices me sitting at the end of the bar, but she recovers quickly and stops to deliver the pints to Mike and Jerry, who, like Fran, Gertie, and me, always eat here on Thursday nights.

She spends a couple of minutes chatting with each set of customers before she finally ends up in front of me. She smiles, but it's strained and doesn't reach her eyes. "Hey, stranger. I was about to give that seat away. Can I get you the usual?"

"Yeah, that'd be great." I don't have a chance to say anything else because she's already heading back down to the other end of the bar. I should've expected the frosty reception. I should also apologize for ghosting her this week, but the middle of a bar isn't very private, and groveling isn't normally something I do in public.

Teagan is clearly not in a rush, seeing as it takes twelve minutes—yes, I look at my phone to time it—for my root beer float to arrive. And it's not delivered by Teagan.

Louis sets it down in front of me, one eyebrow arched, shaking his head slightly. "I don't know what you did, but your presence has sucked the sunshine right out of my bartender. It's like watching a damn thunderstorm roll in."

I glance at Teagan, who's down at the other end of the bar, pouring pints for Aubrey, the server.

"She ask you to serve me?"

"Not in so many words." Louis leans on the bar. "Don't think I didn't notice you weren't here last night and Teagan was, or the fact that the past few weeks you've been driving her home."

"Why is everyone always up in my business around here?"

"The problem with living in a small town is that you can't screw up and hide out for very long, so it might be a good idea to fix whatever you did wrong."

He's right. The good and bad part of small-town life is that everyone knows everything about you. Or at least they think they do. And you can only keep secrets for so long. Although I've been keeping mine for a lot of years. From everyone in Pearl Lake. And one of the ways I've been managing to do that is by keeping most people at arm's length. People can't get the dirt on you if they aren't close enough to go poking around.

This entire situation with Teagan shines a bright light on that. But I can make this work. It's not like she's going to fall in love with me or anything. She's here to figure her life out, and when she's done, she'll go back to the city, and I'll stay here, where it's comfortable. For some reason that thought seems empty, but I brush it aside, not willing to face the fact that I'm clearly lying to myself when it comes to how I feel about her.

Teagan manages to avoid my end of the bar until she brings my burger over. Her arms are full of condiments, which means she only has to make one trip. That fake smile is stretched across her face, and her actions are slightly stilted and jerky.

"Here you go, today's special with a side Caesar and barbecue sauce. Can I get you anything else?" Her eyes don't quite meet mine, staying on my mouth.

I duck my head, trying to get her to look me in the eye. "Uh, yeah, actually."

"Another root beer float?" She adjusts the napkin holder on the bar in front of her.

"Can we talk when you're done with your shift?"

"I'm closing tonight. It'll be late." She keeps fidgeting with the straws, moving the box that they're in around.

"I can wait."

She sighs and tips her chin up, looking at the ceiling. "If that's what you want to do." And with that she spins on her heel and sashays down the bar.

I spend the rest of the evening watching her smile and laugh with all the other customers and completely ignore me, apart from when she absolutely has to speak to me. I've definitely managed to put myself in the doghouse.

It's after midnight by the time she finally finishes up. And it seems like she's stalling, wiping things down more than once and spending a long time in the back room. I sit at the bar until Louis tells me I need to go so he can finish closing. So I wait by her car.

And of course, because this night isn't shitty enough, it starts raining.

Teagan comes out a few minutes later, rushing across the parking lot, chin tucked into her chest, purse over her head, trying to protect her from the rain that's coming down faster and harder with every passing second.

Her head is down, so she doesn't notice when I step in front of her, blocking her way to the driver's side door, and she crashes right into me.

"Oh!" She stumbles back a step, and I grab her around the waist to prevent her from falling into the pothole she jumped over.

She shields her eyes with one hand and tips her head back, her lips thin. "I thought you'd gone home."

"Louis told me I had to go so he could close up, so I waited out here for you."

"Right. Well, maybe it would be better to talk another time, when it's not pouring." She brushes past me, and her headlights flash as she unlocks the driver's side door. I rush to open it for her, and she mumbles a reluctant thank-you. I close the door, blocking out the rain, and bust my ass around the hood, yanking on the passenger-side door. Which is still locked.

I bend down and knock, giving her what Dillion calls my puppy dog eyes. It's the look I often use when I'm trying to get her to give up the last apple fritter. It rarely works where food is concerned for Dillion.

Her shoulders sag, but she hits the unlock button. I open the door and drop into the passenger seat. It's really coming down out there now, rain battering the windshield, blurring everything outside.

She smells faintly of perfume, stale beer, fries, shampoo, and a summer storm. I stare at her profile, trying to figure out what I'm going to say without telling her everything. "I fucked up," I blurt.

Her throat bobs and her head drops before she tips her chin up and stares out the windshield. "Fucked up how?"

"I did something I shouldn't have this week." I did a lot of things I shouldn't have.

"I thought you weren't sleeping with the women on the other side of the lake anymore."

"What?" I'm confused because this conversation has taken a swift left turn down a hill and into a ditch.

"I guess we never discussed exclusivity, so it's probably my fault for assuming that we were." Teagan grips the steering wheel, and her chin does that trembling thing, like it did that first day when I was less than pleasant with her.

"Whoa, whoa. Hold on a second. I know I have a reputation, but I haven't slept with any of the women from the other side of the lake in a long time, and I don't plan to either. Why would you jump to that kind of conclusion?"

"You were gone this weekend, and then Monday and Tuesday you worked late. You weren't out with the guys on Wednesday, and you blew me off all week. And the first thing out of your mouth was that you'd fucked up, followed by doing something you shouldn't have. What other conclusion is there? Other than you're having second thoughts about this whole thing." She motions between us.

"Wow. Okay. I can see where I went wrong there. I mean I fucked up by blowing you off this week. When I said I was working on projects on the other side of the lake, I meant exactly that; it wasn't a euphemism for anything else."

She's quiet for a few seconds before she finally asks, "Why did you blow me off, then? Did I do something wrong?"

I run my hands down my legs. "No. You didn't do anything wrong. I had some family stuff I had to deal with this weekend, and I wasn't in a great frame of mind when I got home. I didn't want to put that on you, because my family shit isn't a problem you should have to deal with."

"You could have told me that. I would have understood if you needed space."

I rub my bottom lip. "Yeah. I see that now. I wasn't kidding when I told you I don't have a lot of experience when it comes to actual relationships. When I'm in a mood, I generally try to avoid people so I don't subject them to it."

"We all have good days and bad ones. You can show me all your sides, Aaron. It's not going to scare me away."

I want to believe that's true, but there are parts of my life and my past that are the kind of ugly even I can't face. And if I can't deal with it, how can I expect someone else to?

CHAPTER 16
LITTLE SIGNS

Teagan

After spending hours putting together the proposal, I get town approval
to go ahead with the farmers' market. We decide end of summer would
be the best time to host it, and if that goes well, I'd like to petition to
have one closer to the holidays. But first I need to get this one off the
ground. I don't account for quite how much work it is, even with a
handful of volunteers. It's a lot different from planning events for a
financial firm with lots of overhead and a team of people who are getting paid to help run things. Regardless, I'm determined to make this
happen and for it to be a success.

As spring rolls into summer, Aaron and I fall into a comfortable
routine. We alternate between nights at my place and nights at his. We
go to the summer beach parties together; he teaches me new things,
like how to drive a boat and water-ski. We go on hikes and take day
trips on the weekends. We don't go for dinner in Lake Geneva again,
but we frequent the local restaurants, and on the rare occasions when
we go out for a nice dinner, it's often tacked onto one of our day trips,

far outside Pearl Lake, where he's not likely to run into women he's previously slept with.

And once a month he's gone for a weekend. Every time he returns, he's quiet and distant for a few days. He hasn't said who he goes to see, and I don't want to force it out of him, but I don't understand why he won't tell me. I've tried to bring it up casually with his mom when we're working at Harry's together; she seems to think he's going to see friends from college. But that time we had the blowout, he said it had to do with family. It makes me think he's lying to one of us.

Often it's on those weekends that I make the trip to visit my dad and Danielle.

And while I don't love the silence that follows Aaron's weekends away, it's a reminder to keep my feelings for him in check. As much as I like Aaron, and as much as he seems to like me, becoming too dependent on him isn't a good idea, especially when I know he's keeping a part of himself closed off from me. And by Wednesday, Aaron is back to his usual self.

It's a Friday afternoon, and I'm counting down the hours until the end of the day. Aaron and I have plans to head to the drive-in tonight for a movie. He has an air mattress, sleeping bags, and pillows ready to go so we can sit in the back and watch under the stars.

We've gone a couple of times over the summer, and it's fun. Plus, we fool around under the sleeping bags—PG-13 version—which leads to R-rated sex later, when we're back at his place.

At four in the afternoon, an hour before I'm done for the day at Bernie's, my phone lights up with a call from him. "Hey! I was just thinking about you."

"Hey, babe."

"Can I tell you how excited I am for movie night?"

"About tonight."

I can already feel the disappointment settling in. "You have to cancel."

"I'm sorry, Teagan. Some family stuff came up that I gotta take care of."

"Oh no. Is everything okay?"

"Yeah. I mean, it'll be fine. It kinda came out of left field. I'm sorry I have to bail on you, but I'll make it up to you next weekend, okay?"

"Sure. Of course. Give your mom a hug for me." I want to remind him that next weekend is the one he's usually gone visiting family, but obviously whatever's come up has him occupied. "If you need anything, just give me a call, okay?"

"I will. I'm sorry, babe. I'll talk to you on Sunday."

"Okay. Sounds good." I end the call and wilt into my computer chair.

So much for my Friday-night plans.

It's a necessary reset, though. A reminder that I should watch how attached I'm getting.

Plus I have another project to work on for the Stitches, and the farmers' market is coming up next month, and there's still so much left to do.

At the end of the day, I hop into my car and head downtown to hit up the grocery store. I pick up all sorts of appetizers, hoping Dillion, Allie, and Tawny will want to get together for drinks and snacks sometime this weekend. Although Tawny has been dating a guy from the next town over, so there's no guarantee she'll be available.

I park in the public lot and rummage around in my purse. I need to withdraw some cash since I'm down to my last five-dollar bill. I try not to use my credit card at the local stores since they charge a fee to the store owners every time. Except I don't have my wallet with me.

For a moment I panic. Until I remember that my purse tipped over last night at Aaron's, and the thunk I heard must have been my wallet hitting the floor. It's probably under his bed. I don't have a key to his house, but I know where he keeps the spare. I'm not sure when he's planning to leave for the weekend or if he's already gone, but if I stop by now and grab my wallet, I can steal a goodbye kiss to tide me over for the weekend.

My stomach does flips and somersaults on my way to his place. I shouldn't be nervous, but I am. Worried he's not being honest with me about this weekend. That's how it started with Troy. Canceling plans last minute, showing up late to pick me up. I shake off the fears. Aaron isn't like Troy. He wouldn't do something like that.

I pull down the gravel road that leads to his house and consider sending him a message, but if he's already left, he probably won't see it until later. I pull up to his driveway.

It's long and tree lined, but I can see his house at the end. There's also a blue SUV that I don't recognize parked behind his truck.

I pull forward, park on the side of the road, and walk up the driveway. The car has an Indiana license plate. Which is where he went to college. The sound of voices filters up from the lake.

My stomach feels like a lead weight has been dropped into it as I step up onto the deck and his dock comes into view. Sitting on the edge of the dock is a woman in a bikini. She turns her head, and I get a glimpse of her profile. She's close to the same age as me. I fight the urge to jump to baseless conclusions. He's been introducing me as his girlfriend for weeks. She has to be a friend of his. Maybe a cousin.

The woman laughs and ducks her head as Aaron cannonballs into the lake, splashing her and a little boy wearing a life jacket. When he pops back up out of the water, the little boy jumps in after Aaron, shrieking excitedly.

Aaron picks him up by the waist and holds him out of the water. "That was a perfect ten, little man!"

When he brings him back down, he kisses the boy on the cheek, and the boy wraps his arms around Aaron's neck. Even from here I can see the resemblances.

He has the same smile as Aaron.

When he sets the boy on the edge of the dock and pulls himself out of the water, I can also see that he has the same nose.

Which can only mean one thing. Aaron has been keeping a big secret.

And that secret is a family I know nothing about.

I don't stop at the grocery store on the way home, mainly because I don't have my wallet. In fact, I don't even remember the drive home, period. I think I'm in a state of shock. I keep going over and over the scene in my head.

How comfortable he was with them. The way that little boy wrapped himself around Aaron, like he never wanted to let him go. How bright Aaron's smile was. The way he called him *little man*.

It could be family. Or a family friend. But then why wouldn't he tell me that? Why not explain that friends from out of town were coming for the weekend?

Because he didn't want you to know.

Because he has something to hide.

My hands are shaking as I slip the key into the lock. My mind is going a million miles a minute, to the point that my thoughts are jumbled and all I can see is Aaron hugging that little boy on a loop. He was Aaron's spitting image.

Not once has Aaron said anything about having a sibling. And I can't imagine that Dillion wouldn't mention something like that. It seems too important a piece of information.

I head straight for the bathroom and open my medicine cabinet, pulling out my prescription. The antianxiety medication is a take-as-needed prescription, but I try not to use it too often. If there was ever a time I needed a little assistance to calm down and think rationally, it's now.

I pop the tablet under my tongue and let it dissolve on my way to the kitchen. I open the freezer door and pull out my bottle of vodka. I need a good stiff drink. Probably more than one. I also need my head to stop spinning and my worst-case-scenario button to stop going off.

I manage to make myself a martini without spilling half the vodka on the counter. I drop into my reading chair, sipping my drink, staring at the wall, trying to make sense of what I saw.

My phone pings with messages, but I don't check to see who it is. I'm contemplating making another martini when there's a knock at my door. I'm calmer than I was when I first got home, my worries covered with a soft, fuzzy, protective blanket of serenity.

I push out of the chair, find my balance, and cross the room. Dillion is standing on the landing, phone in hand. "Hey. I thought you were out with Aaron tonight."

"I was. He had to cancel."

She looks me over, brow pulling together, and her gaze darts past me, to the kitchen counter, where the vodka and shaker are sitting. "Did something happen? Are you okay?"

"Aaron's an only child, right?"

"Uh, yeah, why?"

I tap my lip and blow out a breath. "I think he's keeping something from me. Or someone."

"What do you mean, someone?"

I step back, allowing her to enter. While I make us both a drink, I tell her what happened, starting with Aaron canceling our plans and ending with me forgetting my wallet and stopping by his place, only to find he had company.

"That boy looks like him, Dillion. Exactly like him. Same mouth, same nose."

"I honestly don't know what to think, Teagan. I've known Aaron my entire life, but I spent the better part of a decade living in the city, so there are a handful of years where we didn't see much of each other. I'd like to think I'd know if he had a kid, though."

"And I'd like to think the same, but if it's not that, then why wouldn't he tell me he had friends or family coming to visit? The only reason to omit something like that is because he's got something to hide. And maybe that something is a someone. What if he has an entire family I don't know about?"

Dillion rubs her temple. "I just can't see it, Teag. I guess it's possible, but he's so loyal. I don't know. In some ways it would explain him coming back when he did. Maybe him and the mother aren't involved anymore? Do you want me to ask Tawny or Allie if they know anything?"

"No. I don't want to start gossip."

"That's fair." Dillion raps her nails on the counter. "Then I think the only thing you can do is confront him and hope he has a good explanation."

I don't attempt to contact Aaron for the rest of the weekend. Instead, I focus on putting together design plans for the newest Footprint Construction renovation project and work on the farmers' market, since a number of things need my attention. I have emails with questions from the twenty-five vendors that have signed up. There are a lot of balls in the air, more than I thought there would be. But I want this to be a success, need it to be, so I keep juggling them.

On Sunday night I go to bed, promising myself I'm not going to reach out to Aaron first. After a fitful night's sleep, I realize that I can't physically consume enough coffee or energy drinks to stay alert, so I grab an old bottle of caffeine pills from the medicine cabinet and toss them into my purse. It's been a while since I've had to resort to caffeine in pill form, but I need to get through my shift at the diner without falling asleep.

I'd like to say I'm surprised that I don't hear from Aaron, but based on his monthly disappearances and the way he takes a few days before he reaches out, I'm not.

By Tuesday evening I'm exhausted from the constant anxiety and lack of sleep, and I'm tired of waiting. It's become clear that Aaron is dodging me, especially since Tuesdays are my Footprint Construction consulting days and he's nowhere to be found. He calls and says he has to take care of things on another project and doesn't bother to stop by the office at the end of the day.

So instead of going home after work, I drive to Aaron's house because I can't take it anymore. I also need my wallet back. All I have is my credit card saved on my phone, and most of the stores here don't have that kind of payment option like they do in the city.

Aaron's truck is parked in the driveway, so I pull in behind it and cut the engine. I take a few deep breaths. My fingers and toes started going numb the second I made the decision to finally confront him, but it doesn't dissuade me. I took my antianxiety medication like I'm supposed to when that happens and came here anyway.

It takes a minute for him to answer after I knock. He's shirtless, wearing a pair of freaking gray sweatpants, hair wet, as though he just came from the shower.

"Hey. I was gonna call you." He smiles, but it looks like a lie.

He also looks tired. Like he didn't get a whole lot of sleep this weekend.

I huff a laugh and cross my arms. "I call bullshit."

Aaron's brow furrows, and his tired, stormy eyes flicker with a hint of panic. "What?"

"Who was here this weekend, Aaron?"

"I don't know—"

I hold up a hand. There's only one logical explanation for what I saw on Friday. Only one reason for him to leave once a month and keep it a secret from me and everyone else. "Stop lying to me. Why wouldn't you tell me you have a son?"

CHAPTER 17

THE TRUTH OF THE MATTER

Aaron

I've fucked up again.

It's something I'm good at, apparently. And I keep doing it with Teagan.

"There's no point in denying it, Aaron. I saw you with him on Friday, and before you accuse me of snooping, I left my wallet here on Thursday night, and I wanted to stop by and grab it before you left for the weekend. Imagine my surprise when I see an SUV in the driveway."

She's not angry. That much I can tell. It would be so much easier if she were. But the hurt that's etched itself across her beautiful face makes me want to kick myself in the nuts.

Teagan has been nothing but patient and understanding. It's been me putting labels on us, me pulling her closer and then taking a step back when it gets to be too much. She's never pushed for more, for an explanation. Until now.

And she has every right to be upset and hurt. Because I'm the one who's been holding back.

"It's not what you think."

"He looks exactly like you, Aaron." It's not an accusation. Just a simple statement of fact.

"I know." I close my eyes and nod. When I open them again, I see her wary mistrust, and all I want to do is erase it. And my history. I want to be less messed up. I want to be the kind of guy she *thinks* I am, instead of the one I am. I open the door and step aside. "Come in and I'll explain."

It's days like these that I wish I still drank, because I could sure use a stiff one now.

Teagan is careful not to make contact as she brushes by me. Jamie's bin of crayons and his drawings are still on the kitchen table, which is exactly where Teagan's eyes go. There's no point in hiding them anymore, not now that I have to explain.

She takes a seat on the far end of the couch, and I give her the space she seems to need by sitting on the opposite end. The giant LEGO fighter plane Jamie and I built over the weekend is still sitting on the coffee table. I tried to convince him to take it home with him, but he was adamant that it stay here, with me.

"Jamie isn't my son, he's my nephew." Might as well lay the truth out there. This is the easy part, anyway.

Her brow furrows. "I thought you were an only child. That's what you led me to believe."

I nod. She's not wrong. I did lead her to believe that, and for all but a handful of years, I also believed it to be true. "I'm sure you've heard some stories about how my mom raised me on her own."

"Dillion may have said something about that, yes."

"My mom had an affair with a married man."

"From the other side of the lake?" she asks.

"Yeah. She used to clean the houses over there. I guess she got all starry eyed over him, and she was a bit of a sad story. Young woman

180

from a poor family, trying to find a way to make ends meet. Man in an unhappy marriage. You see where this is going."

"She ended up pregnant."

"Exactly. The story I got was that she told him she wanted to keep the baby and he ended up staying with his wife."

"But that wasn't the truth?"

"It was and wasn't. There are always two sides." I lift my ball cap and flip it between my hands to give me something else to focus on while I get the story out. "When I was applying to colleges, my counsellor suggested I try Notre Dame because I had a 4.0 GPA and got a high SAT score and they have a great football team, so maybe I'd get a scholarship or something. I figured it was worth a shot."

"You got in."

"I did. But tuition was expensive. I'd been working since I was fourteen, and even with my savings and scholarships, I could barely afford one year, let alone four. But my mom, oh man, she was determined to make that dream a reality. She wanted me to have all the opportunities she didn't."

"Did she contact your dad?"

"Yup. He was a doctor. Is still a doctor. Makes lots of money and could afford to help out, but I didn't just want his money, I wanted to meet him. And tell him he was an asshole for bailing on us and leaving my mom to do it all on her own."

Her expression softens as the puzzle of my past starts to come together for her. "And did you get to do that?"

"Oh yeah, and I made a huge ass out of myself, because I found out that he'd wanted to have a role in my life the entire time, but my mom cut him out." Not that I blame my mom. She was scared and alone, and he had money and a family. "I also found out that his wife had gotten pregnant a few months before my mom did, so not only did I have a dad who wanted to be part of my life, but I also had a half brother. At first I didn't believe him—I mean, why should I take his word over my mom's, right? I figured I'd be fine with taking his money and telling him to fuck the hell off."

Teagan tucks her feet under her and shifts so she's facing me, her posture relaxing. "What happened to change that?"

"I met my half brother, Devon. We had similar interests, and my dad was determined to give me every damn opportunity he could to succeed. Devon and I ended up in the same dorm, on the same floor, down the hall from each other. We both played for the school football team. We were in the same year and even had a couple of the same classes together. We couldn't avoid each other. He became my best friend."

She stretches her arm across the back of the couch, fingers close to my shoulder but not quite touching. "How did your mom react to that?"

"I'd only ever planned to take my dad's money and get the education I needed so I could have a better life, like she wanted me to. But then I got to know Devon and my dad. It was . . . so different than what I'd been led to believe." I'd wanted to hate Devon, for having everything I didn't—a father, an easy life—but it hadn't been like that at all. He'd suffered, too, through his parents' divorce, the custody battle. We both had our crosses to bear. "It was like my dad was trying to make up for eighteen years of missed opportunities, always trying to buy me stuff. Make me comfortable. Give me experiences I'd never had before. I went on a spring break vacation with him and my brother. It was amazing, but it also felt like a betrayal to my mom."

Her expression shifts, sadness settling behind her eyes. "You never told her?"

"I didn't want to hurt her like that. At the beginning I honestly believed I'd cut ties when I was done with school." But the more time I spent with them, the more I realized that my mom had been wrong about them, or at least things had changed since she'd gotten pregnant.

"But you didn't finish your degree." There are questions lurking in her eyes. Ones that are hard to answer.

"They made me part of their family." I swallow down the bile as I fight to keep my voice even. "And then Devon died."

"Oh, Aaron." Teagan covers her mouth with her palm, and her eyes take on that soft, watery quality, as though she's fighting not to shed tears. "I'm so sorry."

"Yeah, me too. His girlfriend at the time, Lydia, was pregnant. It was fucking tragic." And it was my fault.

She covers my hand with hers, and I allow that moment of comfort, even though I shouldn't. "You all must have been so devastated. What happened?"

"We were. He died of hypothermia. It was . . . I couldn't handle it. So I ended up dropping out and coming back to Pearl Lake. But I go visit them every month. And my mom thinks I'm seeing college friends. I never told her that they're still part of my life. Or how close I was to my half brother."

"She didn't know they were here last weekend?"

I shake my head. "I usually go to them, not the other way around, because I didn't want to upset my mom. No one in Pearl Lake knows about my family in Indiana. I've avoided having them here because then people would ask questions. I didn't tell you because I didn't want you to have to keep that secret for me." And I didn't want her to see me for who I really am. Selfish, thoughtless, unworthy.

"What changed to make you want them here?"

"It was Jamie's birthday this weekend, and he wanted to come to the lake, and I couldn't keep saying no to him." It's almost a relief not to have to guard this secret from Teagan anymore. "There's a birthday party for him next weekend, so I'm going back up. You can come if you want, meet my dad and Jamie and Lydia, who would have been my sister-in-law if we hadn't lost Devon."

"I don't want to intrude on family time," she says softly.

"It wouldn't be an intrusion. They all want to meet you."

"You told them about me?" She seems surprised.

"Yeah. They were pretty ridiculous about it. Mostly because I haven't had a girlfriend before. Not since college, anyway."

"I'd love to meet them."

CHAPTER 18
PIECES OF THE WHOLE

Teagan

Over the past several months I've learned a lot about dealing with Aaron. Every time we take a step forward, it feels like it's followed by another half step back. So I don't push him to talk about his brother, Devon, even though I'm very aware that there's far more to the story than he's shared up to this point.

Not telling his mother about his relationship with his dad, or the fact that he spent four years developing a strong bond with his half brother, only to lose him, tells me that there's a lot more damage than Aaron maybe realizes.

So I accept what he offers, and I wait for our weekend with his family, when I'm sure I'll get more pieces of the story, such as how his brother died and why Aaron has spent the years since then existing but not really living.

I'm very familiar with what that looks like. I watched my dad do the same thing for nearly two decades. It took losing Bradley—in a way—for him to finally start living again.

Aaron puts up a carefree front, but under that is a very vulnerable, broken man. And I'm hoping this weekend will shed some light on why that is. And maybe, if he'll let me, I can be someone he leans on for support while he heals. Just like he's been someone I can lean on while I figure out who I am, sometimes without even knowing it.

"I should tell you that Lydia has no chill, and she's probably going to embarrass the heck out of me as a result."

We're an hour outside Chesterton. We took my car in part because it's better on gas and Aaron doesn't want to put the miles on his work truck.

"How is she going to embarrass you?" I ask.

"By fawning all over you and telling you how happy she is that I finally have a girlfriend. I'm just preparing you for it."

He looks nervous, so I give his thigh a squeeze. "It's going to be fine. And I'm excited to meet them too."

Aaron's father's house is massive, which is not a surprise. It looks like a much larger version of the houses on the rich side of Pearl Lake. It reminds me of the kind of house I grew up in. Except we had a pool and a tennis court.

"This is beautiful."

"My entire house in Pearl Lake could fit in the garage twice. It's easy to lose people in this place."

"Do Jamie and Lydia live close by?"

"Yeah. They're only about ten minutes away. They used to live here when Jamie was a baby, but Lydia got her own place once Jamie was in kindergarten. They still spend a lot of time together, though."

"It's good that they're still so close."

"Yeah, I think my dad was disappointed when she got her own place, but she needs to be able to move on with her life, and living with your deceased fiancé's father doesn't make that easy."

"I can imagine there would be a level of awkwardness if she brought home a boyfriend."

"Exactly."

We're not even out of the car, and the front door swings open and a little boy who looks to be about six years old comes racing across the driveway. Aaron crouches down and stretches his arms out. Jamie launches himself at him, and Aaron lands on his butt and rolls backward. "You're getting so strong you knocked me right over! You must be eating all your vegetables!"

"I get to see you two weekends in a row, Unca A-A! I love birthdays!"

Aaron stands up with Jamie still wrapped around him like a koala bear. "That makes two of us, little man. I barely even had time to miss you."

"I know! And I loved coming to visit you! The lake is so fun. Do you think I can come back again soon, even though it's not my birthday anymore?"

"We can definitely make a plan for that." Aaron sets Jamie back on the ground but happily takes his hand. "Do you want to meet my girlfriend?"

"Yay! Mommy said you might bring her!"

"I did, and she's pretty excited to meet you."

I get out of the car and smile down at the little boy who looks so much like his uncle. "Hi, Jamie, I've heard so much about you. I'm so glad I get to meet you! I'm Teagan."

He ducks his head, suddenly shy. "Hi, Teagan. You're even prettier in real life."

I laugh. "Well, thank you, and you're even more adorable in person!"

"Unca A-A has lots of pictures of you on his phone. Probably more than he has of me." Jamie's eyes are wide, and he's grinning.

"Ah, come on, man, don't go throwing me under the bus like that." The tips of Aaron's ears turn red.

"I don't see a bus." Jamie shrugs and takes my hand. "Come on, I want to introduce you to my mommy and Grampy."

I glance over my shoulder and smile at Aaron, who shakes his head and hits the release button on the trunk before retrieving our bags. He packs light. Backpack light. Jamie has no intention of waiting for Aaron; instead he pulls me along and bursts through the front door.

"Unca A-A is here, and he brought his girlfriend!"

More than one set of footsteps can be heard coming down the hall from different directions.

"You must be Teagan." The woman I saw on the dock last weekend doesn't offer me her hand, instead pulling me in for a hug. "I can't tell you how great it is to meet you. Aaron can't say enough wonderful things about you. Thank you for coming. I know how much it means to him."

"Thank you for inviting me. It's so wonderful to meet you too." I want to tell her I've heard all kinds of great things about her, but last week was the first I'd heard of her existence, so that would be a lie.

Aaron's father comes down the stairs, and I can see exactly where Aaron gets his height and broad shoulders from. Aaron looks very much like his father. Just like Lydia, he hugs me instead of shaking my hand. "It's so great to meet you. I had hoped that Aaron would bring you along one of these times."

"It's wonderful to meet you, too, sir. You have a lovely home."

"Just call me Arnie, and this place is getting to be far too big. I keep telling Aaron he should subdivide his property and let me build my own little cabin so I can retire up there."

Aaron snorts a laugh. "Little cabin my a—butt. You'll build some monster home and steal all my afternoon sun on the dock. Besides, I don't live on the right side of the lake for the kind of place you'd want to build, and I can't subdivide my property. I can set up a nice tent trailer for you, though."

Arnie shrugs and gives me a wink. "Guess I'll have to look at some listings and see if I can't find my own slice of heaven out there on Pearl Lake."

Aaron and his dad are quickly pulled away by Jamie, who wants to show them his new LEGO set.

"Are you okay for a bit?" he murmurs, kissing my temple.

"Of course. I'll help with lunch, and then we'll join you."

"Jamie's a LEGO fiend," Lydia explains. "He's been waiting for Aaron to get here so they can start the new project." She calls out after Aaron's retreating form, "And I'm warning you now that it's probably going to take up a good chunk of your afternoon."

Less than ten seconds later his head appears around the corner. "Fifteen hundred pieces? He's freaking six."

"It says twelve and up. Between the two of you, you should be able to manage."

Aaron purses his lips and gives her an arched brow.

"You pretend to be put out, but we both know you love LEGO as much as he does."

"Come on, Aaron, Jamie's already opened the first two bags," Arnie calls out.

"What? No! One bag at a time!" Aaron disappears into the living room.

Lydia reaches out and gives my hand a squeeze. "I know I've already said this, but I'm so glad you came this weekend. Aaron has been on his own for a long time, and it's so nice to see him putting himself out there again. It's like you breathed new life into him." Her eyes fill, and she shakes her head. "Oh my gosh. I promised him I wouldn't do this."

"Don't worry, I won't tell." I wink and give her what I hope is a reassuring smile.

"Thank you. You know, he puts on this amazing front, but I can see the difference you're making in his life. This is the happiest I've seen him since we lost Devon." She stops arranging crackers on the tray. "They were so close. Losing him was hard for all of us, but especially for Aaron, because he blames himself for what happened."

This is what I've been hoping for—insight into Aaron from someone who knows him better than I do. I glance toward the living room. I can hear Jamie chattering away and Aaron's words of encouragement. "Can I ask about that?"

"Aaron hasn't told you?" Lydia's expression shifts to sadness.

I shake my head and drop my voice. "He said hypothermia, but that was it. I just found out about all of you last week." I explain what happened to precipitate my coming here.

"Oh. I had hoped he'd made the conscious choice to tell you." She leans against the counter. "Aaron has a lot of guilt over how Devon died. There are a lot of layers to him, and to the situation, starting with the way he was raised and what he believed about his dad. I know his mother was just trying to protect herself, and it was a complicated situation, but Aaron was the one who lost out, and Arnie."

Lydia glances over her shoulder. "Aaron came with us on a family vacation during winter break of his senior year. We'd spent the day skiing and then came back and hung out in the hot tub. Arnie was already in bed, and I was exhausted. Devon and Aaron were thick as thieves. They could stay up all night talking, and I knew if I stayed up any later, I'd have a terrible time getting up to ski in the morning.

"The guys stayed in the hot tub for a while longer, and they'd been drinking. I don't know what time they eventually came in, but Devon left his phone outside. He told Aaron he'd be right back, and Aaron fell asleep on the couch. He's always had the annoying ability to pass out in seconds." She smiles softly, and her eyes turn glassy.

My stomach turns to lead as I put the pieces of the puzzle together. "Devon didn't come back inside."

Lydia shakes her head and wipes away the tears as they fall. "Devon was obsessed with the stars. He would stare at them for hours. And he was drunk and not thinking right. He must have fallen or tripped or something. We'll never really know what happened, but the next morning Aaron found him about fifty feet from the cabin, lying in the snow. It had been so cold."

She doesn't need to say more. He hadn't survived, and Aaron had been the last person to see him alive and was the first person to realize he was gone. "I can't even imagine how awful that was for all of you. I'm so, so sorry." I would be devastated if something like that happened to Van or Bradley.

"It was hard on all of us, but I think Aaron has suffered the most. I had his dad to lean on, but Aaron shut himself off from everyone for a while. And his mother doesn't know that he kept up the relationship with his dad and brother. He was living these two very separate lives. We didn't blame him for what happened. If anything I should have made them come inside. I knew what they were like when they were having fun." She wipes away another tear. "He blamed himself. He dropped out of college and moved back to Pearl Lake. I think he planned to cut himself out of our lives entirely, but I found out I was pregnant. I think Jamie gave him a piece of his brother to hold on to. He comes to see us every month."

"And his mom still has no idea you're part of his life," I muse.

She shakes her head. "We've never pushed him to tell her, mostly because we're worried that he'll cut us off again, and I don't want that to happen. He's stuck between two different worlds."

"He really is. I can't imagine how difficult it must be for him." And now I understand so much better why he is the way he is. And why he reacted to me the way he did in the first place.

I don't need complications in my life, and you're becoming one.

Letting someone in meant giving me access to the pieces of himself that he's kept hidden from everyone who thinks they know him. His life is truly divided into two distinct halves. I know only too well what it's like to be pulled between two people you love, not wanting to hurt or disappoint either one. I'm caught between Van and Bradley the way Aaron seems to be caught between his mom and his family in Indiana.

191

I need to tread carefully with Aaron. And I also need to be prepared for him to shut me out after this weekend, because he's letting me into his world, bit by bit, and for him that's scary.

Lydia and I bring the snacks into the living room, where Aaron, his dad, and Jamie are busy putting together a LEGO creation.

One wall is covered in framed photos. There are pictures of Aaron and Devon everywhere. It's easy to see that they're brothers. They're so similar that they could almost pass for fraternal twins. Their smiles are big and bright, arms slung over each other's shoulders, their friendship clear in their stance. Lydia is often in the pictures as well, and if she isn't, then Arnie is. It's clear they have a close bond. They're his second family.

How hard it must have been to gain a sibling so late in life, only to have him taken abruptly a few years later. It breaks my heart.

We spend the day with his dad, Lydia, and Jamie, and I get to see a very different side of Aaron. He's a devoted uncle and a wonderful, caring son. His loyalty shines through, and still, I can feel the walls around him, the ones that I'm sure he's built to protect himself from the guilt he carries with him.

CHAPTER 19
A LITTLE CLOSER

Aaron

Part of me regrets bringing Teagan to meet my family before she knows the truth about what happened to Devon. How he died. How it was my fault. I know what Lydia will tell her, and in some ways, it absolves me of the responsibility.

I know as soon as she walks into the living room that Lydia has filled in the gaps. The ones she can, anyway. I can see it in the soft way Teagan looks at me. But it's not pity, not exactly. Which is good. I can't deal with the pity.

I fucked up. And my fuckup cost us all my brother. I don't deserve people's sadness or their pity. What I do deserve are the nightmares I still have, and the constant reminder of what I had and so carelessly let slip through my fingers.

"I really like her," Dad says when Teagan goes upstairs to change into her bathing suit.

"So do I, but I don't know if it's gonna be a long-term thing," I warn him.

"Why would you say that?"

"I'm not sure how long she's planning to stay in Pearl Lake or if it's temporary." But I know I don't want it to be. And that's messing with me. I want her to stick around. The more time I spend with her, the more I want. She's like an addiction. But far worse, because quitting her would have repercussions that I can't escape.

He leans on the railing overlooking the putting green. Yes, my dad has a putting green in his backyard. "Can I say something, son, without you getting defensive?"

"You can try. I can't guarantee you're going to be successful, though."

He chuckles. "I know it's hard for you to let people in, Aaron, and it's a big step bringing Teagan here to meet us, but at some point I think you're going to have to stop splitting your life in two. You can't hide from your past, and you can't let your past rule your future."

"I know. I just . . . it's hard, you know? I want this to work with Teagan, but I'm worried once the truth sets in she's going to see that I'm a mess and want nothing to do with me."

"It doesn't seem likely from where I'm standing, but I think you need to give her a chance, and yourself." He claps me on the shoulder, his smile a little sad and a lot knowing.

The sound of footfalls coming down the stairs ends the conversation.

I spend the rest of the day watching Teagan work her magic on Lydia, Jamie, and my dad. She's warm like the sun, effervescent like soda pop, and it's so easy to imagine what it would be like to fold her into my life, to have her here on Christmas morning, to make her my date for every single event my dad invites me to. And it scares the shit out of me.

At the end of the day Jamie pulls us into his bedroom, where he's set up a campout. He fights to stay awake when Teagan reads him a story. Once he nods off, we head back downstairs and sit with my dad and Lydia until they're yawning and apologizing, promising breakfast in the morning before we leave for Pearl Lake.

And then it's just the two of us and my truth hanging between us like a garlic-scented burp. Impossible to ignore.

"Hi," Teagan says, voice soft, eyes the same. Her fingertips drift slowly down the side of my neck. "How are you?"

I lift one shoulder and let it fall. "All right. You?"

"Worried about you."

"I'm not going to freak out," I tell her. But I'm not sure if that's entirely true. My head is full, and when I feel like this, I shut down and shut people out. I know this about myself.

"Okay." She runs her nails up the back of my head, into my hair, and then drags them back down. "I'm so sorry about Devon. That must have been so horrible for you."

I let my head drop forward. I knew this was coming. That this was a conversation I couldn't avoid forever. That she would want to talk about it eventually.

"I think the worst part about the whole thing is all the memories I have of finding him like that." I shake my head and clear my throat. "It overrides everything. All the good memories. And it doesn't fade. I know people say it does, over time or whatever. But I don't even have to close my eyes, and I can see his face. I can see exactly what he looked like. It was him, but so, so wrong. He was this horrible gray blue." I scrub a hand over my face, trying to erase the image in my mind, but it doesn't do any good. It's there, and I can't get it out now. "And like an idiot, I tried to wake him up. He was staring up at the sky, arms spread like he was making fucking snow angels. And the stupid bastard didn't have the common sense to get his ass inside. And I didn't have the common sense to tell him his phone didn't matter." I pinch the bridge of my nose. "I'd give anything to go back in time and fix it."

"I'm so sorry you have to carry that with you, Aaron." She keeps doing that thing with her nails.

It's soothing, and I don't want it to be. I don't want to be soothed. I want to hate myself because that's what I deserve. Not her. Not this. "I stole him from his family and took them as mine."

"Oh, baby, no." Her palm comes to rest against my cheek.

"I did, though, Teagan. He should be here. I wish he was still here." I would trade places with him. Give up everything if I could. "I wish you could have met him."

"Me too. Then your heart wouldn't be so heavy all the time," Teagan says softly.

It scares me how clearly she sees me. How much I want this. Her. Even though I deserve none of it. "I can't—" I shake my head. "I can't talk about this anymore, tonight. Can we just . . . I don't want to think."

Teagan's teeth sink into her bottom lip. "Is this one of those times when it's better just to feel?"

I lick my lips, my mouth dry. "Yeah, it's one of those times."

"Okay." She stands and extends her hand. "Let me help you with that."

She leads me upstairs, and behind closed doors she distracts me from the demons living in my head. But I still dream.

Because those demons might quiet every once in a while, but they never go away.

CHAPTER 20
THE FIGHT TO GET IN

Teagan

We don't leave for Pearl Lake until late in the afternoon on Sunday. I can feel his walls going back up over the course of the day. Shutting himself off like he does. I want to find a way to slip through the cracks, but I don't know how yet. He's quiet for the first part of the drive.

"You okay?" I ask.

"Yeah. Leaving is always hard."

"Because you miss them or because of the memories?" I've been tiptoeing around him all day, worried I'm going to set him off.

"Both, I guess."

"It must be hard for you, coming here and then having to go back to Pearl Lake and pretend like everything is okay when it's not." I want to find a way to show him I understand. "I know it's not the same thing, but it's tough when Bradley calls. I want to be there for him, but it feels a lot like a betrayal to Van. You're caught between two worlds, and you don't want to let anyone down."

"Do you even want to talk to Bradley, or is it that you don't want to turn your back on him?" Aaron asks.

I consider that for a moment before I say, "Everyone makes mistakes, and no one should be alone. He's already isolated as it is; I don't want to have a hand in making him worse when I'm already part of the reason he is where he is." I want to find a way to relate, to show him I see him and that he's not alone either.

"You're not the reason he's behind bars. He tried to frame your brother," Aaron points out.

"But I feel like I'm part of the reason. I helped put him where he is, and whether or not he deserves it, I still feel bad, just like you."

He's quiet for a few seconds before he says, "Lydia likes to paint me in a much nicer light than I deserve. I know you want to believe I'm this good guy, Teagan, but your brother being behind bars isn't the same thing. I'm the reason my brother is dead." He looks out the window, his face obscured by his ball cap.

I want to tell him to give himself some grace. It's not his fault that Devon died, but I know better than to say something like that to him, aware that his guilt is stronger than anything else. Just like my dad's guilt over losing my mother ruled him for nearly two decades. He still blames himself for the way Bradley turned out, and I think he probably always will, even though Bradley made his own choices, much like Devon and Lydia did that night. And I'll always feel some guilt over where Bradley is, even if it isn't my fault.

"Do you truly believe that?"

"Yeah. He'd still be alive if I'd gone out with him to find his phone."

"You couldn't have known he wouldn't make it back inside," I say gently and reach across the center console to touch him.

He yanks his arm away. "It should've been me. I should have gone out there. Then Jamie would have a fucking father and Lydia wouldn't be a single fucking mom and my dad wouldn't be minus a goddamn son!"

"I'm sorry." I don't know what else to say to make it better, and I have a feeling that no matter what I say, he's going to find a reason to beat himself up.

"Sorry isn't ever going to bring him back, so it's a pretty fucking useless thing to be."

I don't try to coax him to talk for the rest of the drive home. His comment stings, but I know it's not me he's angry with. It's himself. For letting me in. For losing someone he loves. For sharing a piece of himself and making himself vulnerable in the process.

I barely have the car in the driveway, and he's already hitting the release on his seat belt, and his hand is on the door. "Thanks for the ride."

"Aaron." I grab his wrist.

"I can't do this with you, Teagan. It was a mistake to bring you this weekend."

His words feel like salt in a fresh wound, but I steel myself, aware that this is him working through his own emotions. "I know that you're going to shut me out, Aaron, and that I'm probably not going to hear from you at all this week. I understand that you need time and space, but I'm not the enemy. And I will be here when you're ready to talk."

"There's nothing to fucking talk about." He yanks his wrist free and bolts from the car, leaving his backpack in the trunk in his haste to escape. I leave it on the front porch and head home, my heart heavy.

One step forward and half a step back. Every single time.

I don't want to believe I'm setting myself up for a broken heart. Not when I can see so clearly that this shattered man doesn't feel deserving of the love he so desperately wants.

I go straight to my apartment when I get home, not in the mood to talk to Van or Dillion, since this weekend started off great and went south fast. I expected it, but it still hurts. And I have to wonder if I'm fighting a losing battle when it comes to him.

I dig into work to take my mind off my woes. I have thirty new emails to weed through. And that was just in a twenty-four-hour period. Over a weekend.

I'm sitting in my chair with my laptop on my outstretched legs, eyes starting to droop since I took my sleep medication earlier than usual, when I'm startled by a knock at the door. I glance out the window, noting that the lights in the house are out, which makes sense since Dillion and Van both get up around six in the morning.

At first, I think I must be hearing things. Or that maybe there's a bear outside. But the knock comes again, followed by the muffled sound of my name.

I set my laptop aside, pad over to the door, and throw it open to reveal a very disheveled-looking Aaron standing there.

"I'm sorry I was a donkey," he blurts.

I smile at his phrasing. "It's okay."

"It's not, though." He gives his head a shake. "I brought you to meet my family, and then I treated you like crap because I couldn't handle the way I feel about you and the whole fucking situation."

I step back and pull him inside, closing the door behind him. "It's hard to let people in." I take his hand and lead him to the couch.

"Why do you have to be so fucking perfect?"

"I am far from perfect, Aaron."

"You're patient and kind and giving and understanding. I don't deserve you, and one day you're going to figure that out, and then I'll be right back where I started." He knocks his hat off his head and runs his hands through his hair, gripping the back of his neck and resting his elbows on his knees. "It was so much easier when I could keep everything separated."

I settle my hand on his back. I want to say so many things. I want to fix all his broken pieces. "I know you blame yourself for what happened to Devon, but at some point, you're going to have to learn how to forgive yourself so you can move forward with your life. You deserve to be happy, to be loved, to be cared for, and I know that you don't believe that right now, but I'm going to be here to keep telling you that until you do."

He shakes his head, and I shift, sinking to the floor in front of him, taking his face between my hands, forcing him to meet my gaze. "I will love you even when you can't love yourself. I'm not going anywhere, Aaron."

His expression is pained and yet hopeful. "I don't feel like I deserve to be happy."

I stroke his cheek. "I know. I'll be here to keep reminding you that you do, until you're ready to accept it as truth."

He kisses me, ending the conversation.

Because sometimes it's easier to feel than it is to think.

Aaron doesn't push me away again. Instead he lets me in, a piece at a time. He shares college stories about his brother. We stay up late some nights, lying in bed—his or mine—just talking. I love that he relies on me, that he trusts me, and that he comes to me when he needs me.

Over the weeks that follow, I take on more design projects for the Stitches and get ready for the first farmers' market at the end of August. I manage to entice all my employers to participate in the market. Harry's Hardware has a booth set up with small DIY woodworking projects; the diner has take-out lunch boxes; Bernie's law office is participating because it's National Make-a-Will Month, and they're offering their services for free; and the Town Pub managed to get a liquor license and a beer tent set up with a cordoned-off area for the plus-twenty-one crowd. The majority of the local businesses are participating; even Tucker Patrick from the real estate office has a booth.

The farmers' market falls on a Saturday, and I'm kept busy making sure things run smoothly by going booth to booth, ensuring everyone has what they need. I'm also handing out bottles of water because it's a hot, sunny day.

I've just passed out water bottles to the Boones booth—I went into the shop with the intention of begging them to participate but didn't need to, as they were more than willing—and when I turn around, I'm surprised when Van is standing right in front of me, with my dad and Danielle flanking him.

"Hey! I didn't know you were coming for a visit!" I throw my arms around Dad's waist and then hug Danielle as well.

Dad beams with pride. "Honey, this is amazing."

"Thanks! I had so much fun organizing it. Come on, and I'll introduce you to all of my bosses." I thread my arm through his and take him on a tour, my cooler of water bottles emptying as we go.

We stop at the pub booth, and I grab an iced coffee while I introduce Dad to Louis. "You've got a wonderful daughter, Mr. Firestone. She's a real bright light around here, and we're happy to have her as part of the community." He pumps my dad's hand vigorously.

They chat for a few minutes before I take him over to Harry's Hardware, where I introduce him to Harry and Aaron's mom, Noreen, who are running the booth. "Your daughter is so talented. I can't tell you how lucky we are to have her around here. Bee would be so darn proud of everything Teagan and Van have done to help this town."

I can feel my cheeks heating up as Harry wraps an arm around Noreen's shoulder and the two of them talk about the day I was hired and how lucky they were that someone called in sick.

My dad and Danielle have met the Stitches before, when Van and Dillion had their engagement party—it was a backyard barbecue. Aaron is helping out at the Footprint booth, and I'm unsurprised to see a group of teen girls wearing shorts and bathing suit tops talking to him.

His eyes flare when he sees me, silently begging me to help him. I offer him a bottle of water, and he grabs my wrist, pulling me into him and laying a very non-PG kiss on me. After which he introduces me as his girlfriend. And then I get to introduce him to my dad—although they've also met before, at Dillion and Van's engagement party, just not as my boyfriend.

The event is a huge success, and by the end of the day I already have requests piling in for another event in the fall. It makes all the late nights and too-little sleep worth it.

And the icing on the cake comes after the event, when we're all sitting on the dock later in the evening and my dad announces that he and Danielle are engaged. It feels like things are finally falling into place. So I don't know why my anxiety seems to be worse, not better. But I push it down and tuck it away, chalking it up to the overwhelming day.

A few weeks after the event, Aaron is spending the night at my place. It's the middle of the week, so he needs to go to bed at a reasonable hour which often happens to be earlier than my bedtime. He passed out ten minutes ago, and I'm lying here, thinking about the fall farmers' market. I have double the interest this time, and a bunch of the families from the McMansion side of the lake want to participate as well. I also have the support of the hockey wives, and those ladies love to get involved. Apparently they have a lot of experience with events and event hosting, so they're fantastic to have on board, but they also seem to have a lot of time to devote to things like this, and when they're in, they're all in. So I've been getting a lot of texts and emails that I'm trying to stay on top of.

I also need to read over my proposal and cost list for the newest renovated pool house and outdoor fireplace so I can send it to Dillion to vet. The family wants to get started on it next month, which means we need approval sooner rather than later.

I wait until Aaron's been out for twenty minutes before I carefully get out of bed. I've learned that's about how much time he requires to hit the deep-sleep stage, at which point I can sneak out of bed and work for a few hours before I take my sleep medication and join him again.

I grab my laptop from the kitchen counter and tiptoe across the room. I'm glad I added the folding room divider. I set my laptop up and adjust the divider to block the glow of my screen. I pour myself a glass of red wine—I don't want to open the fridge to get my bottle of white because it's too bright—and settle into the corner of the couch so I can answer emails and work on my Pinterest board. My shift at the Town Pub doesn't start until four tomorrow, so I don't need to worry about getting up early.

I work through all my emails and create three different Pinterest boards, including one for a brand-new account. That email came in yesterday at six in the evening, and I figured it's a good idea to get a head start, since this weekend is going to be busy. Especially since I'm supposed to go to Chicago to visit with my dad and Danielle. And I have a care package I'm sending with my dad for the next time he goes to see Bradley. He needs more books, and newspapers. The last time I spoke to him, he mentioned the prison soap isn't great for his sensitive skin.

The sound of Aaron's alarm pulls my attention away from the screen.

"Babe?" The bed frame creaks with his movement. It drives him nuts that he can't figure out where that one creak is coming from.

I realize that the sun is coming up and I've been working all night. I close my laptop and place it carefully on the coffee table, trying not to make a lot of noise, and then pad across the floor. "Morning, sleepyhead." I slip around the divider and find him lying on his stomach, sprawled across the mattress, hugging my pillow.

I slip under the covers and snuggle up next to him. "Why're you up so early?" he mumbles into my neck.

"I had some stuff I wanted to take care of. Can I make you pancakes for breakfast?" I run my fingers through his hair.

He shakes his head.

"No? What about bacon and eggs, then?"

He shakes his head again, nose dragging along my neck, lips following. "I want you for breakfast." He bites the edge of my jaw and pulls my mouth to his. He tastes like mint, likely because he always has those Listerine tabs handy so he doesn't have to get out of bed and brush his teeth in the morning. "Open for me, please," he murmurs against my lips.

I comply, and his tongue slips inside my mouth, stroking softly. His knee finds its way between my legs, and his hand roams over my curves.

"What is that?" he mumbles, still half-asleep, judging from the rasp in his voice and the lazy way he's touching me.

"What's what?" I drag my fingers down his stomach, over the ridges and solid planes of muscle.

"That taste in your mouth. You're fruity?" He pulls back, blinking a few times.

"And you're minty." I pull his mouth back to mine and wrap my fingers around his length. That's all it takes to distract him.

Afterward, I make coffee and pancakes for him. He pulls me down into his lap. "Aren't you going to eat with me? Where are your pancakes?"

"I'll eat later." I try to get back up, but he wraps his arm around my waist.

"You need to eat, Teagan." He stabs a butter-and-maple-syrup-drenched bite of pancake and brings it up to my mouth.

"I don't really like pancakes."

"Who doesn't like pancakes? These are delicious. Just have one bite so you know how amazing they are."

I give in, not wanting to start an unnecessary argument. Then I steal the fork from him and start cutting up the pancakes so I can feed him one piece at a time.

His gaze meets mine while he chews, and I look away so I can spear another piece. "That one's for you."

"It's huge. I'll have the next one." I poke his lip and he eats it, albeit reluctantly. I use the side of the fork to cut a chunk off a large piece and pop it in my mouth. My stomach is off, probably because I pulled an all-nighter and accidentally polished off a bottle of wine while doing it.

He watches me as I chew. His brows pull together, and his thumb brushes along the hollow under my eye. "You look tired. How much sleep did you get last night?"

"I can have a nap after you leave for work." I feed him another bite, and he glances over his shoulder, toward the couch, where my empty wineglass sits.

"Did you even sleep at all?"

I don't want to lie to him. "I had a lot on my mind, and I forgot to take my medication because I was busy having orgasms. I'll catch up tonight, and I'll be fine."

He exhales heavily, questions in his eyes.

"I told you I have insomnia sometimes, remember? It usually only lasts a few days, and then I'm good again." I'm off my routine, and I've needed to work extra hours while he's asleep, which means I haven't been taking my sleep meds every night, and I've needed more help staying awake than usual. But once I get the Stitches' proposals under my belt and my emails under control again, I'll be fine.

"I didn't realize that means you don't sleep at all."

"I'll be able to nap and then reset tonight." I shift so I'm straddling his lap. "If you want to help, you can tire me out before you leave for work."

CHAPTER 21
CLOSE, BUT NOT TOO CLOSE

Aaron

The thing about spending a lot of time with one person is that they get to know your habits, and you get to know theirs.

Devon used to have this terrible tell when we would play cards. Every time he had a good hand, he would get this look on his face. It was how I always knew when to fold. He also used to snap his fingers when he was nervous. It amped up when he first started dating Lydia. Every time they had a date, he'd sit on the couch and snap his fingers until it was time to leave. It drove me up the wall. I'd give just about anything to have him sit beside me and snap his freaking fingers again.

I'm guessing it's the same with most relationships. Things that don't bug people in the beginning can turn grating. Quirks that are cute in the beginning can sometimes become annoying. From what I've witnessed, it's often a sign that the relationship is going south. I've seen it happen enough times with my friends to get a gauge on how relationships work, even if I haven't spent much time on my own.

With Teagan, it's different. Her patterns and the things she does tell me something about how she's feeling. Or what she's avoiding. Like how she rolls up on the balls of her feet when she's excited, as though there are springs under her, ready to launch her into the sky.

At first, I didn't think much about the insomnia, maybe because I don't typically have problems sleeping. Except after Devon died. For a while I had constant nightmares. I used to dream that I could see him lying in the snow, making snow angels—something he loved to do even at the age of twenty-one—and I'd watch this wall moving toward him. I'd be stuck in the chalet, unable to open the sliding glass door, screaming his name, but he couldn't hear me. And that wall of frozen air would sweep over him. He'd stop making snow angels, his smile fixed in place, arms outstretched, eyes wide and unseeing.

Those dreams aren't all that frequent anymore. But when they happen, it's typically around the anniversary of Devon's death, and occasionally after I've seen Lydia and Jamie. So at the beginning I didn't pay much attention to Teagan's sleeping habits.

But over time I start to notice things. Like the way she compulsively checks her purse for her medication.

Or how she always makes me an elaborate breakfast but often has a few bites and tells me she's going to eat later and opts for coffee instead. And then there are the times that I wake up at five in the morning and she's already up, working away on her laptop, one of those nasty energy drinks on the table beside her, perky to the point of being jittery. I assumed she was an early riser, but now I'm starting to wonder if that's the case, or if she's not going to bed at all. Pulling all-nighters.

I used to do it in college every once in a while, when I had a huge assignment due and I'd procrastinated until the last minute. But I'm worried that it's more than that with Teagan. I sleep like the dead, so she could literally be up all night, and I'd never know.

To test that theory, I set my alarm for two in the morning and tuck my phone under my pillow the next time she stays over. I wake up with a start and stifle it quickly. I run my hand over Teagan's side of the bed.

It's cold, and not because fall is closing in but because Teagan most definitely has not been in bed for a while.

I lie there for a minute, waiting to see if I'm wrong and she's gone to the bathroom, or if she heard my alarm go off, but there's no immediate sign she's awake. Although if I listen closely enough, I catch the soft click of her keyboard. Which means she's working. She's been taking on more and more projects for the Stitches lately. And she's taken on the fall farmers' market in early November, which looks like it's going to be twice as big as the one in August. Both of those things might be manageable on their own, but with her still working five days a week at five different jobs, I think she's biting off more than she can chew. A lot more. And she's trying to balance it all by cutting out sleep. Which is a dangerous and slippery slope.

I carefully slide out of bed, watching my step so I don't hit any of the creaky floorboards. I find her in the living room on the couch, laptop in her lap, typing away.

"Babe, you should come to bed."

She startles and looks up from her laptop. "Oh, hey, did I wake you?"

I shake my head and run a hand through my hair. "I had to go to the bathroom, and you weren't all snuggled up beside me."

"I remembered I had an email I needed to manage."

"It's two in the morning; that must have been one hell of an email." I notice the can on the table, one of those freaking energy drinks she's been guzzling like water lately.

"Is it really? I must have lost track of time." She smiles, but her eyes dart away. "I'll finish this up and come back to bed."

"I'm gonna use the bathroom."

"Okay."

I shuffle down the hall, use the bathroom because I'm already up, so I might as well. Instead of going back to bed and waiting for her, like I'm sure she expects me to, I return to the living room and stand at the end of the couch.

"Just one more minute."

"Those emails aren't going anywhere. And no one expects you to answer them in the middle of the night. Come back to bed, please."

"I'm in the middle of a thought, just a second," she snaps.

Teagan never snaps. Apart from at the beginning, when I was being a donkey and hurt her feelings. I stand there for a few seconds, debating my options. I won't have a problem going back to sleep, so I could literally stand here for an hour while she clacks away on her keyboard—and possibly fall asleep while remaining upright—but I'm thinking that's not going to go over well.

So I do something I'm not proud of but will likely get the result I want, which is Teagan in bed beside me. Not burning the candle at both ends. I take a seat beside her on the couch.

"I swear, Aaron, I'll be in bed in two minutes. You don't need to monitor me."

"I know. I just . . . I need you."

That gets her to stop with the typing. She glances over at me. "Are you okay?"

"I had a dream about my brother." It's not entirely untrue. I did have a dream about my brother, but it wasn't tonight. Occasionally I dream about him after I see Jamie or talk about Devon. But that was weeks ago.

"Oh, baby." She closes her laptop and sets it on the coffee table, then shifts so she's facing me. She runs her fingers through my hair. "Do you need to talk about it?"

I shake my head, feeling like an asshole for manipulating her. "I need you beside me so I know you're safe." I send an apology up to heaven, where I'm sure Devon is, looking down on me with judgment over using his death to coerce my girlfriend not to pull an all-nighter.

"Of course. Let's go to bed."

She takes my hand, and we head back to bed. She rummages around in her purse in the dark, and I hear the tinkle of pills being shaken out of a bottle. She takes a sip from the glass on the nightstand and slips under the sheets. I slide my arm under her and pull her against me.

"I'm sorry I wasn't here when you woke up."

"It's okay."

"I promise I'll be right here beside you the next time you wake up." She settles her palm on my chest, and I cover her hand with mine.

I fight to stay awake long enough to make sure she does go to sleep, but I suck at staying conscious when I'm lying down. In the morning she's still tucked into my side. She doesn't move at all when I get out of bed, and I stand there staring down at her sleeping form.

I want to think this is a onetime thing, but I don't know if it is.

I glance at the nightstand, where her glass of water sits. And two different prescription bottles. I pick them up and read the names. I have no idea what one is, but it says she's supposed to take it at night. The other is a name I recognize. Adderall. There were always kids in college looking for this kind of thing to help them focus better. I didn't know Teagan had any issues with attention, although that probably makes sense if she's taking these every day.

The bottle is mostly empty, and there are refills on the prescription. I can't see a doctor prescribing something she doesn't need. But I'm also the type of guy who doesn't take Tylenol unless absolutely necessary, so I generally avoid prescription medication whenever possible.

Teagan is still out cold by the time I'm ready to leave for work. Her shift at the Town Pub doesn't start until later in the afternoon, so I press a kiss to her temple and leave her to get what I'm expecting is some much-needed sleep.

I stop at Boones on the way to the office. I hadn't wanted to make a lot of noise and risk disturbing Teagan's sleep, so I skipped out on breakfast and coffee at home. I grab fritters and coffee for everyone and head for Footprint Construction.

I dole out coffees and fritters, and we go over the schedule for the week. We're working on two different McMansion renos at the same time, and we've had to hire a few local guys to help. While Jack doesn't do much of the grunt work anymore, he does spend a lot of time going between the projects, making sure things are running smoothly, and helping where he's needed. It means that I've stepped into a foreman-type role when it's me and a few of the younger, less experienced guys.

John, Jack, and Billy take their coffees and fritters to go, leaving me and Dillion in the office. We need to go over one of the plans for an addition, which is perfect because it means I can ask her a couple of questions in private.

"How many projects do you have Teagan working on right now?"

"A few. I can't even tell you how awesome it's been having her help. With all these huge renos, we needed someone with an eye for design, and it's not something anyone local has a lot of experience with."

"Yeah, she really does have an eye for design." She rearranged my living room, and now the space looks twice as big. "Can I ask you something?"

"Yeah, sure. What's up?"

"It's about Teagan, and it's kind of personal."

"Is everything okay with you two?" Dillion's expression shifts to concern.

"Yeah. We're good." I flip a pencil between my fingers, needing to do something with my hands.

The tension in her shoulders eases slightly. "Okay. That's good. You two seem like a bit of an unlikely pair, but I'm glad you work together."

"Me too." I nod a couple of times. "I'm worried about her."

She stops leafing through her day planner and gives me her full attention. "Worried how?"

I bite the inside of my cheek. I don't know how much I should or shouldn't say, but any kind of advice I can get is better than nothing.

I tell Dillion about what happened last night and how I have a feeling it's not the first time.

"She told me she has insomnia sometimes, but I don't know. I worry that she's bitten off more than she can chew. She's working five different jobs, she's putting together all these design plans, and she's taken on the entire fall farmers' market on her own. The last two on their own would be a lot, but with everything else . . . I don't know. I'm concerned she's overwhelmed but she doesn't want to disappoint anyone?" It's framed like a question, because that seems to be something Teagan might do.

Dillion leans back in her chair, realization dawning. "Oh shit, Van warned me that she's terrible at saying no, and I've been handing her new projects, thinking he was joking."

"I don't know if she recognizes that she's taking on too much. I keep finding her in the living room working on emails first thing in the morning or the middle of the night." I scrub a hand over my face. "She has a bunch of prescriptions; one is for attention issues." I don't want to talk about her behind her back, but I want to see what Dillion knows.

Her expression is pensive. "Oh yeah, Van mentioned that before. I think she was diagnosed as a kid or something? They never made a big thing about it because they didn't want her to feel stigmatized or like it defined her as a person."

"Okay. That makes sense." And Dillion understands what that's like, since Billy was diagnosed last year with bipolar disorder. It's part of who he is, but it doesn't define him as a whole person. "I just . . . the whole not-sleeping thing worries me a lot. She's always hopped up on those energy drinks, which I don't think is helping her at all. And her not being able to say no is probably making it all worse."

Dillion taps her fingers on the desk. "She's always been the kind of person to put herself last. Her job, her living situation, even her ex-boyfriend."

"You mean the asshole who cheated on her?"

Dillion nods. "She started dating him because her dad thought he would be a good, stable partner. And then she kept trying to make it work even though she wasn't invested because her dad liked him."

"I didn't know that." But I'm starting to think there are a lot of things Teagan is hiding. And under that sunshine-and-smiles facade is a woman facing a lot of demons. I wish she understood she doesn't have to face them alone.

Dillion makes a face, like she's concerned she's crossed a line. "I don't know how much I should or shouldn't say. I don't want to get into your personal business, Aaron, but she's been through a lot, and I think she's still trying to figure things out. And maybe taking on too much in the process."

I hold up a hand to stop her from having to step into the awkward territory of my relationship nonhistory and what exactly I'm doing with Teagan. "We're well past the fling stage. I know I don't have the best track record, but I'm serious about her."

"Okay. That's good. I hoped that's where you were at, since the two of you are always together, but I wanted to make sure." Dillion blows out a breath. "Van worries about her a lot. She was only six when her mom died, and the coping strategies in that house weren't great. Their dad is a good guy, but he has the money-managing skills of a teenager on a shopping spree. He used money as a substitute for actual parenting. Add to it her brother going to jail for fraud, her feeling like she's part of the reason her brother is in jail, her ex breaking it off and dating her former best friend, and having her entire family's financial status shift— that would be a lot for anyone. Her entire world has been thrown into upheaval, and now she's on this soul-searching mission."

"I wonder if her talking to Bradley isn't helping things, either," I muse.

"She's talking to Bradley?" Dillion's eyes are as wide as saucers.

Half of me wants to backtrack, because based on her expression, Teagan hasn't told Dillion or Van that she's talking to her brother in jail. "I think he calls her sometimes."

"Shit. Did she initiate it, or did he?"

"I don't know. I probably shouldn't have said anything."

"Bradley's a manipulator, and Teagan can't say no." She scrubs a hand over her face.

"Maybe it's not malicious on his part?" Dillion's feelings about Bradley are tainted by Van's experience.

"Maybe, but I think we've all learned that the word *no* doesn't seem to be in Teagan's vocabulary."

I don't know if there's ever been a time in our relationship when Teagan has been anything but agreeable. And that's . . . unnerving at best. "Do you think she's afraid of letting people down? Or she's looking for approval?" I think about the ways I dealt with losing Devon. I couldn't focus in school. Nothing I read was absorbed. My head was a spinning mess of guilt and pain. I tipped over the edge and found an escape in alcohol, looking to numb the feelings. I failed a bunch of assignments and moved back home, to Pearl Lake.

I got a job with Dillion's dad, worked long, grueling hours. Wearing out my body was the only way I could settle my mind enough to be able to sleep. And I needed that break from all the noise in my head, because the drinking was only making things worse, not better.

"Maybe? I can lighten her load up for the next little while, at least until she's done with the projects she's currently working on."

"I don't want to take things away from her, but if you can keep an eye on her, that would be great. The not sleeping worries me. It's not a sustainable way to live." Exhaustion leads to poor decision-making.

"Do you think she'd be willing to quit one of her jobs?" Dillion asks.

"She probably needs to. I'll see if I can work on getting her to do that." Although based on what I'm learning about Teagan, I'm not sure how easy that's going to be.

"Okay." She flips a pen between her fingers. "Do you want me to talk to Van, see if he knows anything about the medications she's taking?"

I shake my head. "No. I don't want to put you in a weird position or do anything to make Teagan think I'm not on her side. I can do some research. I don't want to make him worry more than he already is. I'll keep an eye on her and see if cutting back the demands helps." I lace my fingers behind my neck. "Can we keep this between us for now? I don't want to betray Teagan's trust or give her a reason not to confide in me."

"Yeah, I can do that. You'll let me know if you think there's anything else to worry about?"

"For sure. I'm hoping she's just overwhelmed with everything and that we can take some of the pressure off."

CHAPTER 22
OOPS

Teagan

I have to change my routine up because Aaron keeps insisting I come to bed at the same time as him every night. If I don't take my sleep medication before I snuggle up with him, he mentions it, so I do something I shouldn't and switch them out for caffeine pills sometimes so I can get work done after he passes out.

And he always wants to spoon. Which I love, but he wraps himself right around me, like an octopus. Half the time I wake him up when I try to wrangle myself out of his hold, and then I have to wait for him to fall asleep again before I can get up and tackle a few emails, set up a design board, or make sure everything is ready for the fall market.

I don't want to let anyone down. I've managed to get over forty vendors to sign up for the fall market. Even some of the summer families are participating. A few of the hockey wives have great skills. One of their daughters is an avid sewer with a sense of humor. She makes these pillows called Butt Pucks to sit on during hockey games, and I thought it would be a great thing to sell, especially with winter on the way.

I make sure I'm in bed well before Aaron gets up for work. Besides, I need at least a few hours so I can manage my shift at Harry's tomorrow. I get anxious every time I see Noreen, knowing that Aaron is keeping secrets from her, and now so am I. Sometimes it makes my sleep the night before a shift even more spotty. My alarm is set for seven thirty, but I hit the snooze button five times. I don't even have time to shower or make a coffee before I leave for work. Instead, I grab an energy drink from the fridge. I need to stock up on those, since I only have one left.

I'm forced to throw my hair in a ponytail and take my travel makeup case with me so I can dab concealer under my eyes on the way in. I've never been late for a shift, and I don't want to start now.

I'm fishing around in my purse for my bottle of caffeine pills because I'm still feeling groggy when I end up taking one of the turns too quickly. The gravel road needs to be graded, and it's turned into a washboard on the bend, making it hard to get any kind of grip with my tires. I skid out and try to correct, but I overcompensate and end up in a ditch.

I get out of my car, glad that this isn't a highly traveled road, and survey the damage. It doesn't look like I've done much to the car, apart from a few scratches and a couple of small dents. My hands are shaking, though, and I can feel that familiar panic rising, making my toes and fingers go numb. I quickly root around in my purse, debating whether it's a good idea to add antianxiety medication to the mix, but I decide I'm too shaken to be able to deal without it.

The incline is too steep to be able to back the car out of the ditch. Van is in Chicago today at the office. I don't want to call Dillion. She'll tell Van, and I don't want him to worry about me. Last week he mentioned that I seemed to have a lot on my plate and that I looked tired.

Aaron is definitely out. He's already concerned about my sleep and how much I'm taking on. I also don't want to upset him or cause an argument. I don't want him to know how irresponsible and careless I was.

Calling a tow truck could work, but then someone might say something to someone else. I can't leave my car here, though. I scroll through my contacts until I reach Billy's name and number.

He was in a DUI accident last year. If there's anyone who understands how much it sucks for people to know your business, it's him. I cross my fingers and hit the call button. He answers on the second ring. "Hello?"

"Hi, Billy, it's Teagan, Van's sister."

"Oh, hey. Hi. How's it going? You need to talk to Dillion and she's not answering her phone or something?" he asks.

Billy and I haven't spent a whole lot of time together. He comes to the pub and plays pool with Aaron, and sometimes he'll come for dinner at the cottage, but he's a quiet guy. Nice but quiet.

"Um, no. I'm sorry to call you out of the blue, but, uh . . . I have a bit of a situation, and I could use a hand."

"A situation? What kind of situation?"

"I'm having some car trouble, and I wondered if maybe you could help me out." I might be downplaying it, but again, I don't want to alert anyone I don't have to about this.

"Oh. Well, yeah. Of course. Where are you?"

"I'm halfway between Van's and downtown."

"Is that close to the S-bend?"

"That's it exactly. Would you mind coming to get me? If you're working or it's inconvenient, I'll figure something else out."

"Nah, it's cool. I was just on my way out the door 'cause it's a late start for me. I should be there in less than ten, that okay?"

"That'd be great. I'll owe you one. If you have tow equipment, it might help."

"Right. Okay. I'll be there soon."

I call Harry's and tell them I have a flat but that I should be there in an hour or so. Of course, they offer to send someone to pick me up, but I tell them I'm okay and that I already have it under control.

Less than ten minutes later the Footprint Construction truck comes around the bend and pulls over to the side of the road. Billy is tall and lanky with a mop of curly blond hair and blue eyes. He hops out of the truck, and his brows lift. "Oh, wow, what the heck happened?"

"I tried to swerve to avoid a chipmunk," I lie.

He surveys the road, eyes shifting between me, the skid marks, and my car in the ditch. "You sure you weren't taking the bend too quick? You really gotta slow down this time of year, 'cause they only grade the road at the beginning of the summer and then a little later in the fall."

I bite the inside of my lip. Lying again seems silly since it's clear he knows what actually happened. "I guess I learned that the hard way, huh? Do you think you can pull me out?"

He doesn't say anything about my lie. Instead, he walks around the perimeter of the car. "I should be able to. Might end up with a few extra scratches and dings, though."

"That's okay. I can deal with scratches and dings."

He rubs the back of his neck. "Okay. Let me get the tow rope hooked up, and we'll see what I can do."

Twenty minutes later my car is back on the road with minimal damage. I'm grateful that no one has driven by.

"Thank you so much, you have no idea how much I appreciate your help, Billy." I clasp my hands together to keep them from shaking. I'm sweaty, and my heart feels like it's trying to pound its way out of my chest.

He tucks his thumb in his pocket. "No problem. You might want to take it to the garage in town to make sure the frame isn't bent or anything."

"Okay. I can do that."

"Can I ask you something?" Billy rubs the scruff on his chin.

"Sure. Of course." I fight not to fidget or bite the inside of my cheek until it bleeds. I don't know that the caffeine-and-antianxiety combination was such a good idea. I want to simultaneously run a marathon and take a nap.

"Why'd you call me and not Aaron?" His eyes meet mine and narrow the tiniest bit.

One thing I've learned about Billy is that he generally tells it like it is. Dillion is much the same way. I glance at my car so I don't have to focus on him. "I figured if anyone would understand how much it sucks to have people talking, it would be you. And I didn't want Aaron to worry."

He rubs the scruff on his chin. "Does that mean I should be worried?"

I give him what I hope is a reassuring smile. "I was just driving too fast because I was rushing."

He's quiet for a few moments. "You're sure that's all it was?"

"I'm sure."

He exhales through his nose. "Be careful, Teagan, all right? And take it easy on these roads. You're important to a lot of people around here. I wouldn't want anything bad to happen, and this could've been a lot worse." He motions to the scratches and small dents on my car.

"I understand. I promise I'll be careful. Can we keep this between us?"

His eyes search mine. "Am I going to regret doing that?"

"No. I promise I was distracted and rushing. I don't want to upset Aaron or my brother."

"That's the part I'm worried about. Just . . . be more careful with yourself."

"I will. I gotta get to Harry's, but when I get home, I'll make you some muffins or biscuits, okay?"

"Okay, take it slow." He lopes back to his truck, and I climb into my car and turn the engine over.

He follows me most of the way to town, then turns one street before me and heads up the hill toward the McMansions. The tension in my shoulders eases once he's no longer behind me. I hope I can trust him not to say anything to my brother, Dillion, or Aaron.

Everything is going so well; the last thing I want is for any of them to make a big deal about a fender bender. I need some time to catch up on all the projects I have going on, and then things will settle down again and I can get back to my normal routine. It's going to be fine. It has to be.

CHAPTER 23
NO MORE SECRETS

Aaron

"I don't want to put you in a difficult place, Aaron, but Jamie's been asking if we can come for a visit. We could always stay in a hotel in the next town over. Or maybe we could rent a place on a neighboring lake if that would be easier?" My dad's tone is gentle, not pushing, because he never does.

And maybe that's the problem.

He's not the kind of guy to push his own agenda.

And I can see my own role in making it this way. My inability to come clean with my mother about my relationship with my dad. The way I've tried to separate my life into two distinct halves that never cross paths. As I sit on my couch, with Teagan beside me, her eyes full of questions and concerns—likely at my expression—I have to wonder who I'm hurting most by trying to keep them separate from my mom.

"There's no reason for you to rent a place or stay at a hotel, unless you're not a huge fan of sleeping in my two-bedroom shack." I cringe as soon as the words are out. "I meant that as a joke, Dad, not in that I believe you care about how big my house is."

He chuckles. "I know that, son. I just don't want to inconvenience you."

"It's not an inconvenience at all. And we're finishing up a project this week, and then we'll have a couple of days off early next week, so if you can make it a long weekend, that would be great."

"You're sure about this? I know how tricky the situation is for you."

"I'm sure. I'll see about getting my old trailer set up, and if the squirrels haven't made a home out of it, maybe Jamie and I can have a campout while he's here."

"He'd love that. Will Teagan be around?"

"She absolutely will." I reach out and squeeze her hand. "I know Jamie's been asking about her nonstop."

"He's enamored, like you. I'll call you later in the week to firm up the details, then?"

"That sounds good."

We say our goodbyes, and I end the call. Tossing my phone on the coffee table, I exhale a breath and try to shake off the anxiety.

"Your dad is coming to visit," Teagan says.

"Yeah. I can't keep making excuses as to why they can't come here." Or why we have to go two towns over whenever we go anywhere. "And frankly, I don't want to anymore."

"Do you think your mom will still be upset? When was the last time you tried to talk to her about it?" Teagan has gotten to know my mom because they both work at Harry's. They have lunch together in the break room sometimes. My mom adores her, which is great because I do too.

I was worried after she met Jamie and Lydia and my dad that she would accidentally mention them to my mom, and then I'd have to explain or deal with the guilt. But I can see what *not* dealing with this has done to me. How it's made me closed off and set me up for a lifetime of meaningless one-night stands with women who only see me as a means to an orgasm. Until I met Teagan.

Teagan, who always puts herself last.

Teagan, who's fighting ghosts and struggling to let me in. And I'm putting her in an impossible position, forcing her to keep my secrets.

I'm so in love with her it's almost painful. And if I can't face down my own demons, how in the world can I expect her to face hers?

So I'm willing to take this step in order to help her see that she's got her own healing to do too.

"Yeah. I have to. I've been putting it off because I don't want to hurt her feelings, but honestly, the only person whose life this doesn't affect is hers—at least it hasn't, because I've been keeping her in the dark. I've spent all these years blaming myself for Devon's death, all this time hiding the relationship I've had with my dad, and all it does is breed resentment. And now you have to keep this secret from her too. It's not fair to you, or me, or anyone. I don't want to live two separate lives anymore. I can't." I'm hoping that if I take this step, I might be able to help her take one of her own. Get her to drop some of the obligations she's been taking on, and maybe convince her to talk to Van about Bradley so it doesn't weigh so heavy on her shoulders.

"Then you should talk to her. Tell her what you need. You've been sitting on this pain for a lot of years. Let her take some of the burden, then maybe you can both heal."

I wish she could take some of her own advice.

The next night I head over to my mom's for dinner. Teagan sends me with biscuits and muffins. I half wanted to invite her along so I'd have the buffer, but it's Thursday night and she has to work, and putting her in the middle of this situation more than she already is isn't fair.

My mom lives in a one-bedroom apartment on the first floor of a fiveplex. Everything in it is tired and in need of updating, but she refuses my help financially and always has.

"Hey, Mom." I give her a hug, her small frame dwarfed by mine. She's wearing a pair of jeans and a loose sweater.

"It's good to see you, come on in. I wasn't sure if you were bringing Teagan or not." She seems disappointed by her absence.

"She has to work tonight, but she sent along some treats. You'll have to come over for dinner one of these days. She can cook like nobody's business."

"That sounds lovely. She's such a nice girl. And always on the go!"

"That she is. She's not a fan of idle time." To a fault, maybe. But I keep that to myself.

I help her prepare dinner, nerves making it hard for me to focus.

"Is everything okay, Aaron? You seem distracted," she says as she pulls a root beer from the fridge and pops off the cap.

"I need to talk to you about something."

"Of course. You can talk to me about anything, you know that." She offers me a small, concerned smile.

For the most part it's not a lie. She's always been there for me. She did the best she could as a single mom. Made the choices she thought were best for the both of us. But that's the thing about choices—we make them framed in our singular experience, not always taking into account time or current circumstances. But there has always been one topic that wasn't open for discussion, and I'm about to broach it in a way I never have before.

"It's about my biological dad."

Her expression shutters. From one second to the next the mood shifts completely. "You know I don't have contact with him. I haven't spoken to him since you went to college."

"I know." I take a deep breath, feeling like a teenager who stole the car and crashed it into the bushes—something I never did. "Please don't be mad, Mom."

"Mad about what? What could I possibly be upset with you for?"

"I've been in contact with Dad."

"What?" She stops mashing the potatoes to gape at me. "When? Why would you do that? He's a cheater and a liar!"

I raise a hand. "I know how you feel about him, but I need you to hear me out."

She crosses her arms. "He abandoned us!"

"He made mistakes, Mom. We all do, because we're human. And I'm not excusing him for what happened between the two of you, but there are two sides to every story, and somewhere in the middle of that is the truth. He *wanted* to be part of my life."

She rolls her shoulders back and turns her head, looking out the window instead of at me. "He could have taken you away from me, and I wasn't going to let that happen."

"I know you were trying to protect us." And standing here, in the middle of her tiny, worn apartment, I can see that's exactly what she was doing. Especially growing up in a small town and having fallen for a man who was in a much better position financially. Not to mention significantly older than she was. My dad has a good decade on my mom. She was the young home-wrecker. He was the wealthy doctor, married to another doctor, both of their lives so busy with work that they never had time for each other. "But I'm an adult, and I don't need protecting anymore. What I do need is to be able to have a relationship with my father, even if you don't."

I lead her to the couch, needing to sit down so I can explain the rest. About having a relationship with him for the past nine years, about Devon, about losing him, about how difficult it's been to keep those two parts of my life separate from each other and that I can't and don't want to do that anymore. It's too hard, and it's not good for me, her, or my dad.

She tries to blink back the tears, her trembling hand at her mouth. "Oh, Aaron. I am so, so sorry. This is all my fault. I can't believe you've held on to this for almost a decade."

I take her other hand in mine, my emotions frayed, but I'm aware this needed to happen. "It's no one's fault, Mom. Or if there needs to be blame, it's everyone's fault. Dad could have pushed to have a relationship with me, you could have done things differently, I could have said something years ago, but I didn't. And all I was doing was creating a rift that I wasn't going to be able to fix if I kept going this way. I thought I was protecting you, but really, it was hurting all of us." And it took Teagan coming into my life to make me see that.

"You're not at fault, Aaron. I'm the parent here; I should have recognized that you needed more than financial support from your father, even if I didn't." Her shoulders curl, as if the weight of her guilt is dragging her down. "I'm so sorry you didn't feel like you could share any of this with me, and that you had to go through all of that without having anyone to lean on."

For a lot of years I believed that I was responsible for the loss of my brother. And that in keeping my relationship with my dad from my mom, I'd somehow tipped the balance, and the universe had taken away someone I loved to even out the score.

But now that I've come clean, I feel so much better, the guilt and fear I've been carrying around with me for years lifting. I know I have more work to do, but this feels like a start. A good one.

"They're coming down for a visit this weekend. Jamie, Dad, and Lydia."

"Lydia?" Mom's brow furrows.

"Jamie's mother. She would have been Devon's wife."

"Oh. What about Arnie's wife?"

"They're not together anymore. They haven't been for a long time." They divorced when Devon was seven or eight. It wasn't a messy divorce; they just weren't meant to be married to each other. And sometimes I wonder if maybe my dad had never gotten over what happened with my mother.

She clasps her hands together. "I didn't realize that."

"I know it's a lot to get your head around, but maybe when you've had some time to process, you can meet Jamie? He's a big part of my life, and I think you'd love him. No pressure, though."

She gives me a small smile. "Do you think Arnie would be okay with that?"

"Oh yeah, he asks about you all the time."

She blinks several times. "He does?"

"Pretty much every time I talk to him."

"Oh. Well, he's probably making polite conversation."

"Eh, I don't know about that. I get that you might not be ready, but you're both my parents, and I would love it if eventually you could be civil with each other. You're always going to be my number one, Mom."

It's late by the time I leave my mom's, and Teagan has already texted to say she's off work earlier than expected, if I want to meet her at her place. She likes to shower after a shift at the pub. Sometimes she'll come to my place, and other times she'll take the night for herself, in part because half the time I'm already passed out by the time she gets off work. But tonight I want to see her, despite the fact that I'll be underslept tomorrow.

I feel like I unloaded a hundred-pound backpack of personal baggage with one conversation. One long-overdue conversation that has the power to change my entire family dynamic. I'm cautiously optimistic about my dad's visit this weekend. My mom seemed to warm to the idea of meeting Jamie over the course of dinner and mentioned reaching out to my dad before the weekend to feel things out. It seems like miles of progress in one afternoon. I know better than to assume there won't be any bumps in the road along the way, but at least we're moving forward.

I pull into the driveway, beside Teagan's car. She usually parks on the right side, but tonight she's on the left side. I hop out and notice a bunch of scratches on the passenger side. Teagan's car is in pristine condition, so the scratches must be new. I hope whatever happened doesn't have anything to do with why she got off work early.

I make my way up the stairs and knock on her door. I could probably let myself in, but I like watching her face light up when she opens the door. Which is exactly what happens a few seconds later.

"Hi." She loops her arms around my neck, pulling my mouth down to hers. She's freshly showered, long hair still wet, skin still warm. Her kiss tastes like vodka and lemon.

"Can I get you something to drink? Are you hungry? I can whip something up for you if you are."

"Just a glass of water would be good," I tell her.

She flits over to the fridge and grabs the water jug, filling a glass for me. I take her in as she moves around the kitchen. She looks tired. Her cheekbones seem more prominent than usual. Or maybe I'm looking for things to be wrong. And she just finished a shift at the pub. It's always busy on Thursday nights, and she's usually wiped out at the end of her shift.

She pulls me over to the couch, moving her laptop aside so we can sit. Her martini is half-full, but there's an empty pick sitting on the coffee table, which means she might very well be on her second drink.

"Did you know there are a bunch of scratches on your car?" I ask as I settle next to her and stretch my arm along the back of the couch.

Her eyes flare for a second, and she waves a hand around. "I parked too close to the trees today, and it was windy. I'm sure I'll be able to get it buffed out no problem."

The way she can't quite meet my gaze has me questioning how honest she's being. "If you need to take it to a garage to have it looked at, I can follow you there. Carter's is in the next town over, but they're better with the bodywork than the guy in town here."

"Sure. That'd be great. I'm not in a rush, though, and bodywork can be expensive." She takes the glass from my hand, sets it on the table beside me, and straddles my lap. "I missed you at the pub tonight. How was dinner with your mom?"

I settle my hands on her hips, trying to figure out what's going on with her. She's usually a bubbly person, but tonight she seems wound up. "It was good."

"That's good." She lifts my hat from my head and runs her fingers through my hair and drags her lips up the side of my neck.

"I told my mom that my dad's coming to visit this weekend."

"Oh?" She lifts her head. It takes a few seconds for her eyes to focus.

"And basically everything else too."

Teagan shifts back to the cushion beside me, maybe realizing I need to talk this out. "How did that go?"

"She was surprised. Maybe a little hurt at first, and then guilty—it's a lot to process, and I know that one conversation isn't going to fix everything, but for the first time in years, I feel like I can finally breathe," I admit.

Her smile turns soft, and she takes my hand in hers. I notice for the first time that her nails are bitten to the quick. That's not typical. "That took a lot of courage, Aaron. I'm so glad you were able to talk to her and that she was so receptive."

"Me too. I went in prepared for the worst, and I think this is the best possible outcome. I want her to have a relationship with Jamie. And there's some relief in knowing that I don't have to keep those parts of my life separate from each other. I didn't like that you were forced to keep secrets for me."

"You didn't force me, that was me supporting you. You needed to tell your mom on your own time."

"Still. It wasn't fair of me to do that to you." I thread my fingers through hers. "I wish it hadn't taken me this long to finally do something about it, but at least I can see that there was a problem and I was part of it, you know?"

"Everyone played their own role in how things turned out. It's not all on you, Aaron."

"I know that. But I also know how I contributed to it." I want to say something more about her car, her hectic, punishing schedule, that she's keeping the fact that she's talking to Bradley from Van, but today has been emotionally taxing on a lot of levels, and getting into it tonight doesn't seem like a good idea. "Do you think you could come over this weekend when they're visiting? My dad would love to see you again, and you're pretty much all Jamie can talk about. And it'd be good to have the support."

"Of course. You know I'm always here for you."

I wish she'd let me do the same for her. "You know, I'm always here for you too."

She gives me a small smile. "I know. Watching you go through everything with your mom made me realize that we're going through similar things. You and your mom, me and Van. The secrets."

"Do you think you'll talk to Van about what's going on with Bradley?"

She sighs before answering. "I'll tell him eventually. I just know how hard it's been on him, and I don't want him to feel like he has to forgive Bradley."

"It puts you in an awkward position, though."

"I can handle it for now. And we don't need to worry about my stuff." She waves a dismissive hand in the air. "I'm so glad you were able to talk to your mom. You must feel so much better."

"I do." Better than I thought I could feel. Like I've let go of some of the ghosts of my past.

She leans in and kisses me. And even though I shouldn't, I allow myself to get lost in the feel of her mouth and her hands and her body.

Afterward I watch as she washes down her medication with whatever's left of her martini. For once, she's out before I am. She's curled up beside me, body tucked against mine, skin cool to the touch. I run my hand down her spine, feeling the ridges, trying to decide if they're more prominent or not. I want her to be okay, but I don't think she is.

And now, she's starting to remind me of myself after Devon died. But I drowned myself in alcohol and punished myself through work. This isn't the same, but it also doesn't seem that different.

I see her nearly every day. I know the contours of her body, the curve of her hips. She has bruises on her arms and a few scratches that look fresh. It makes me question whether she's lying about whatever happened with her car. If it were an isolated incident, I might not be too worried, passing her reaction off as embarrassment, but there are too many other things piled on top of that sundae for me not to be concerned.

I carefully slip a pillow between me and Teagan and slide out of bed. I grab my phone and wait a full minute, watching her back rise and fall, before I pad across the loft to the bathroom. I close the door with a quiet click and turn the lock before I open the medicine cabinet. I've looked in here a few times in the months I've slept over, noted her prescriptions and the random over-the-counter medication. None of it seemed like a red flag, mostly allergy meds and painkillers. I took an ibuprofen once because I'd stupidly missed a nail and hammered my finger. It was throbbing pretty good. That was probably a month ago.

Since then the cabinet has been filled with a slew of bottles. What I do next is something I'm not particularly proud of. I've already looked up her prescriptions. One is for attention deficit, which I already knew from talking to Dillion. Teagan has never mentioned it to me, but then maybe she doesn't feel she needs to. There are two other prescriptions. The Valium is for anxiety and says *take as needed*. There's also a warning about driving and drowsiness. The third prescription is a sleep aid and is the one she always takes before bed. But there are other prescription bottles in here. One is a painkiller that belongs to her dad and is two years old.

On top of the prescriptions are a bunch of over-the-counter medications, some herbal, some not. There are bottles of NyQuil and other over-the-counter products that cause drowsiness, and there are also over-the-counter sleep aids. Those seem like a bad idea for someone already taking prescription sleeping pills. And then there are the caffeine pills. Those, combined with the energy drinks and her constant coffee habit, aren't a good sign. This is a recipe for crashing and burning.

And I can't believe I haven't put it together until now. I want to be wrong, but I worry I'm right.

I'm afraid of the possibility that she might reach for something stronger when the pills she's taking stop doing their job. I count the pills in the antianxiety prescription. It was filled a little more than two weeks ago and is already missing most of its contents and is supposed to be a use-as-needed medication. It has one refill left on it. Which means she's taking these often, on top of all the other things.

I take a seat on the edge of the bathtub and drag a hand down my face. I can't ignore this. It's more than a few red flags. It's verging on an entire minefield waiting to go off.

Teagan has always been very open about the fact that she takes medication, that she has trouble sleeping. In a lot of ways, she normalized the behavior until I accepted that she was comfortable with me and wasn't ashamed that she sought medical treatment to help her manage her mental health.

After Devon died, I took over-the-counter sleep aids for a while. And for a short time they worked. But this seems bigger. Much bigger. And possibly more serious. She has an arsenal of medication that she takes regularly. And she's drinking on top of that. I don't even know how much or how often. I don't think there has ever been a night that she's been with me that she hasn't taken something or multiple somethings.

I drop my head in my hands.

What if I'm in love with an *addict*?

I may not be an addict, but I know what it's like to fall down that rabbit hole, from when I numbed the pain of losing Devon with alcohol. Though I didn't have an addiction, it was still hard for me to change my habits. Alcohol trumped everything else, including the people I cared about. I couldn't see past myself to what I was doing to the people I loved and who loved me. I saw a therapist to help me get back on track and quit drinking altogether.

I don't want this to be Teagan's road. I want to help her see that we're all here for her. That whatever is going on, we can get through this.

I don't get much sleep after that. And I call John first thing in the morning and ask if it's okay for me to come in a couple of hours later than usual, with a promise that I'll make up the time. He tells me not to worry about it, since I routinely pull ten-hour days.

Before anyone else gets up, I take another look at her car and discover that there are more than a few scratches. There are a bunch of dents, and the undercarriage looks like it's been dragged over rocks. Which means she definitely lied and was in an accident. Possibly as early as Wednesday.

Teagan's alarm goes off at seven thirty and continues to beep for a full three minutes until she finally reaches for her phone, slapping blindly at it until she gets it to stop. I'm sitting on the edge of her bed, dressed for work, all the medication from her bathroom sitting in a pile on her comforter.

Yesterday's conversation with my mom was hard, but I have a feeling that this is going to be a lot different. I don't want this to be the problem that it is.

As upset as I am about the lie she fed me about what happened with her car, I'm more worried about how she's going to react when I confront her about her stash of medication. Teagan is a pleaser. She thrives on being needed and winning people's approval. She's carefully crafted this reality and made the pills part of her everyday life. If I threaten to take that away from her, there are going to be consequences. Ones I might not like.

I stroke her cheek and bend to press my lips to her forehead. She makes a noise and rolls over, curling into my leg. The weight that lifted yesterday settles in my gut.

"Babe, you need to wake up. We need to talk."

She blinks once, twice, and her eyes roll up and flutter shut again.

I swallow down the anxiety. An image of Devon pops like a bubble in my head. How his skin had turned gray blue. How his eyes had frozen open, staring blankly at the sky. How he hadn't even realized that he was hypothermic, or maybe he had and it had been too late, muscles seized, unable to get up and come inside, voice lost in the cold night.

Because we drank too much.

Because I passed out on the couch.

Waking up one morning and finding Teagan like that from an overdose could be a real possibility if she's combining the wrong things. It's a reality that I don't ever want to face. And it solidifies my resolve.

I give her shoulder a gentle shake, but all she does is groan. "Teagan, I need you to wake up." I have no idea how much medication is floating around in her system. And that scares the hell out of me.

It takes me a full five minutes, and I finally resort to spritzing her with the spray bottle she uses to water her cactus to wake her up.

She scrubs a hand over her face. "What the hell?" She blinks a bunch of times and sits up. Her eyes are sunken. She looks exhausted and confused. "What are you doing? What time is it?"

"It's seven forty."

She frowns and glances at the clock. "Shouldn't you be at work?"

"Yeah, but we need to talk."

That seems to put her on alert. "Did something happen?"

I motion to the pile of boxes strewn all over her comforter. Some of the labels are from Chicago, but the majority are from the local pharmacy, or the one in the neighboring town.

Her frown is back in place. "What is this?"

"You tell me, Teagan."

"Did you go through my medicine cabinet?"

"Yeah." There's no point in lying when the evidence is in front of us.

Teagan runs a hand roughly through her hair. "Why would you do that? Why is this stuff all over my bed?"

"Because I'm worried about you, and I think I have a right to be."

"Why, because I'm stocked up on generic over-the-counter medication?" She scoffs but swallows thickly. "There's nothing for you to be worried about, Aaron. I know you've got issues with alcohol, and I get it, but I don't go around pushing my personal choices on you, so you can't go putting yours on me."

"This isn't the same thing, Teagan. My brother died because we were both too drunk to recognize that him going back outside to find his phone wasn't a good idea. And while I'm working on making peace with that, I'm not going to put myself in a position where that could happen again. And this"—I motion to the boxes and bottles littering her comforter— "isn't about me pushing my choices on you; this is me worried because I think you have a problem."

She throws off the cover and tries to scoop up an armful of boxes. "I don't have a fucking problem, Aaron. Just because I take medication doesn't mean I'm fucking crazy! I moved to Pearl Lake so I could deal with my issues, which is a lot more than I can say for you. You've been living two separate lives for the better part of a decade and sleeping with all of those women on the other side of the lake so you don't have to feel anything for anyone because you're the one who's too scared!"

This isn't the rational Teagan I'm used to dealing with. She doesn't do confrontation, and she doesn't like conflict. It's why she's a yes person.

"You're right," I tell her. "I was living two separate lives, hiding one of them from my mother because I didn't want to deal with the potential fallout. But I was only going to cause myself and her and the rest of my family a world of hurt if I kept it up. And the reason I saw that I needed to change it was because you came into my life, and I didn't want to put you in a terrible position like that, where you were forced to keep secrets too. I wanted to be able to share you with them and them with you, and the only way I could do that was to finally deal with my shit. And it's hard, Teagan. Really fucking hard, but this"—I motion to her defensive posture and the way she's holding the fucking boxes like they're her precious—"this isn't you dealing with things. I think this is a Band-Aid for a bigger issue. You lied to me about your car. You were in an accident, and you tried to brush it off as nothing. Did you hit another car? What the hell happened?"

"I took a corner too fast, and I knew you'd overreact, so I didn't say anything," she snaps.

"You could've been hurt!"

"But I wasn't. I'm fine. And you're making a bigger deal out of this than you need to, which I knew you'd do," she spits back.

I grab the back of my neck, willing myself to stay calm and rational, trying to decide if I'm overreacting or not. "Do you really believe that it's not a big deal? Look at you, Teagan. You're lying. You look like you're on the verge of a panic attack."

"You attacked me the second I woke up!" She scrambles off the bed and rushes toward the bathroom. She throws the boxes she's holding inside and slams the door shut, standing in front of it. "You know what? I don't need this negativity or you putting a savior complex on me. I want you to leave."

"Teagan, please. You have to see how dangerous this is. You could have been hurt. You could have hurt someone else, and let me tell you from experience, it's not something you want to have to live with."

"I'm fucking fine! I need to get ready for work, and you need to get out of my space."

She tries to come back for another armload of pills, which proves my damn point. Especially when I step in front of her, blocking her way. "Let me help you," I say softly.

"I don't need help! I need you to get out! Get the fuck out!" She spins around, stalks to the bathroom, and slams the door behind her. I hear the click of the lock.

I can't decide if it's me overreacting or her. I don't think it's me, but I'm not going to get anywhere with Teagan when both of us are heated.

I grab my backpack and shove everything on the bed into my bag. If she wants it back, she'll have to deal with me.

CHAPTER 24

HOW DEEP IS THIS HOLE?

Teagan

I feel like I'm trying to breathe underwater. My chest is tight, and my head is a mess of thoughts I can't hold on to. I'm scared and angry. How dare Aaron come here and throw accusations around, telling me I have a problem, making me feel bad about needing help to manage.

I search the boxes and bottles on the floor for my Valium. I have to work today, and I won't be able to do that if I'm this upset. I don't understand why he would do this. We were great last night; he seemed like he'd had a good conversation with his mom. Maybe that's what this is all about—maybe the conversation with his mom brought up fears and worries about what happened with Devon, and he's projecting them onto me.

I'm grateful when I find the bottle next to my foot. I shake out one pill and count what's left. I should have enough for a couple more weeks. Then I'll have to call in a refill. Which is okay. I can make them last that long.

By the time I'm calm enough to get ready for work, I don't have time for a shower. I wash my face and apply makeup, trying to keep my emotions in check so I don't start crying and make my skin all blotchy. I also don't have time to grab a coffee, and Aaron took my caffeine pills. I have one energy drink left, though, and that should get me through until lunch. I can make it until then.

I get in my car, not loving the new clunking sound that only happens when I'm in reverse. I keep reminding myself to breathe and relax all the way to work. I pull into Harry's Hardware, and I'm halfway across the parking lot when I realize I'm not wearing my store shirt and that it's not Wednesday, it's Friday, and I'm supposed to be at Bernie's. I arrive with five minutes to spare, which is a heck of a lot better than late.

My stomach is a mess, and I can't seem to get a handle on how much my hands are shaking, but I manage to make it through the day. I know I'm off; I can see it in Bernie's concerned gaze. He lets me go home an hour early, telling me to get a head start on my weekend.

When I get to my apartment, I realize I left my bed unmade, which is totally not like me at all. And I lost it on Aaron, also very unlike me. I'm half-embarrassed by the way I acted and half-angry that he would come at me like that before I even had a chance to wake up.

I smooth out the covers and frown when I notice the rest of the contents of the medicine cabinet are no longer strewn about the comforter. This morning feels like a million years ago. The whole thing is a haze. I look under the bed and find a mostly empty bottle of my attention deficit medication but nothing else. I rush to the garbage can, but all it contains is an empty bottle of vodka and the half loaf of bread I threw out because it was stale.

I tap my lips, panic starting to take over. "He couldn't have taken them," I murmur to myself, but as soon as the words are out, I have to wonder if I'm wrong about that.

I rush to the bathroom and open the medicine cabinet. Which is when I discover that it's totally empty. All that's left are the bottles I tossed in there this morning when I was in the middle of my temper tantrum. My hands are shaking as I pick them all up and spread them out on my bed. Which still smells like Aaron's cologne.

I grab my purse and my overnight bag and dump them both out, then sift through the contents, pulling out my prescriptions and my backup medications, for those occasions when I forget or am at risk of running out. He can't be right. I don't have a problem. My doctor wouldn't prescribe me medication I don't need. Maybe I need to cool it on the caffeine pills, but other than that, everything else is harmless.

I try to be logical about this. Aaron is hypersensitive to this kind of thing, considering what he's been through. He wasn't trying to attack me; he thought he was helping. I know he cares about me the same way I care about him. At least I think he does.

I have an extra bottle of my attention deficit medication, leftovers from before my doctor increased the dose because it wasn't as effective. And I have an extra week's worth of the prescription for sleep, but it's also at a lower dose. And even the current dose hasn't been working all that well. Not recently. So I've had to take some over-the-counter stuff to help. I can up those if I need to, at least until I can get in to see my doctor. I'm lower on my antianxiety meds than I realized, and that worries me, because the more anxious I am, the more likely I am to struggle with sleeping. It's a vicious cycle. One I had under control. And now everything is fucked up.

I force myself to take deep breaths. I need to stay calm. I can't afford to burn through the rest of my Valium this weekend. Not because Aaron thinks he knows what's best for me. At least I have my prescriptions. The rest is over-the-counter stuff that can easily be replaced.

I avoid his calls. Despite trying to be rational, I'm too upset to talk to him. I spend the night in my jammies, drinking martinis and trying to work on one of the new projects for the Stitches. I can't focus on anything, though, and I can't remember if I took my attention meds this morning or not.

On Saturday my brother comes knocking on my door at noon. I'm still in bed. I'm not sleeping; I'm just lying there, staring at the ceiling.

Van isn't dissuaded when I tell him I'm not feeling well. In fact he lets himself in. The annoying part about living in the loft above my brother's garage is that he can pretty much do as he pleases. Usually he gives me space, but I've blown him off since yesterday, and obviously he feels compelled to check on me.

"I'm not feeling good. I just want to suffer by myself." I hug my pillow and snuggle deeper under my covers.

He doesn't say anything, but I hear him cross the room and feel the dip of my mattress as he sits on the edge.

"I want to be alone."

"Aaron's pretty worried about you."

"Aaron's being dramatic, and he's putting his own fears on me."

"I'm worried about you, too," he says softly.

I huff, annoyed that everyone is overreacting. "I'm fine. I've had a lot on my mind, and I've been having trouble sleeping, that's all. I need a reset and I'll be good."

"Really, Teag, because the state of your car tells a totally different story. Did you think no one was going to notice all the dents and scratches?"

"I tried to swerve around a chipmunk and ended up in a ditch. It's not a big deal."

"You told Aaron that you took a corner too fast."

I throw my hands up in the air. "What does it matter? It's a few scratches and a couple of dents."

He's quiet for so long that I finally drag my gaze from the ceiling to his face. "It could have been another car that you hit, or a person. I know you've been struggling to figure yourself out, but the medication you're taking isn't the answer to the problem. It's designed to help, not to fix things."

"You think I don't know that? I'm just going through a rough patch. Things have been intense lately, and I needed a little extra help, but I'm fine. I promise. I'll prove it to you. I'll only take my prescriptions. You can take everything else."

"Maybe you should make an appointment with your doctor and see if things need to be adjusted."

"I'll call on Monday."

"What if you call today and leave a message?"

"What's the difference if I call now or on Monday? No one is in the office until then, anyway." I hate that Aaron's paranoia is affecting my brother now too.

"Maybe you should consider dropping a job. I know you don't like to tell people no, but you're working five days a week, and then you've got the design projects with Dillion, and you're taking on the entire fall market. It's a lot. Maybe too much."

"I can give some of the market stuff to the hockey wives. They're always happy to help."

"It's not just that, though, Teagan. You look exhausted, and you've lost weight. You need to take better care of yourself. No one is going to be upset if you need to take a few things off your plate. They'll understand."

"It's been busy. But I'll think about dropping a job." I have everything under control with my projects, now that the planning phase is out of the way. I don't want to give up any of my jobs. I like them all, and everyone tells me how amazing it's been having me around.

He's quiet for a few seconds. "Are you going to call Aaron?"

"Not today. He has family obligations." It's the truth, but even as I say it, I feel bad, because I was excited to see Jamie and I hate that I'm letting him down, even though I'm frustrated with Aaron.

He calls on Saturday and Sunday, but I let the messages go to voice mail. I want to talk to him, but I can't do that with his family there. And I'm determined to prove to Van and Aaron that I can handle everything on my plate and that all I need are the prescriptions from my doctor. That I don't need the energy drinks or the caffeine pills or the over-the-counter sleep medication.

But even with my regular prescription, I don't sleep much on Saturday night. I expect it. The first couple of days when I stop taking the over-the-counter stuff are always rough. But Sunday night is just as bad, and it feels worse because Aaron isn't there for me to curl up against.

I need to remember not to rely on anyone for my happiness but me. I don't *need* Aaron. I'm fine on my own.

Monday is hard. I make mistakes at the diner and get people's orders wrong. I hate letting people down. But I know in a couple of days I'll be okay again. I need to hit the wall, and then I'll be good. That's what it's always like.

I get a couple of hours of sleep on Monday night, but I wake up at three in the morning, and I can't fall back to sleep. I have a long shower and fall asleep on the couch while I'm checking my email. Which means I'm almost late for my shift at Harry's.

I make it with a few minutes to spare, rushing to the office to punch in. I give Chloe a bright smile. "I didn't know you were working today."

She gives me a funny look. "Are you filling in today?"

"Filling in? Maybe. Who's sick?"

The intercom in the office goes off, paging her to customer service. "Gotta run. See you later."

I follow her out and head for the cashier stands. I get a couple more questioning looks. Usually I'm on cash four, but Chuck is there today. I stop at the customer service desk, where Noreen is filing returns. I haven't seen her or Aaron since things blew up on the weekend. I adopt a bright, cheery smile. "Morning! Looks like cash four is taken; where would you like me?"

"Oh, hi, Teagan! I didn't know you were on the schedule today. Are you filling in for someone?"

"Not that I know of. I always work Wednesdays."

Her brows pull together and she bites her lip, her gaze dropping from my face to my shirt and up again. "It's only Tuesday. Are you okay, honey?"

At first I think she's joking. Until I glance at her computer screen and see the date in the right-hand corner. I slap a hand over my mouth. "Oh my gosh! I can't believe I got my days mixed up. I guess that explains why everyone is looking at me funny. Well, I guess I better hightail it out of here!" I check my planner; I have a meeting with a client on the other side of the lake in less than an hour. And now I need to go home and change.

It isn't until I'm in my loft that I notice my Harry's Hardware shirt was inside out.

I tell myself that I'm fine, just frazzled and stressed out. A good night's sleep and I'll be back on track.

I make myself another coffee and head to the meeting, stopping at the convenience store to grab an energy drink as well. I know I said I was going to quit them, but I'm going on no sleep, and I need to stay alert, at least until this meeting is over. Normally I'd drive in with Dillion, but I don't want to risk running into Aaron. Not yet. Not until I have things under control again.

I notice a few typos when I'm presenting to the new clients. Usually, I'm so much better at catching those, but I forgot to send it to Dillion to look it over. I wait until we're out of the house before I say anything.

"I'm so sorry about the typos."

"It's okay. I should have asked to see it yesterday, and it slipped my mind. A few typos aren't going to stop them from hiring us." She gives my shoulder a squeeze. "Is everything okay? I don't want to stick my nose where it doesn't belong, but Van's worried about you."

"Honestly, I'm fine. Everyone is making a bigger deal out of things than they need to." I hate that everyone is on me now. I feel like I'm being watched. Like I'm a kid who needs babysitting.

"Okay. If you say you're fine, I'm going to believe you. I told Van I was Switzerland and that I wasn't taking sides and I wasn't going to push you for information."

"Thanks. I appreciate that." I honestly do too. Because I have a feeling if Dillion joined the harp-on-Teagan brigade, I'd probably end up losing it, and I don't want that to happen. She doesn't deserve that.

I expect that I'll finally be able to get some sleep tonight, but even after three martinis I'm wide awake.

In the morning I head to Harry's with a headache, feeling more than a little fuzzy. I haven't slept for more than a couple of hours since Friday. I know the wall is coming. I can feel it. I wish I'd hit it so I can get some actual rest and press the reset button like I need to.

At lunch I usually sit in the break room with everyone else, but today I desperately need caffeine, so I offer to pick up coffees for everyone and head down the street to Boones. I don't drive because it's a crisp day and I could use the fresh air. I order a dozen fritters and coffees, then manage to trip on my way back to Harry's and lose one coffee. At least it's just a black one, so I tell everyone that I drank mine while I waited for the fritters. At the end of my shift I'm beyond exhausted. So tired, in fact, that I lean my seat back and take a fifteen-minute power nap before I drive home.

Except I must have passed out for longer than fifteen minutes, because a knock on my window startles me awake. The sun is sinking toward the horizon. It's Billy.

I quickly swipe the back of my hand across my mouth to make sure I'm not drooling, then try to roll down my window, except the key isn't in the ignition and the car isn't on, so nothing happens.

I turn the engine over, nearly pee my pants at the loud music, turn it down, and then roll down the window.

His wide blue eyes dart around the inside of my car before they land on me. "Hey, are you okay, Teagan?"

"Yup! Just fine. I was waiting for a message, and I must have fallen asleep. Guess that's what I get for bingeing an entire season of *Stranger Things* last night." Why am I lying? I can't seem to help it.

"Do you need me to drive you home? We can pick your car up tomorrow," he offers.

"No, no. I'm okay." I wave him off. "Thanks for making sure I didn't spend the night sleeping in the parking lot."

"Are you sure you don't want a ride home?" He glances at the passenger seat. The contents of my purse are strewn about, and there are a couple of empty energy drink cans on the floor. Normally my car is clean and doesn't look like the inside of a garbage can.

"I'm sure. I'm good. Thanks, though." He steps back, and I put the car in gear and drive home, feeling pretty awful after that nap. I hate napping. It makes me feel out of it for hours afterward, and getting a decent sleep tonight will be virtually impossible.

My day goes from bad to worse when I get home and find Aaron's truck parked in the driveway.

It annoys me that the first thing I want to do is hug him. I want to curl up beside him and close my eyes and listen to the sound of his heart beating until it lulls me to sleep. But he's the reason I'm feeling like this in the first place. If he hadn't pushed me and made everyone worry about me unnecessarily, everything would be fine.

He steps out of his truck as I pull in beside him. He's parked to the right, which means I can't get to the door without passing him.

"I can't deal with this right now." I hate that I'm snappy and emotional. I try to brush by him, but his legs are way longer than mine, and he steps in front of the stairs leading to the loft.

"How long are you planning to dodge my messages?" His voice is soft.

"I don't know. As long as it takes for me to get over what you did, I guess." I stare at his chest.

"I get that you're upset, Teagan, and maybe I should have broached this differently, but I care about you, and I just want you to be okay."

"Does that mean you're bringing back all the stuff you took?" He has my extra antianxiety medication, and I can't fill the repeat for the one I have for another week. I'm down to my last two pills. If I had that, then maybe I'd be able to calm my mind enough to get a decent night's sleep. I want things to go back to the way they were last week, before everything imploded.

"Really, Teagan? That's what you're focused on?" He drags a hand through his hair. "I don't understand how you can't see that this is a problem."

"The problem is you coming in trying to be a savior and then telling my brother you're worried about me. Now everyone is on me, all because you think I have a problem. You know, I get why you're the way you are, Aaron, and I've never tried to push you outside of your comfort zone. I kept this light because I knew how hard it was for you to let people in, and what do you do in return? You throw my damn life into upheaval!" I tip my chin up, fighting tears. "As if I needed any help in that department! Everything is fucked up, and you made it worse for me. So thanks for all your concern, but I don't need it or you. I was fine on my own before, and I'll be fine on my own again. We're done. I don't want to see you anymore."

Half of me wants to call those words back and bury them, but the other side of me wants to lash out. I nudge him out of the way, stomp up the stairs, and lock the door behind me.

A minute later gravel pops under his tires as he leaves.

I should feel relief that he's gone.

But all I have is emptiness.

CHAPTER 25
IT'S DARK AT THE BOTTOM

Aaron

Everything I feared would happen is. I keep asking myself if things would have been different if I'd realized it sooner. If I'd seen the problem earlier, before it got to this point. At first I second-guessed myself, but the more I pieced together the puzzle, the more sure I became that I was right. That this is a problem.

So I shouldn't be surprised that Teagan breaks up with me. I should've expected it. Especially if she's on her way down into the spiral and anything in her way is collateral damage, including me.

I stand outside her apartment for a few minutes, debating whether trying to talk some sense into her is going to work. But I can't force her to see that she has a problem. She has to come to that realization on her own.

So I go home.

My place feels empty without her.

I feel empty without her.

And there are little reminders of her everywhere. Pieces of her scattered around in the form of pens and throw pillows.

After sitting on the couch for an hour, staring at the blank TV screen, I finally decide to go to bed. I haven't changed my sheets in more than a week. Not since the last time Teagan slept here. And I won't until the faint scent of her shampoo disappears from the sheets and her pillow.

It takes me forever to fall asleep, and when I finally do, it's fitful and laced with nightmares. In them I keep trying to get to Teagan, but she's at the bottom of a dark hole, and every time I think I can reach her, she falls down again.

The next day I head to the jobsite, unrested and feeling like a bag of shit. I need to talk to Van and Dillion, but he's in Chicago for work today, and Dillion is meeting with a homeowner to talk about a project, so that conversation will have to wait until later.

I'm working on the outdoor electrical at the Winslows' place, finishing things up so we can move on to the next big project, but halfway through the installation I notice that the plate covers don't quite match the switches, which means I need to go to Harry's to pick up a few more.

On my way there, I pass the local pharmacy and notice Teagan's car is parked in the lot. I pull in and find a spot, debating whether I should go in or not. I don't want to have a public confrontation with her, but with what I know, her being at a drug store after what happened last night seems like another red flag.

I cut the engine and head inside. It's not a big store, but one half is dedicated to the pharmacy, and the other half has knickknacks and trinkets and an aisle of cards for every occasion. The card aisle is farthest from the pharmacy counter, so I head over there and busy myself with pretending to look at them.

Teagan is at the pharmacy counter. Her hair is pulled up in a haphazard ponytail, and she's wearing her Town Pub shirt and a pair of jeans.

The pharmacist passes a bag to her, and she checks the contents, her smile pulling down at the corners. "Oh, I think one must be missing. There should be three." She rolls up on the balls of her feet once, then quickly plants them back on the floor.

"Let me check the file." The pharmacist smiles and clicks away on the computer for a moment. Her expression remains placid as she turns back to Teagan. "I'm sorry, it looks like your doctor only called in two prescriptions."

Teagan rolls up on the balls of her feet again. I can see her profile from where I'm standing, and her bright smile widens until it's almost manic. "She must have forgotten the third." She drops her voice and says something I can't quite catch.

The response from the pharmacist fills in the gap. "It's not due for a refill for another two weeks."

"I know. I lost my prescriptions in the lake, and I'm not going to see my doctor until next week. Can't you give me a few until I see her?" Teagan's foot taps agitatedly on the floor with her lie.

The pharmacist's smile drops. "I'm sorry, I can't do that."

I glance around the store, glad that there are only a couple of people milling around—one of them is a woman whose house I've worked on recently, and the other is a local—plus the cashier.

Teagan's voice rises with her irritation. "You can clearly see that I have a standing prescription. I lost them in the water. It's not like it's a big deal for you to give me a few when I'm going to see my doctor next week."

The pharmacist's expression goes stony. "Please don't raise your voice at me, ma'am. Valium is considered a class-four narcotic and is a controlled substance. I'm not permitted to give them to you without your general physician's authority. If you'd like to call and have your doctor send a request here, we can fill it for you."

Teagan glances around the store, maybe realizing she's drawing attention to herself. She plasters on a smile. "I'm so sorry. Of course

I'll call my doctor. I'm sure it was a mistake." She adds generic allergy pills and two energy drinks to her order and pays for her prescriptions, then leaves the store.

She stops short when she sees my truck and whirls around as I head toward it and her. "Oh my God. Are you following me?"

I don't see any point in lying. "I saw your car, so I stopped in. I think we need to talk, Teagan." Close up she looks even more exhausted than she did yesterday, which is unnerving. Her eyes are bloodshot, and her bottom lip looks raw, as if she's been compulsively chewing it.

"Well, I don't think we need to talk. I have to go to work." She sashays past me.

I grab her wrist to stop her. "Are you even okay to drive?"

"I'm fine." Her chin trembles as if she's fighting tears, and she shakes me off. "Just leave me alone, Aaron. You're making a scene." She stalks over to her car.

I don't want to publicly embarrass her, so I let her go, but I follow her through town until she pulls into the pub parking lot before I head to Harry's.

It's already after four by the time I'm done picking up the new light switches, so instead of going back to the Winslows', I head to the Footprint office, hoping that I'll catch Dillion. At this point I'm not worried about making Teagan angry; I'm worried about her health, and the last thing I want is her driving under the influence of a pill cocktail and hurting herself or, worse, someone else.

It appears to be my lucky day, because both Dillion and Van are in the office when I get there.

"Hey, Aaron, you all finished at the Winslows'?" Dillion's smile fades when her gaze shifts from Van to me. "Is everything okay?"

"Not really. Do you guys have time to talk?"

"Yeah. Of course. Take a seat." Dillion motions to the seat across from her. "What's going on?"

"Uh, is it just the three of us in here?"

"Yeah, it's just us. Did something happen with a homeowner?"

"It's not about a homeowner." I drop into the chair. "It's about Teagan."

Van sits up straighter. "Is she okay?"

I shake my head. "She broke up with me last night."

"What? Why?" Dillion's expression turns to shock.

"That's not the issue. I mean, it's an issue for me, but that's not the problem." I fill them in on what happened: the accident she had, her not sleeping, the lying, the medication, even all the calls from Bradley, which Dillion already knew about.

"Shit. I had no idea it was this bad. How long has this been going on?" Van runs his hand through his hair.

"A while. I started noticing that she wasn't coming to bed back before the first farmers' market. I thought it might get better when it was over, but it's only gotten worse. And when I confronted her about it, she lost it on me, and now she's refusing to talk to me." I grip the arm of the chair, hating that I feel like I'm betraying her but knowing that I have to. "I think we need to stage an intervention. I don't like where this is going, and I'm worried she's going to get hurt or hurt someone else."

"I think you're right," Van says. "She's already been in a car accident; what happens if next time there's another car or a person involved?"

"I'm worried about what else she might be hiding."

"Me too."

And of course, because this day hasn't been bad enough, at seven Van gets a call from the pub. Teagan apparently fainted and hit her chin on the sink on the way down and needs to be taken to urgent care.

The three of us head there, Dillion and Van together and me in my own truck. I doubt she'll want to see me, but I want to see how bad the damage is.

When we arrive, she's sitting on the floor behind the bar, a wad of paper towels pressed to her chin. They're soaked with blood.

"What happened?" Dillion and Van flank her, helping her up off the floor.

"I fainted. It's not a big deal." Teagan tries to stand on her own, but she wobbles and sags against her brother. Her eyes are slow to track, and when they finally land on me, her brow furrows. "What are *you* doing here?"

"He came because he's worried about you. We all are." Van wraps his arm around her waist. "Come on, let's get you to urgent care."

"We'll call you in a bit." Dillion squeezes my hand on her way past.

Half an hour later Dillion messages to tell me Teagan didn't need stitches and that they used Steri-Strips. She passed out because of dehydration and exhaustion, and they're taking her home, so the intervention will have to wait.

CHAPTER 26

ON THE ROCKS

Aaron

The problem with a small town is that word gets around pretty damn fast when something gossip worthy happens. So I might not have a front-row seat to Teagan unraveling anymore, but I'm hearing the whispers.

Guilt is a heavy hand on my shoulder, making me feel like I'm reliving Devon's death all over again. I should have done something sooner. I should have tried a different tactic. And now she's shut me out and I'm paralyzed. I can't help at all. The only thing I can do is watch from the sidelines as she does a swan dive into dark waters and hope like hell she finds her way back to the surface.

I knew it would get worse before it could get better.

For me, I only realized my problem when I saw what it was doing to my dad. He'd already lost one son. I'd be a special kind of selfish bastard to rob him of another. I moved back to Pearl Lake, pulled myself together, quit drinking, and saw a therapist.

People think addiction is reserved for things like illicit drugs or alcohol. But it's not. The worst kinds of addictions are the ones that sneak up on people and pick away at them, little by little. Prescription drugs are particularly dangerous. Because they're given and monitored by a professional. Someone who generally has the best interests of their patient in mind.

Her prescriptions should be safe to take. As long as they're not combined with the wrong things or used in place of managing the underlying issues.

I'm not surprised when I overhear a couple of people in Boones the next morning, talking about that Firestone woman and how she's not looking good these days. "Too thin" is whispered, "such a pretty girl, but she's starting to look strung out." Someone else mentions the incident when she yelled at the pharmacist because she wouldn't fill her prescription. They tsk and shake their heads, because we've all seen it happen before.

Sometimes it's one of the wives from the other side of the lake, showing up day drunk in the grocery store. Then a few weeks later she's at the local pharmacy picking up prescriptions, stopping to buy vodka on the way back to her mansion, huge sunglasses in place to hide her bloodshot eyes.

And then there's Bob, who sits at the bar from the minute it opens to the minute it closes, eating free peanuts and spending his disability check on beer. Eating the occasional meal someone buys him but mostly drinking himself to death to manage the PTSD.

Any one of those could have been me, and they're a reminder to stay on track and away from the vices that can rule me.

But with Teagan it's different. She's no longer the rich girl from the other side of the lake, and she's not Bob, whose time in the war has scrambled his brain, and the only way he can survive now is to drown the memories. She's become part of this town, brushstrokes in a painting that give it light.

She's getting close to the bottom, and I want to do something to ease the fall.

On Monday I get confirmation that Teagan is on the rocks.

I'm working on the framing for the Wesleys' outdoor bar. The pool is closed for the season, but their college-aged daughter and her friend have found a reason to prance around in bikinis. They're taking these thirty-second videos and then jumping in the hot tub to warm up. It's a special level of ridiculous, but I do my best to ignore them.

Their mom comes out, and I'm hoping she's going to tell them it's time to come inside, but she doesn't.

"Aaron?" She stands at the door, questioning smile firmly in place.

"What can I do for you, ma'am?"

Her left eye twitches once. It happens every time I use the word *ma'am*. "The designer from Footprint Construction needs a word."

It takes me a moment to make the connection that she's talking about Teagan, who appears behind her. I haven't seen her since Thursday. She looked worse for wear then, but it's got nothing on how she looks now.

Her eyes are sunken, the hollow dark, and she looks like she's lost even more weight. Which is saying something because she didn't have weight to lose in the first place.

She thanks Mrs. Wesley and heads my way, a huge, fake smile plastered on her face. She waves to the girls in the hot tub with a little too much enthusiasm to look natural. "Hey! I'm so glad I caught you!" She gives me a hug, which is . . . unexpected.

I wrap my arms around her, feeling a lot like I'm hugging a potentially rabid bunny. Teagan looks harmless, but I'm very aware of what's on the other side of that sunshiny smile and what happens when her defenses are up.

"Can I talk to you for a minute?" she whispers in my ear.

I release her and step back. I take her in, how exhausted she looks, how her eyes are slow to track. She looks frail. "Yeah, of course. Is this Stitch related or us related?"

"Us related." She twists her fingers and glances over her shoulder. "I know you're at work. I probably should've waited until you were off today, but I missed you. I know I made a mess of things. I've had some time to think, and I see that now. There are a few important things I need to tell you."

I tuck a few strands of her hair behind her ear, wanting to believe what she's telling me but worried about her motives. "I missed you too. And you didn't make a mess of things, Teagan. No one's perfect, and every relationship has bumps. We can get through this. I'll be done in an hour. Unless it can't wait."

"I guess it can wait. I know I interrupted in the middle of your workday." She keeps chewing on the inside of her lip, to the point I'm starting to worry that she's going to break the skin.

"I just . . . maybe I could wait for you at your place? I could borrow your key?"

My house key is in my truck, where I always keep it during the workday.

"I could meet you at your place if that's easier. Then you don't have to wait around."

Her jaw works. There's a small clear Band-Aid on her chin, and the skin around it is purplish and bruised. She reaches out and links her finger with mine. "I thought maybe I could pick up some of the stuff you took from my medicine cabinet when you were upset with me."

The small seed of hope that she's here because she wants to work things out withers and dies. I know that she cares about me, but I also know she's struggling and that her need to find a way to cope is trumping those feelings. It doesn't make it hurt any less. I cross my arms. "So this actually isn't about us at all."

Her face crumples with confusion. "What do you mean? Yes it is. You were mad at me for not taking care of myself, and now I am. I'm going to see my doctor on Monday. I just need some extra help to get me through the weekend. I have to drive to Chicago, and I'm not getting enough sleep. I always sleep better next to you." Her hand comes to rest on my chest, and she smiles up at me. "When I can feel your heartbeat."

I feel like I'm going to be sick as I place my hand over hers. I hate that I didn't see this sooner. That I didn't see how hard this all was for her or the path she'd wandered onto. What I'm about to say next is going to determine a lot of things. Like how deep in the hole she truly is. "You can come over, and we can talk, and if after that you still want to stay, you're more than welcome, but I don't have any of that stuff I took."

Her smile drops into a frown, and her cheek tics. "What do you mean, you don't have it? What did you do with it?"

"I got rid of it all. The prescriptions were a year out of date. They're not even any good anymore after that. I brought them back to the pharmacy." That way someone couldn't dig them out of the trash and use them.

Her lip curls into a sneer, and her eyes flare with ire. "You had no right! Those were mine, and I needed them, and you threw them away?" Her voice rises, scaring a few squirrels and birds in the nearby trees.

"You need to keep your voice down, Teagan."

"Don't tell me to keep my voice down! You *stole* from me!" And now she's full-on shouting.

I grind my teeth together, fighting to stay in control. I take her hand and pull her toward the gate.

"What are you doing? Let go of me!"

"You are making a scene, and you're embarrassing yourself." I drop my voice, but it shakes with my anger and frustration. Anger that these pills have such a hold on her. That they override her logic. Frustration that she can't see what her addiction is doing to her. How it's breaking her down. That I'm losing her, and I can't fix her or make her better.

I throw a glare toward the girls still sitting in the hot tub, eyes wide, phones in their hands, and call out, "Don't even think about it." The last thing Teagan needs is someone recording her having a public meltdown and accusing me of stealing from her. I can imagine the kind of gossip that would result.

That seems to stop her, at least until we get to the driveway. "Why would you do that to me? Why would you throw away my prescriptions?"

"They were past their expiration, Teagan."

"So? There was nothing wrong with them! And it wasn't your place."

I raise my hands. "Okay, you're right. I shouldn't have thrown them out, but honestly, Teagan, me tossing them isn't the real issue, and you know it."

"Like hell it isn't!"

"The fact that you would seek me out at a jobsite and use wanting to talk as a thinly veiled excuse so you could get to your precious freaking pills is the goddamn issue. You look like you haven't slept in days. When was the last time you ate a meal?"

"Why are you doing this to me? Why are you trying to make me feel bad? I'm doing everything I can to be better, Aaron. What more do you want?"

I scrub a hand over my face. "I want you to face reality, and I want you to get help."

"Forget it. This was a mistake. I should have known better." She spins around and heads for her car, stumbling across the driveway.

There are people walking down the road, and a couple on the balcony across the street.

I go after her, aware that we have an audience, and that it's growing the longer we're out here, fighting like this. But there is no way I'm letting her drive. She's too upset, and I'm responsible for putting her in this highly elevated state.

I rush ahead of her and step in front of the driver's side door.

"Now you're not going to let me leave?" She throws her hands in the air.

I take her face between my palms and appeal to the piece of her that so desperately needs to be needed. Manipulating her back the way she just tried and failed to manipulate me. Even though it hurts like hell, I'm aware that she's not rational, and she can't see what this is doing to her or me. Not now. "You're not okay to drive, Teagan. And you can hate me as much as you want for what I've done, but I have enough ghosts haunting me. I barely survived losing my brother. If something happens to you, I will never recover. Just let me drive you home. If you need to shut me out again after that, fine. But I'm the reason you're this upset. I won't be the reason something bad happens to you too. Just, please, Teagan."

Her bottom lip trembles, and two tears slide down her cheeks.

I hate that I have to use one of her best and worst qualities against her.

Thankfully Teagan stops fighting with me and gets in my truck. The only sounds she makes are quiet sniffles, and she stares out the passenger-side window, wringing her hands.

"I know you're angry with me, Teagan, but I love you too much to let you keep putting yourself at risk like this."

She makes a sound but doesn't respond otherwise. A little squeak comes from her, and she presses her hand over her mouth, like she's trying to keep the sounds in. I want to reach over and touch her, hug her, console her, but I don't think she can accept the affection.

I pull into the driveway, and Teagan swipes away her tears, then fumbles with her seat belt as I park in front of the garage. Her breathing grows increasingly labored, and her hands are shaking so badly she can't manage to hit the release latch.

I cut the engine and hop out before rounding the hood and opening the passenger-side door. I reach across and cover her shaking hand with mine. "Let me help you, Teagan."

"I'm fine. I h-have it." She tries to push my hands away, but her movements are jerky and uncoordinated, and her breath comes faster and faster, sucking in air between heavy gasps.

"I messed things up," she whispers. "Everything is messed up. I'm a failure. I messed it all up."

I brush tears from her cheeks, but they keep falling. "You're not a failure, babe." I release the latch, and she tumbles out of the truck and into my arms.

She struggles to stand, to hold on to my arms, but the shaking is worse.

"Teagan? What's happening here?"

Her head lolls back and her eyes roll up to the sky. She's a rag doll in my arms, and I worry that this might be an overdose.

And it feels like Devon all over again.

I can't be too late again.

If Teagan doesn't survive this, I don't know if I will either.

I call out for help, struggling to hold on to her shaking, limp form.

"Aaron, what's going on? Teagan? Oh shit. What the hell happened?" I hear Van, but he's a million miles away, and I'm stuck here in this hell, where I'm afraid I'm losing another person I love.

"We need to get her to the hospital. Now."

CHAPTER 27

A PINPRICK OF LIGHT

Teagan

A steady beep is the first thing that registers, followed by the unpleasant smell of bleach. My eyelids feel like they weigh a thousand pounds. I don't try to open them right away. Instead, I absorb the smells and sounds and feels. The sheets are scratchy, not like the soft ones in my bed. They don't smell like home, or Aaron.

Aaron.

Just the thought of him makes my chest hurt. I miss him.

If something happens to you, I will never recover.

My stomach rolls at that memory. I can't quite connect it to anything else.

Did I go to see him?

Fragments of memories float around like bubbles in my mind, but as soon as I feel like I can grasp them, they pop and fade away. I remember his hands on my face, his sad voice and matching sad eyes. I remember sitting in the passenger seat of his truck.

Not being able to breathe.

Familiar cologne registers, along with the creak of a chair. "Teag? You waking up?"

Not Aaron.

I finally crack a lid. The room is dimly lit, but it's still a lot brighter than the backs of my eyelids. I blink several times before Van's face turns from fuzzy to clear.

I glance around the room. "Where am I?" My voice is a hoarse whisper. My mouth is dry. It's a silly question. It's very clear that I'm in a hospital. "What happened?"

"You're at Lake Geneva General." Van grabs the plastic cup from the nightstand and brings the straw to my lips. "Small sip, okay?"

I do as he asks, taking small sips until I finish the drink.

His eyes meet mine. "You had a seizure."

"A seizure?" The word feels foreign in my mouth.

"You were severely dehydrated. That combined with lack of nutrition, an electrolyte imbalance, the insomnia, and the stress your body was under is what caused it, but the doctors want to run a bunch of tests to make sure there isn't more going on." He takes my hand in his. "You scared the shit out of all of us."

"I just needed some sleep," I croak, but even as I say it, I know it's not true.

Van's expression crumples. "This is bigger than needing sleep, Teagan. What if you'd been driving when that happened? You've been hiding things, lying to everyone, especially yourself." He gives my hand a squeeze. "I know about the car accident and you calling Billy instead of anyone else, and that you asked him to keep it a secret. And he didn't have to come out and tell anyone for us to figure it out, either, since your car is scratched all to shit."

"I didn't want you to be upset with me." And I knew he would be. And that he would have a right to worry, because I was pushing way too hard. Not only hiding things from the people I love but hiding from myself.

"You didn't want me to ask questions, and you didn't want to face the truth and acknowledge that you have a problem." He closes his eyes for a second and exhales a slow, deep breath. "I'm not mad at you, Teagan, and I know it hurts to hear this, but you're trying to bury your problems under a mountain of prescriptions. You've been working five different jobs and taking on more and more projects, because you can't or won't say no. It's more than anyone can reasonably handle. That alone would have caused anyone to have a breakdown."

"I wanted to prove I could do it, and I didn't want to let anyone down." The words sound hollow and weak, and like another useless excuse.

"I know. You never want to let anyone down. But you keep piling it on and not taking anything off your plate. You don't even give yourself time to breathe. You need to find some balance, and this isn't the way to do that." Van's expression is pained, his tone imploring.

I look down at our clasped hands, not wanting him to be right but knowing that he is. "If I stop, then I have time to think."

"Why is that such a bad thing?"

Because then I have time to reflect on my choices. That I've spent my whole life trying to be what everyone else expected instead of accepting myself for me. That I wanted to fit into an ideal instead of just being me. And when I got to Pearl Lake and managed to get these jobs, I wanted to prove that I could do all of it. That I could handle everything. I lost sight of the goal, and instead of figuring out what I want, I tried to juggle everything, liking the feeling of being needed. Until it all came crashing down.

There's a knock on the door, and Aaron appears, holding two white paper cups. He looks exhausted. "You're awake. Thank God."

"I'm going to give you two a few minutes." Van pushes to his feet, and Aaron takes his place in the chair beside my bed.

He sets the cup on the night table and folds my hand between both of his. "Hey."

"Hi," I whisper. I don't know where to start.

"I thought you had overdosed." He bows his head and presses his lips to the back of my hand. "I thought I was going to lose you."

"I'm so sorry," I whisper. And I am. More than words can express. Especially knowing his past and everything he's been through when he lost his brother. "I didn't mean to hurt you."

"I want you to get help, Teagan. I don't want you to feel like you have to keep taking on the weight of the world. And I know it's not going to be easy, but I will love you even when you can't love yourself, okay?" He gives me back my own words.

Lying here, in this hospital bed because my body and brain told me what I've been refusing to see all this time—that I'm pushing myself to my breaking point—I can finally see that it's not everyone else I'm letting down; it's myself. And in doing that, I'm causing the people I love pain. I can see it on Aaron's face, and it breaks my heart.

Over the next forty-eight hours I undergo a slew of tests, including an MRI and a CT scan. I'm terrified that there's more going on in my brain and my body that I don't know about. But it turns out the seizure is a result of exhaustion, dehydration, and a general chemical imbalance in my brain. My body literally shorted out on me. And it scares the hell out of me.

Enough that I agree to a thirty-day treatment program where I can detox from the pharmacy of medication I've been swallowing on a regular basis to make it through my days. I almost back out, afraid of what people are going to say and think, worried about all the people I'm letting down and the projects that aren't going to be taken care of while I'm gone. But my family rallies around me, and despite everything I've put him through, Aaron is there to offer his support. He even drives me to the treatment center.

We pull up to the estate house. It's a beautiful sprawling home on twenty acres of property. It even has its own man-made lake. It's expensive, and going here will eat pretty much all my savings. We did the research, though, and this place has a high success rate. And it's only about an hour away from Pearl Lake. Van offered to pay for it, but there was no way I would allow him to foot the bill for this. I needed to own this, and I needed to take control of my own life, starting with putting myself through treatment.

Aaron parks the car but doesn't make a move to get out.

"Tell me that I need to do this."

He reaches over and squeezes my hand before slipping his fingers under my hair, his palm curving around the back of my neck. "You need to take care of yourself, and this is one huge step in the right direction."

"You're right. I know that. I'm just scared."

"Scared of what, exactly?"

I give voice to my fears. "What if it's too hard? What if I can't do it? What if it doesn't work?"

His thumb sweeps along the column of my throat. "You have to want it to work, Teagan. And you can't go back to the way things were."

"Maybe you should give me an ultimatum." I drag my attention away from the white house. "Tell me that you can't be with me if I go back to the way I was before."

His smile is sad as he brushes his thumb across my cheek. I realize he's wiping away a tear. I've shed a lot of those over the past few days. That Aaron hasn't run screaming for the hills tells me I'm pretty damn lucky to have him in my life.

"You know I can't do that," he says softly.

"You can't stick around if this doesn't work." I motion to the house.

"I'm not sending you in there with that hanging over your head, Teagan. That's like tossing someone into the ocean without a life jacket and expecting them to tread water for the next thirty days without support. This is one day at a time. I'm not expecting you to be perfect, and neither should you. Give yourself the grace you give everyone else." He cups my cheek and presses his lips to mine.

I sink into the kiss, dragging it out as long as I can. There won't be more kisses like this for a while. We've decided that we're going to take a step back while I'm in treatment. It means we're on pause while I get the help I need. And I hope like hell that when I come out on the other side, I'll be able to stand on my own, and we can find a new us.

CHAPTER 28
A NEW DOOR TO OPEN

Teagan

The thing about addiction is that you don't know how big of a problem it is until the things you're addicted to are taken away. One of the first things the doctors at the treatment center do is reassess my medication. It means lots of questions, some questionnaires, and a slew of assessment tests.

I was six when my mother passed away. Six years old when she went in for outpatient surgery and never came home. And the month after she passed, I started first grade. I was overwhelmed, scared, confused. And motherless.

I don't have a ton of memories from that time. But I know school was hard, and different. I had to sit in a desk all day for the first time. There were new rules. Lots of kids. People to talk to. My teacher was older. She reminded me of a grandma, and she had more rules than Grammy Bee did.

I was diagnosed with attention deficit hyperactivity disorder and put on medication. My dad was overwhelmed with the loss of my mother. Van was only eight and Bradley was four. There was a lot going on in the house. I remember the first time I took the medication. How I could sit for hours and color or complete pages upon pages in my spelling workbook. And I loved the praise I would get from my dad when I finished something and got most of the answers right.

Food tasted different, though. Not quite right. As if someone had put something metallic in it. My appetite at school didn't exist, and by the time I was nine, I'd learned to share my snacks with my friends so I wouldn't come home with a full lunch bag. But at night it was like a black hole opened in my stomach and food suddenly tasted right again. And I would eat and eat and eat.

Bedtime was always hard. It took me forever to fall asleep. And even when I did, sometimes I would wake up in the middle of the night and couldn't go back to sleep. My dad would give me melatonin, and most of the time that worked. Except it gave me vivid dreams. Sometimes bad ones.

By the time I was a teenager, my grades were stable and I was managing okay. But when I went to college, things started to shift. We had to up my dose because I was struggling to focus in my classes. I started having panic attacks, and I wasn't sleeping. So we added a sedative, which helped with the sleep. And when the stress got to be too much and the panic threatened to take over, I had an antianxiety medication that I could take.

I was handling what life threw at me. At least I thought I was. Until I wasn't anymore.

And the sleeping pills stopped cutting it. I added melatonin to the mix, because it was natural and could tip me over the edge. But those stopped working, too, and then the energy drinks came, and the excessive coffee, and when I was having an exceptionally challenging day, I started on the caffeine pills.

Until my body literally couldn't handle it anymore.

A few days into my treatment, I meet with the psychologist and the doctor to discuss the results of all the tests. The therapist is a woman in her forties named Edith. She and Dr. Storey sit in comfy chairs across from me.

We've talked about the medication and when and how it started and when it got out of control. Since I've been here, there have been adjustments to my medication, doses lowered, and the sleeping medication has been changed to one meant specifically for anxiety that's also supposed to help me sleep. So far it's been successful.

It feels like so much has changed in such a short time.

"How are you feeling today, Teagan?" Edith asks.

"I'm good. I slept well last night."

"I'm glad to hear that; the foreign environment and all the changes can make it difficult for some people."

The first couple of days were the hardest, being alone in a place I didn't know, shining a spotlight on all my issues. "I know it's necessary, though. So I can get the space I need to regain control of my independence."

"This is very true." She crosses her legs and laces her fingers together. "I wanted to talk to you about some of the diagnostic tests we ran when you first arrived."

"Okay." I take a sip of my water, suddenly nervous.

"We've had some time to observe you and review your full medical history. I believe you were misdiagnosed as a child."

"Misdiagnosed how?"

"I don't believe that you fit the profile for attention deficit," Edith says.

"But I couldn't pay attention in school." I remember feeling lost back then, unable to handle the separation from my dad, afraid one day I'd come home from school and he'd be gone, too, just like Mom had been.

"You were a child grieving the loss of your mother, and you lost her weeks before the school year began. It was a lot of change, more than you could handle. And considering the way things were at home after she passed, it makes sense that you were struggling with the demands of school. On paper it looks like the medication was doing its job, but when we look critically at all the data, I believe the diagnosis is incorrect, which means the Adderall contributed to the worsening anxiety and created the sleep disturbances."

"What does that mean?" I've been on some form of ADHD medication for nearly twenty years, and we switched to Adderall when I started college.

"We're going to wean you off the Adderall and monitor you closely for side effects while you're here."

"What will that look like?" I've been sleeping okay over the past week, despite it not being my bed. And the lack of Aaron to snuggle with. That's one of the things I miss the most.

We review the potential side effects, talk through my fears and concerns, and come up with a plan on how we're going to wean me off the medication I've been dependent on for the past two decades. It's not a high dose, so Edith believes I'll be able to wean off the drug in my remaining time here.

We work on reducing my dose during my stay. It isn't a fun process, and I have good and bad days, but as the drug leaves my system, I slowly start to realize the impact it was having on my body and my brain. That instead of making the anxiety better, the medication heightened it. It also contributed to my sleeping problems, and it made my concentration and memory worse instead of better.

Two weeks into treatment, Van and my dad come to visit. I've been able to talk to them daily, but we don't have access to our cell phones most of the time, apart from an hour in the evening.

My dad pulls me in for a huge hug and then steps back and holds my shoulders, his eyes roaming over my face, taking me in. "You look great. How are you doing, sweetheart?"

"I'm good. I'm glad you could come."

He steps back, and Van moves in. His hug is longer and tighter. "I'm sorry I didn't see what was happening," he murmurs.

"It's okay." I squeeze him back. "I didn't see the problem until it was too late either."

And I truly didn't.

I take them on a tour of the grounds so we can talk with some privacy.

"How is everything going?" Dad asks. "How is treatment?"

"It's good. A lot of work, but good." We take a seat on one of the picnic benches. Fall has settled in, and the leaves have started to create a colorful landscape. I wanted to wait until I saw them before I told them about my new diagnosis. "The doctors did a bunch of tests when I first got here, and they believe I was incorrectly diagnosed with attention deficit disorder."

Dad's eyes flare. "Incorrectly diagnosed? What do you mean?"

"I don't have issues with attention. A general anxiety disorder, yes, but not attention deficit." I explain what my therapist and my doctor explained to me. How the changes and the loss affected my ability to manage school.

Dad reaches out and covers my hand with his. "Teagan, sweetheart."

I see his guilt, and I wish I could take it away for him, but I know that he needs time to process this, just like I did. "I don't blame you, Dad; you were struggling to raise three kids on your own, and you lost your wife. I was six and constantly afraid one day I was going to come home from school and you'd be gone too."

Van puts his arm around my shoulder. "I remember how upset you'd get if Dad was late coming home from work."

"I was always worried something was going to happen to him. My therapist says I have abandonment issues. Which makes sense. And I look so much like her, and you used to tell me that all the time." I give Dad a small smile.

"You do, still. You have her smile and her eyes and her personality." He squeezes my hand.

I nod. "I have some great memories of Mom, but I have some not-so-great ones too."

"What do you mean?" His smile falls.

"I remember she used to drink 'water' with lemon or cucumber slices out of fancy glasses. And she always napped at the same time of day as me, and she always made us fun dinners, but she never ate with us, saying she was going to wait for you." I bite the inside of my cheek.

"I remember that, too," Van says softly, as if he's putting it together for the first time and seeing how all the pieces fit.

I turn back to Dad, whose expression is crestfallen. "We don't blame you for what happened to Mom. And I think being here, I've learned a lot about what it must have been like for you. And I'll never know why she was the way she was, but she loved us with her whole heart, and you, and sometimes I think maybe she didn't leave enough room in her heart for herself."

"She was so selfless, just like you. Always doing things for other people. She loved you kids so much. You were her whole world." His eyes pool with tears, and I feel like I didn't bring enough tissues for this conversation.

"I know how much you loved her, Dad. You were always taking care of her, giving her whatever she wanted. I remember you telling her she was beautiful and she didn't need to change a thing." Tears slide down my cheeks, and I pull a tissue from my pocket. I've shed my fair share of them since I started down this path to healing.

Dad covers his mouth with his hand, fighting with his own emotions. "I didn't want her to have the surgery. I tried to talk her out of it."

"I didn't know that," Van says. He's been quiet so far, observing.

"I loved her so much, maybe to a fault. I wanted her to be happy, but sometimes she struggled with that. When she suggested the surgery, I told her it wasn't necessary and that I loved her exactly as she was, but she told me it would make her feel better about herself. She'd been through bouts of postpartum, and I'd hoped it would give her some-thing to feel positive about. And then we lost her."

This isn't something we've ever talked about as a family. Sure, Dad sent us all for counseling, but not together. When we were kids and Mom had passed away, Dad blamed himself. Saying he shouldn't have let her take the risk. And instead of letting us all know the truth, that she had been the one who wanted the surgery, he allowed us to believe it was him because he didn't want to tarnish her memory. And in his mind, he'd failed our mother and deserved to shoulder the blame.

And as he breaks down, as we all do, I feel like we're finally on the road to healing.

As we talk and share stories, I tell them that they aren't to blame for me ending up here. "You've both always been so supportive of me, and sometimes what I was told wasn't always what I heard. A lot of the pressures I felt were of my own making."

"I should have seen that you were taking on too much," Van argues.

"Now that I'm no longer in it, I can see what it was doing to me. All of those jobs were a distraction from the real issues. It started as me trying to figure out what I liked and quickly spiraled into me trying to take on the world and not wanting to disappoint anyone. They made me feel important, essential. At least on the surface."

"No one would have faulted you if you wanted to quit a few of those jobs," Van says softly.

"I know, but they were a diversion from the real work that needed to be done. And that work needed to be done on me." I squeeze his arm. "Sometimes we need to dig out all the bullshit so we can get to the heart of the matter. Which is what I'm doing now."

"Will you come back to Pearl Lake when the program is over?" Van asks.

"You know you're always welcome back at home, if you think Chicago would be better," Dad offers. "I know I haven't been the best dad, or the most present, but you always have a place with me."

This is one of the things I've talked through with my therapist over the past couple of weeks. Where I plan to go when the program is over. I've done a lot of reading while I've been in treatment and listened to all the stories of the other people who are here too. They all say the same thing, that I need time to recover, to stand on my own. And I'm not sure Pearl Lake is the right place to do that. At least not yet. Eventually, yes, I want to make it my home. But for now living with my dad is probably the better, smarter plan if I truly want to recover and heal.

"I want to come back to Pearl Lake eventually, but I think I might need a few months to work on me before I can do that."

"You can stay with me for as long as you want," Dad says.

"And you can visit me and Dillion whenever you feel like it. The apartment above the garage is yours." Van hugs me for what has to be the tenth time.

I feel like I'm taking steps in the right direction.

But the next one is going to be a lot harder than this.

CHAPTER 29
WAIT FOR ME

Teagan

After thirty days my therapist and my doctor believe I'm ready to start my new life. I've been weaned off the Adderall completely. I have a new prescription for the anxiety that is much better for me, and I've kicked my energy drink and caffeine pill habit.

I feel like a very different version of myself, but I'm aware that inside the protective walls of a treatment center I'm insulated and secure, outside them not so much. So I decide that I'm going to move back to Chicago for a few months, at the very least.

I'll still consult on designs for the Stitches and go to Pearl Lake once a week, but I'll be working remotely otherwise. And I'm still managing the fall farmers' market, but I have lots of help this time.

There's one other thing I need to manage, though, and it's going to be hard.

I know Aaron and I are on a "pause," but I shouldn't be in a relationship. Not for the foreseeable future.

While this isn't a typical "addiction," what I'm going through still fits under that umbrella. And my therapist suggests I spend the next six months focused on myself. Or maybe even longer, depending on how things go outside the walls of the treatment center.

So when I tell Aaron that I'm going to stay in Chicago for a few months, he asks if he can pick me up and drive me home. Of course I say yes.

This isn't a conversation I want to have over the phone. He's far too important to me, and he deserves better.

I haven't seen him since he dropped me off and I tried to make him give me an ultimatum. Which was so unfair of me. I see that now, but I couldn't see it then. I was scared of the path I was going down. And scared to lose him. I'm still scared. Because my therapist isn't wrong. I need to be a better me before we can be an us again. And I don't know how long that's going to take.

I don't have any makeup with me, not even mascara, so all I can do is shower and smell good. They confiscate most personal effects, apart from our own clothes. We're not even allowed to use our own shampoo, because sometimes people will try to smuggle in pills in Ziploc baggies. I only found that out when I saw it happen the second week I was here.

Aaron and I have talked as much as they'll allow while I've been here, but seeing him is different from a phone call. I don't know if things are going to be the same or different.

Well, I know they'll be different, but I don't know to what extent. Aaron has seen me at rock bottom. He knows what it looks like when I'm falling apart, and part of me understands that with everything he's already been through, I might be too much for him. That a pause with no real definitive end date might not be something he can manage.

I have to come to terms with the possibility that moving forward, there might not be an us.

It makes sense that I had trouble with breakfast this morning. Normally when I'm this stressed out, I'll avoid food altogether and go for coffee. I might spend hours on a Pinterest board to escape my own brain.

But this morning I drank a fruit shake and spent two hours on meditative yoga. Caffeine has been limited to one coffee a day. I typically drink it with breakfast but skipped it this morning because I was already jittery enough. I don't run from my fears today. Instead, I face them down and accept that whatever is going to happen is out of my control, but I decide how I'll deal with whatever is coming.

I pack my things and thank the staff and my team, and then I wait for him to arrive. I'll miss the serenity here, but I'm ready to get back to my life and the people I love, no matter what that looks like.

When he pulls up in his truck, my heart skips a few beats. And when he steps out, his smile wide and warm, it kicks into a full gallop.

This is going to be hard. Harder than I thought.

He jogs up the front steps and folds me into his embrace. He buries his face in my hair, and I feel his lips on my neck.

"I missed you so fucking much, babe," he murmurs against my skin.

I return the embrace, breathing in the scent of his cologne and absorbing the feel of his arms wrapped around me, blanketing me in his strength. "I missed you, too, so much."

We stand there for a long time, just holding on to each other. Long enough that my nerves take over and I feel a few chips in my resolve. But I remind myself that we can't go back to how things were. That I need to be able to stand on my own before I can stand beside him.

Eventually he releases me, but he takes my face between his cold palms, and that smile he's wearing fades. "Babe, what's wrong?"

"I'm just emotional. Today is big. Thank you for coming to pick me up."

He must see something in my expression, because instead of dipping down to kiss me, he presses his lips to my temple. "I'm here for you, whatever you need, however you need me."

The drive from the center to Chicago is only about half an hour. We talk about Pearl Lake, and he points to a card on the dash that's been signed by at least a hundred people. He tells me about his last visit with Jamie, and how he thinks he might be convincing Lydia to move out toward Pearl Lake, and how his dad has been actively looking for his own place on the lake.

"He came down last weekend and stayed at my mom's."

"Really? How did that go?"

"My mom was blushing like a teenager every time he so much as glanced at her, so that was awkward as hell, but good, you know? They both deserve to be happy. Kinda makes me wish I'd had that discussion with her a long time ago. Maybe things would have been different if I hadn't sat on it as long as I did."

"Hindsight is always twenty-twenty, isn't it?"

"Seems that way."

When we reach the outskirts of Chicago, I suggest we stop for a bite to eat. I want more time with Aaron before we get to my dad's place. And I need to talk to him about what the next few months are going to look like for us.

We stop at a diner and take a seat in one of the booths. After we order, Aaron places his hand on the table palm up, and I slip my hand into his.

"You know, when you come to Pearl Lake next week, you're more than welcome to stay at my place." His thumb smooths back and forth along my knuckles.

My stomach flips. I don't want to say no, but I have to. "About that." I don't know if I can do this without getting emotional.

"Is everything okay? Are we okay?" Aaron's gaze shifts to the side, and he swallows thickly.

"We're okay." I give his hand a squeeze.

"Your expression says something a lot different," he says softly.

"I didn't want to have this conversation over the phone," I tell him.

His jaw works, and he pulls his hand back, sliding it under the table. "This sounds like the beginning of a breakup speech."

"It's not," I whisper.

"You look like you're gonna cry, Teagan."

"That's because I am." I fish around in my purse for a tissue.

"Should we leave?" Aaron's face reads panic.

I shake my head. "One of the steps in recovery is learning not to be dependent on other people. And I know it's not like a typical addiction, but it still hits all the same notes, you know? My therapist said I shouldn't be in a relationship right now, and she's right."

"So you are breaking up with me, then." His voice is hoarse and low, and when I glance up at him, his expression nearly shatters my resolve. He looks almost as heartbroken as I feel. Which is how I know what I'm about to say next is the right thing.

"More like hitting the pause button. Again." I blow out a breath. "I don't ever want to go down the path I was on again. I don't want to do that to myself, or you, or us. And for there to be an us, I need more time to work on this." I motion to myself. "You deserve a better version of me."

"I'll love every version of you."

I smile, but it's weighed down with sadness. "You've been through a lot, Aaron. And so have I. I think we can be great together, but I'm not where I need to be for that to work. And it's going to be a while before I'm there, maybe longer than you're willing to wait."

"How long we talking? Weeks? Months? Years?" He twists a napkin until it tears, then folds his hands on the table.

"Hopefully not years, but it could be a year. It could be less, but I can't set a deadline, because I honestly don't know how long it's going to take for me to get where I need to be emotionally and mentally. I need to learn how to say no and how to stand on my own before I can be someone's girlfriend."

"What does that mean for us?"

"It means we can be friends, and if you're still interested in trying to be more than that when I'm in the right place, then we can try to be an us again. I'm not asking for promises, though, Aaron. I know that's not reasonable, and a lot can change between now and then, especially when we don't know how far away then is."

He rubs his bottom lip. "I don't think I'm going out on a limb if I assume that this is a friends-*without*-benefits situation."

I chuckle, glad for the moment of levity. "You would be correct."

"I guess I should have kissed you when I had the chance, then, huh?" He blows out a breath and gives his head a shake, glancing up at me from under his lashes. "I know you're not asking for promises, but I'll take friends until you're ready for more. However long that takes."

CHAPTER 30
NEW BEGINNINGS AGAIN

Teagan

Over the months that follow, I settle into a new routine.

Living with my dad this time around is different. In a lot of ways, it feels like he's stepping into his dad shoes in the way I need him to. And I'm learning to accept the help and let the roles reverse, allowing myself to be taken care of instead of being the one to take care of everyone else except myself. At first I worry about the impact I'm going to have on his relationship with Danielle, but the more I get to know her, the more I come to see that she's a great partner for him, and while I don't need someone to fill the mom-shaped hole in my heart, she's become someone I feel comfortable with.

I learn how to say no when it feels like I'm putting too much on my plate. It's hard at first, but the more I do it, the easier it gets. I learn what I can handle and when it's too much.

And that's not isolated to my jobs but is also true for the people in my life. I let my dad step in and help mediate my relationship with Bradley, who has also been surprisingly supportive, giving me hope that with time, our family can repair the fractured bonds and be whole again. While Van isn't ready to talk to Bradley and he isn't sure when, or if, he ever will be, he's supportive of my role in our brother's life, which is a relief.

With a heavy heart, I quit all my jobs in Pearl Lake, and I work for the Stitches on a contract basis. I only work on a few projects at a time. And I'm in charge of organizing and running the farmers' market in Pearl Lake, which sounds like a lot, but since it's winter and the market won't start up again until May, I have lots of time to get everything organized, especially since we're holding it twice a month now.

And it allows me to focus on what's important, which is learning how to avoid overwhelming myself by taking on too much. I go to therapy on a weekly basis.

I do most of my work for the Stitches remotely, but once a week, barring bad weather, I make the trip out to Pearl Lake. I don't stay the night most of the time, though. Sometimes I meet Van or Aaron for lunch; other times I have dinner with Dillion and the girls. It's nice. But I always go back home after that.

It's a Wednesday afternoon in April, and I'm answering emails regarding the first farmers' market of the season. When my alarm goes off at three, I finish up my email and close my laptop. Typically I have set hours that I work, but I have therapy on Wednesday afternoon.

Aside from Wednesdays, and with the exception of any emergencies, of which there are very few, I work from eight until six, Monday to Friday. The weekends are reserved for me and my family. It's not always easy, and there are times when I struggle, or wake up in the middle of the night and fight with myself not to get up and jump on the computer. But I'm in a much better place than I was six months ago, and that's what's important.

Little gains and small steps forward are what I strive for.

I make the drive to see my therapist. Most of my sessions are over video chat, since she's outside Chicago, but once a month I head to her home office and we discuss my medication, how I'm sleeping, and how I'm coping.

Her office is cozy, and there's already a cup of chamomile tea waiting for me.

"How are things? The farmers' market starts up next month, doesn't it? Are you feeling any stress over that?" Edith asks.

"Over the market? Not really. I have lots of help from some of the women in Pearl Lake. Some of them have experience running events, so they've been a great support." I've gotten a lot better at delegating. And Stevie and Queenie, two of the hockey wives, have this way about them that makes me feel like nothing I ask is ever too much for them.

"That's wonderful. And what about the Stitches? How many contracts do you have?"

"One is wrapping up, and I have two new ones," I tell her. "It's the busy time of the year there, so I know the next few months are probably going to be a bit more demanding, but we've agreed that I won't take on more than three projects at a time. And that it's okay if things take longer design-wise, because they're willing to wait until off-season to finish up projects."

Edith smiles. "That's great news. Now tell me what *is* stressing you out."

I sip my tea and give her an arched brow. "I can't slip anything past you, can I?"

"I wouldn't be doing my job very well if you could."

"I've been making a point of only going to Pearl Lake for the day, but I'll have to start doing overnights soon."

"What about that worries you? Are you reconsidering whether you want to move back there?"

"No, I'm not reconsidering." That's the one thing I'm sure of. That I want to live in Pearl Lake. Allie and Tawny have become my friends. My brother is there, and Dillion has asked me to be one of her bridesmaids in the fall when they get married. And of course, there's Aaron.

I set my tea on the table and pull the stone out of my pocket, running my thumb over the smooth surface. Aaron gave it to me the first time I saw him after we talked about putting our relationship on pause. It's a pink stone in the shape of a heart. He said it reminded him of me, and I've taken to carrying it with me everywhere. "Aaron."

When I don't say anything else, she raises a single eyebrow. "What about Aaron worries you? Has he been putting pressure on you one way or the other?"

She knows about our relationship and his history. She also knows how hard it's been for me to toe the friendship line. Aaron and I have chemistry. It's been a challenge to ignore it. "No, none. He's honestly been great."

"So is it Aaron you're worried about or *you*?" she asks.

I flip the stone between my fingers. "I guess it's me," I sigh.

"What about you and Aaron worries you?"

"If I'm in Pearl Lake overnight, I'm going to want to spend it with Aaron."

"Are you ready to spend a night with Aaron?"

"My body is ready. It's been seven months."

Edith chuckles and shakes her head. "Fair. Can you handle the emotional ramifications of a night with Aaron? And do you feel like you're capable of stepping back into a relationship with him that is no longer just platonic?"

I scrub a hand over my face. "I want to be."

"Is wanting to be enough?"

I sigh. "I don't know."

"I think the more important question here is this: Does avoiding staying in Pearl Lake make it impossible for you to figure out if you are or aren't ready for the next step?" She takes a sip of her tea and waits for me to digest that.

"Maybe?"

"Let's unpack that a little more."

"If I don't stay in Pearl Lake, I can't end up back at Aaron's, and we can't be alone together."

"But you would like to be alone with Aaron."

I throw my hands in the air. "Of course I would. I haven't had more than a hug from him in months. But if I'm alone with him, I'm worried that I'm going to want to hug him while I'm naked, and I'm worried that he's going to tell me he doesn't want to hug me when I'm naked. Or worse, that he's going to tell me that we should just be friends."

"Is that fear logical?"

"Probably not, since he's always poking me in the stomach with his man-dangle if I hug him too long," I mutter.

That gets another chuckle out of her. "Okay. So here's my next question for you, Teagan. Why is there no in-between?"

"What do you mean, no in-between?"

"Relationships progress. You go on a date; maybe on the first one there's a good-night kiss. There's a second date; maybe that kiss turns into something else, but does it have to be all or nothing? You are doing very well, Teagan. You've made great gains over the past six months. You've put yourself first and made your own goals and needs a priority."

"I don't want to mess this up with him."

"I understand that, but all relationships are a risk. That you're here, talking about your fears and wants, tells us both something, don't you think?"

"It's not about jumping in with both feet."

"That's right. It's not all or nothing. Dip a toe in. Have the discussion with him. Tell him where you are and what you want."

"But not that I want to naked hug him."

"I wouldn't lead with that, since your relationship with him is about more than sex. The first step is staying in Pearl Lake overnight at your brother's. You've established a solid friendship. He's a great source of support for you, and you've been the same for him. If you think you're ready, try going on a date. Allow yourself new boundaries."

"So we should start dating?" I flip the pink stone heart between my fingers.

"If you feel ready, then yes."

I exhale my worries. "I feel ready."

◆ ◆ ◆

On Saturday morning I wake up bright and early and head to Pearl Lake. It was hard not to tell Aaron I'm staying overnight, especially when he seemed resigned to the fact that all he was going to get this weekend was a couple of hours at dinner with Dillion and Van, and maybe a walk by the water, before I drove back to Chicago.

I spend the morning going over all the details for the first farmers' market with the hockey wives. I half expected them to lose steam or interest along the way, but they're as committed as ever. They've been amazing to work with, and they're so much fun.

Afterward, I head to town hall to meet with Bernadette, and once I'm done there, I hop back in my car. All day I've been getting messages from Aaron asking when he'll get to see me, followed by endless hug GIFs.

I message him to let him know I'm on my way to Van's place, and by the time I get there, Aaron's truck is already parked in front of the garage. He's clearly just arrived as well, because he gets out of the truck as I pull my car in beside him.

I barely have a chance to open the door before he's there, wrapping his arms around me. "I'm sorry. I have no chill. I missed you. And everyone monopolizes your time when you're here. I want one really long hug before I have to share you for the rest of the evening."

I allow myself to be enveloped in his embrace. He truly has been so patient and understanding. His scruff tickles my skin as he lifts me off my feet and continues to hug me.

He hasn't shaved since I put us on pause. There was an occasion early on when we first started seeing each other where he hadn't shaved for a few days. I ended up with the wickedest chafed chin thanks to stubble burn. He figured if he didn't get to kiss me anyway, what was the point in shaving? And it seemed to be a mild deterrent for making bad choices that might feel good.

But the truth is, although it hasn't been easy to stay in the friend zone, all I had to do was remind myself that I needed to be a better version of myself before I could go there again with him. I wanted to be a partner in the true sense.

And I feel like I'm finally there.

He sets me back on my feet. "Hey."

I laugh. "Hi. And I missed you too."

His eyes roam my face. "You look beautiful."

"And you look scruffy." I reach up and stroke his beard. I actually like it, but he said he's going to have to shave it soon, because the facial hair is too much for the summer heat.

"How was your day? How was the meeting with the hockey wives? Everything look good for the farmers' market?"

"Everything looks good." I pop the trunk.

"Did you make biscuits, or muffins? The ones that taste like dough-nuts with the jam in the middle?" He rounds the car and stops dead when he sees what's inside the trunk. His gaze bounces from me to the trunk and back again. "Are you staying?"

"For the night."

To his credit, he tries to hide his disappointment. "Okay. That's good, right? Overnight is good."

"I thought it would give us more time to hang out." I move around the car to stand beside him.

"Just the two of us?" he asks.

"Just us."

Aaron grabs my bag from the trunk. "I have a lot of questions."

"I thought I heard a car!" Van's voice pulls our attention in his direction. He glances from me to Aaron to the pink bag in Aaron's hand. "Oh, hey, hey. I'll be in the house." He thumbs over his shoulder and starts moving in that direction while grinning.

I incline my head to the stairs leading to the apartment. "Come up with me?"

"Yeah. Yes. I will. Come. Up with you." Aaron nods a bunch of times and follows me up the stairs.

The air is stale in the apartment, but it looks exactly like I left it the last time I was here. I come up sometimes when I visit. Many of my memories here include Aaron. And for the most part, they're good ones.

He sets my bag on the bed and then moves to the kitchen and leans against the counter. "What does this mean?" He motions to the bed. "You staying the night here."

"I'm not moving back quite yet, but I plan to. Probably once the farmers' market starts up. And things are getting busier for the Stitches, so being here more will make sense."

He crosses his arms. "Okay. That makes sense." He pokes at his cheek with his tongue. "But that's not what I was talking about."

"You want to know what it means for us?" My heart feels like it's going to pound its way out of my chest.

He nods once.

"I guess it depends."

"On?"

"What you want." I had such a great speech planned, but now that we're here, it's gone poof in my head.

He drops his arms, and his mouth goes slack. "What I want? Teagan, babe, I want the same thing I've wanted since you showed up in Harry's buying yellow paint."

"And what's that?" It's hard to believe that was a year ago. So much has changed, except one important thing: that connection we share hasn't diminished one bit.

"You and me. Us."

I exhale a relieved breath, and it feels like my shoulders drop from my ears. "Okay, good. I want that too."

"Were you seriously worried I wouldn't?" He looks flabbergasted.

"I didn't want to presume anything. And it's been more than six months of me making you wait. I know it's a long time."

"Every time I hug you, I poke you with my business end." He motions to his crotch. "I figured that was an awkward enough indicator I'm still very much into you."

"Good point." I laugh and scrub a hand over my face. "Can we try dating before we start sleeping together again this time around, though?"

"Yes. Definitely. I'm absolutely on board with that. In fact, I'd love to take you out for breakfast tomorrow morning, if you're interested."

"I'm interested." I smile.

"Good. That's good. Am I allowed to come up here after dinner and hang out with you?" he asks.

My stomach flutters. "I'd like that."

"Me too. I'd like that a lot." He rounds the counter and comes to stand in front of me. "So we're going to take it slow this time, yeah?"

"I think it would be smart."

"I can get on board with smart. What about kissing you? Can I do that?"

"Kissing me seems reasonable."

"And do I need to wait until after our breakfast date, or is now okay?"

"Now would be more than okay," I whisper.

Aaron's fingers drift up my arm and slide along the edge of my jaw. I tip my head back, anticipation making my heart beat faster. He drops his head, but his lips find my temple first. "I missed you so much, babe."

"Me too. I know it took a long time to get here."

"You're worth the wait." His lips sweep across my cheek.

"I wanted you to have the best version of me."

"I love you, Teagan." He presses his lips to mine.

"I love you back." I loop my arms around his neck.

"And I will love you twice as much on the days when you find it hard to love yourself."

It's a promise sealed with a kiss.

EPILOGUE
THIS MAGIC PLACE

Teagan
One Year Later

"I'm leaving for the market in five minutes. Do you want me to stop at the office and grab the signs for your booth on the way over?"

"That would be great. Do you need anything from your apartment?" Dillion asks.

I switch my phone to speaker so I can rummage through my purse. "I think I have all the important things I need."

"I can always drive over there if you're missing something essential." Aaron crosses from the bedroom to the kitchen, where I'm currently trying to do six things with two hands.

Over the past year the Pearl Lake Farmers' Market has turned into a job that I'm now compensated for. It runs weekly from the end of May to the end of September, and then we have a huge holiday market at the end of November. The town hired me on to help organize and run their other events throughout the year. I love it, and I've learned, with help from my family and Aaron, when to put the brakes on and when to delegate so I don't get overwhelmed.

I'm still consulting for the Stitches on design projects. And in the slow seasons I take design courses. I've discovered a passion for both interior design and event organization. I'm learning how to balance those two things I love without letting either of them take over my life.

It's a beautiful day for the market. The weather looks promising, and there are now a hundred vendors signed up to participate. It means we've had to relocate the market to the main street. It took some work and some permits, but with the help of the volunteer team I've put together, it's all been very doable.

"And don't forget we're hosting a barbecue tonight," Dillion reminds me.

"Super excited for that!" I end the call and glance up at Aaron, who's standing in the doorway of the bedroom, shirtless. "Maybe I should make biscuits for the barbecue."

He arches a brow. "Do you have a clone I don't know about?"

I try to come up with a witty comeback, but he has a point. "Or I can buy some from Boones and support local."

"Seems like the more reasonable thing to do." He pushes off the doorframe and glances at the clock on the wall as he crosses the room. When he reaches me, he wraps his arms around my waist and pulls me against him. I allow myself a few moments to appreciate the warmth of his embrace as I absorb his love.

He's been my rock for the past two years. He's loved me when I've struggled to love myself. He's stood beside me and given me a soft place to land when I fall. There have been hiccups along the way. Times when I've started to take on too much and struggled to pull back. But Aaron and my family have been here to help me course correct.

I'm lucky to have them and this community. Pearl Lake is a magical place, and it's become my home.

When Aaron's hands start to wander, I press my palms against his bare chest. "We need to leave in fifteen minutes, and while you can man the Footprint booth shirtless, I'm not sure you're going to love the attention you'll get." Aaron and Billy trade off every other week managing the Footprint Construction booth. They get as much attention from the college-aged girls as they do from people legitimately looking for project advice. Aaron handles it pretty well, but Billy turns a million shades of red and gets all flustered when they flirt with him. It's pretty funny to watch.

"I'm just hugging you. And it doesn't take fifteen minutes for me to put on a shirt." He drops his head, and his lips brush my ear. "You know what else we can do with the next fourteen minutes?"

I grin against his chest. "We do not have time for that."

"You have such a one-track mind, Teagan."

This time I push hard enough that he lets me go. "You're poking me in the belly button with your less evolved head. Save it for tonight."

"But that's sixteen hours from now."

"Whining isn't sexy, Aaron."

He frowns. "I'm not whining. I'm stating facts."

"I promise I'll make it worth the wait."

"You're always worth the wait, babe. I'm being greedy." He pulls me in again and kisses me softly but doesn't make a move to deepen it, probably because he knows I'll clamp my teeth shut, and getting himself more worked up isn't going to help either of us.

He pours us coffees, and I toast our bagels, slathering his with Nutella—he has the breakfast tastes of a ten-year-old—and topping mine with a slice of cheese and tomato, and then we're out the door and in his truck, on the way downtown.

The sun is cresting the horizon. Saturday mornings are early since the market starts at eight and ends at one in the afternoon.

"What time are Lydia and Jamie going to be here?" I ask.

It's a big weekend around here with the first farmers' market of the season. Lydia and Jamie are coming to visit, and so are my dad and Danielle.

"Before the market ends, for sure. My mom and dad want us to go over to their place for brunch tomorrow, but I told them today is a big day and with everything else going on we'd just have to play it by ear," Aaron replies. "Besides, they're coming for dinner at Van's, so we'll get in a visit."

Arnie managed to buy the piece of property a few lots down from Aaron's, and he hired Footprint to renovate the existing cottage. A few months ago, Noreen gave up her apartment and moved in with Arnie. They're a family now, in the true sense of the word. Something Aaron was missing in his life.

"Okay. That sounds good." It's in my nature to say yes, but Aaron's right: this weekend is a busy one, and as much as I love being with my family and his, I don't want to overcommit myself.

"You gonna stay at my place this weekend so Danielle and your dad can have the apartment?" Aaron asks.

"If you're okay with that." I've been spending more nights at Aaron's place over the past six months than I have my own.

We took it slow when I unpaused us. We went on dates; we had make-out sessions like we were high schoolers. We didn't jump back in with both feet. And I had a chance to fall in love with him all over again.

"You know I love waking up to your beautiful face every morning." He takes my hand in his and kisses my knuckle. "I've been thinking— with summer coming, your dad and Danielle will probably be coming up to visit more often, right?"

"He was talking about taking a couple of weeks off and spending them here, with Van." That's another thing that's changed over the past year; our relationship with our dad has shifted. We've gotten closer as a family. And Danielle is part of the equation. A big part. While she'll never replace my mother, she's become someone I can rely on, and so has Aaron's mom. My life is full of family and love, and I feel so fortunate to have it all.

Aaron adjusts the brim of his ball cap. "Maybe it's time for you to start moving some more stuff to my place. That way Danielle and your dad can have the apartment to themselves."

"Are you asking me to move in with you?" I'm half joking, since I already live with him more than 50 percent of the time.

He pulls into the town hall parking lot and puts the truck in park. He shifts to face me, looking nervous. "You don't have to answer right now, but you stay at my place more than you stay at the apartment. I love you. I want you next to me every night and every morning. I don't want to push you before you're ready, though. You can think about it for as long as you need to, but this is my official invitation for you to move in with me. It's open indefinitely."

"I don't need to think about it."

"Seriously, Teagan, I know it's a big deal, and I didn't mean to spring it on you right before the first farmers' market of the year. You can let it percolate for a while." He brings my hand to his lips and kisses the back of it.

"Can I be honest with you?" I ask.

"Of course. Always." His expression is earnest.

"I only have a handful of outfits left at the apartment."

"Really?"

"And I haven't slept at the apartment in over a week."

His brows pull together. "That was last weekend, when we had dinner with your brother and Dillion."

"And you stayed the night with me," I remind him.

A slow smile spreads across his face. "That's right. You were frisky."

My cheeks heat with the memory, and his expression shifts back to serious. "Does that mean we've been living together for a while and we didn't even realize it?"

I chuckle. "It seems that way."

"So can we make it officially official?"

"We can."

"And you're not just saying yes because you feel like you have to?" I arch a brow.

"Just checking." His palm curves around the back of my neck, and he pulls me in for a kiss. One full of promise.

Aaron is my partner. My person. My rock.

And I know, in my heart, that we'll love each other the most on those days when it's hardest for us to love ourselves.

ACKNOWLEDGMENTS

Kidlet and hubs, your support is unwavering. Thank you for standing behind me every step of the way.

Pepper, thank you for your insight, for your support, and most of all, for your friendship. I adore you.

Kimberly, thank you for helping me make this one the best it could be.

Sarah, you are amazing, and I'm grateful that I have you as a friend and as part of my support team.

Hustlers, I couldn't ask for a better book family. You're my crew, and I love you.

My SS ladies, thank you for being willing to go through the fine details with me. You're amazing.

Tijan, your kindness is a gift. Thank you for being a wonderful friend.

Sarah, Jenn, Hilary, Shan, Catherine, and my entire team at Social Butterfly, you're fabulous, and I couldn't do it without you.

Sarah and Gel, your incredible talent never ceases to amaze me. Thank you for sharing it with me. Lindsey and Christine, thank you for helping me make this a better story with your insight.

To my ARC crew, thank you for always being enthusiastic about my words. Julia and Amanda, your eagle eyes are always appreciated.

Beavers, you're my soft place to land, and you're always excited for what's next. I'm lucky to have you in my corner for all these years.

Deb, Tijan, Kelly, Erika, Marty, Karen, Shalu, Melanie, Marnie, Julie, Krystin, Laurie, and Angela, your friendship, guidance, support, and insight keep me grounded. Thank you for being such wonderful and inspiring women in my life.

Readers, bloggers, and bookstagrammers, your dedication and your love of books, romance, and happily ever afters are inspirations.

ABOUT THE AUTHOR

Photo © 2018 Sebastian Lohnghorn

New York Times and *USA Today* bestselling author Helena Hunting lives on the outskirts of Toronto with her incredibly tolerant family and two moderately intolerant cats. She writes contemporary romance ranging from new adult angst to romantic comedy.

LINKS

Website ⇨ http://www.helenahunting.com/

Amazon ⇨ http://amzn.to/1y6OBB7

Twitter ⇨ http://bit.ly/HelenaHTwitter

Facebook ⇨ https://www.facebook.com/helena.hunting69/

Pinterest ⇨ http://bit.ly/1oQYRVN

Instagram ⇨ http://instagram.com/helenahunting

Goodreads ⇨ http://bit.ly/GoodReadsHH

Newsletter ⇨ http://bit.ly/HelenaHnewsletter

BookBub ⇨ http://bit.ly/BookBubHH

The Beaver Den ⇨ http://bit.ly/TheBeaverDenHH